Through Psychotic Eyes

Presly Phillips

Luna Moon Press—Findlay, OH
ISBN: 979-8-218-19472-7
Library of Congress Control Number: 2023908272
Title: *Through Psychotic Eyes*
Author: Presly Phillips
Digital distribution | 2023
Paperback | 2023

This is a work of fiction. The characters, names, incidents, places, and dialogue are products of the author's imagination, and are not to be construed as real.

Chapter 1
The Camping Trip

My first camping trip with my family is all I seem to remember from my childhood. I woke up to the overwhelming smell of burning material. The popping sound of the flames filled my ears. I looked around to see the flames slowly swallowing my tent. I started crying out for my mother because the fire was surrounding me. Instead of an answer I heard a bloody scream that sounded an awful lot like my mother. That scream is something that haunts me every single day. It was the sound of pure torture and it echoed through the woods. I tried to escape the tent from the zipper, but the flames covered the opening. Next to the zipper was a tool kit my father took with us, so, I quickly scavenged up a pocketknife. I desperately started stabbing through the back of the tent. It created enough of a slit to allow my small body to slip through. I was probably around 6 years old; a little boy who thought he was just going on a family camping trip.

When I got out, the woods were dark and damp due to the rain that was lightly falling. Behind me the fire had swallowed the tent whole and everything inside it. I heard my mother weep again and ran to the other side of the tent to see my mother laying there on the muddy ground. She was crawling away from a figure standing above her. I yelled for her which caused her to look up at me. Her head was bleeding, and her face was black and blue. Her eyes were red and one of them was swollen shut. The night dress she was wearing was no longer white and her face was no longer peaceful.

"Jessie, run!" she pleaded.

I couldn't move and my eyes began to fog with tears as the man lifted his arm. He was wearing a black glove and gripped the gun firmly in his hand. I shouted but he already pulled the trigger, shooting my mother when she was down. In one quick and unbearable second my mother was gone. Anger raced through me and I grabbed a log and ran at him. I hit the man in the stomach with the log and caused him to drop to the ground and drop the gun. After I did, the moonlight shined in his face and I saw who the man was. I picked up the gun and pointed it at him.

"Son, you wouldn't kill your own father," he said, putting his arms up.

"You killed mommy," I cried.

"She deserved it, son," he grinned.

Those words haunt me. If there is one thing, I remember about my mother is that she would never "deserve" any harm. This made my anger become uncontrollable. I looked at my mother who was laying limp on the ground. The red blood was dripping from her head. From the corner of my eye, I saw my father pick up the log. I looked straight at him and saw him raise the log above his head. Before he could strike, I pulled the trigger. I remember the feeling of pulling that trigger and the pressure of the gun when it released. It created a striking pain in my arms as they pushed back into my chest. The look of my father falling to the ground with his hand pressed against his chest will remain with me. He fell next to my mother. I stood there frozen and dropped the gun next to them. There I was standing above my two dead parents. They lay next to each other like they died lovers even though they died enemies. My body felt as cold as ice and I was trembling uncontrollably. I backed up slowly and without looking back I ran through those woods.

The woods had a chilling fog that hovered over the trees like a blanket. It was like the woods were symbolizing what had happened. The cold droplets fell on my face when I looked up. I ran and ran, inhaling the cold air that started to sting my lungs. I didn't stop till I got to our house which was small but looked Victorian. I forgot to grab keys from my parent's pockets, so, I climbed into the living room window that was often unlocked. I got to my room and hid. The blue walls were glowing from the moonlight as it seeped through the windows. I sat in the corner of my closet with my knees tucked by my chest. The images rushed through my mind and began to drive me insane. All I could do was rock myself to sleep and pretend that it was all a dream.

Two days later, I was found by a police officer. He found me in the closet and there were drawings all over it. It all showed what I saw. My mom lying there dead, my dad looking down on her and them lying beside each other dead. I have seen the polaroid of this scene and I could not imagine being the police officer looking in. The drawings were drawn repeatedly, and it covered the whole wall inside the closet. I sat there with my knees pulled up to me and had crazed, watery eyes. I didn't even look at the police officer. They explained it as if I was in a trance. The doctors described it as catatonic. I think I was just trapped in my own nightmare and couldn't find the door to free myself.

Now it is 2013 and I am 35 years old. I sit here in my cell, but it is much better than the padded room and straitjacket I am usually in. I haven't shaved in what feels like forever; my dark brown hair is getting long, and my beard is traveling everywhere. My hair is making me sweat even more than usual. I have dirt all over me and am covered in filth. Before you ask, yes, I smell as bad as it sounds. I have been rotting in a prison for most of my life. The worst part about it is right now I am in the psych ward inside the prison. It is a place where they don't see us as humans; to them we are animals who are misbehaving. Don't growl or they'll hit you with a stick. They also like to send you to a dark padded room with arms locked to your sides and all you can do is hope you don't have to itch your face. In here, it is always stuffy, and it doesn't matter if your nose is cleared or not. Just get used to not being able to breathe. Nobody gets showers until the guards can't take the awful smell of body odor. The cells are small but in the psych ward you at least you have your own room which almost makes it worse because you start thinking the voices in your head are your friends.

I sit there in my corner of the cell and I look around it as I see the walls closing in on me. Sometimes, I can even see them move and I try to remind myself they aren't. *It is just in your mind Jess.* The walls come closer and I try to back up, forgetting that I am already in the corner, and just making scrape marks on the floor. I watch as they shriek and inch their way towards me as if they are trying to tame a wild animal. The cell is so dark and dull. I start to breathe even heavier and my heart begins to race like it is about to burst through my chest. I close my eyes to try and calm down but my mind races back to when I was 6 years old.

It is 1984 and I'm standing in the court room and feeling so small. Everyone is looking at me like I am a strange creature from another planet. The doctors dressed me in a tux that had a light green tie which

3

matched my eyes. I kept my head down while occasionally glancing at the old, wrinkled judge. Her hair was white, and she looked like she was squinting her eyes. I remember thinking that she needed to get herself some glasses. Her lips were shriveled up and her eyes looked almost gray. She watched me with a puzzled look on her face.

My hair was parted and slicked back. Tears were dried to my face and I had almost black circles around my eyes. They started with the evidence first…

"We found various items from the campsite near Mr. Reids' house. We found a piece of wood that is the correct size for the bruise left on the boy's father. The gun that killed both of his mother and father had only his prints on it," the lawyer explained to the jury.

The flash of my father's glove went through my head.

"This boy brutally hurt his mother, attacked his father and shot them both."

I remained silent forever and still stuck in a daze but something about that day snapped me back into reality.

"No, I didn't hurt my mother!" I yelled.

"Quiet Jessie," said the lawyer they appointed me with.

"Please, your honor, he is 6 years old. What 6-year-old would be capable of causing so much damage as this?" said the lawyer.

"I'm wondering the same thing," said the lady who had the evidence, "why would a 6-year-old kill the only family he had."

You see the rest of my family lived in the UK and didn't associate themselves all that much with us ever since my mother moved to the U.S. to look for a life of her own. My mother met my father at a university in the U.S. and that is how I came about.

There was a lot of bickering and I ended up with a plea bargain. If I pled guilty, I would be sentenced 10 years in Juvenile jail with the guarantee that I would get psychiatric help in the facility.

"Jessie Reids, you are sentenced to 10 years in the psychiatric ward of the East Haven Juvenile Detention Center. Maybe we can save this boy," said the judge as she slammed her gavel.

The police officer started walking towards me with handcuffs in his hand while two others were trailing behind him.

"No!" I screamed, hitting one of the officers.

The police officer picked me up while I kicked and screamed.

"He killed my mommy!" I screamed.

"Contain him!" yelled the judge.

I watched the doors close behind the guards as they held me over their shoulders. I remained kicking and screaming until the damp halls became cold and wet rain as we made it outside. They carried me into a van and took me to the East Haven Juvenile Detention Center. The place looked big to me and gates surrounded it. Guards were in towers, looking down on us like we were bugs. Everything about it made me realize I was the villain of the fairytale books. When they walked inside, they started taking me somewhere, but they didn't put me in a jail cell instead they started walking towards a metal door. I screamed again and tried to get out of their hands. More men dressed in gray ran towards me with this strange white jacket. They kept me still and wrapped it around me until my arms were stuck. It was stiff and I felt claustrophobic. I couldn't move and it scared me more.

"Get me out of this! What are you doing? Help me!" I cried hysterically.

The guards looked at me like I was an untamed animal. They all pushed me into the room full of off-white padding. It was cold and dark with cheap padding that had a couple blood stains on them. I screech as they closed the steal door and the darkness of the room consumed me.

I'm sweating through my orange jumpsuit outfit. I start to rip apart my jacket. I finally tear it off so I could breathe again. I sit there in the corner with my legs stretched out and I stare at the ceiling. I finally cool down a little, but the place starts spinning, making me feel like I could hurl at any moment.

"Reids, time for lunch," says one of the guards, opening my cell door.

I slowly get up and the guards lead me down the hallway. The inmates in their cells stare and watch as we walk past them. They all look like a bunch of animals begging for food. Some of them reach us and try to grab the guards. They are laughing and howling but to me all their noises are faint due to the constant ringing in my ears. The lights flicker as they lead me to the mess hall. All the inmates are there picking at their food. The place is filled with nothing but orange. The new inmates sit there in a corner, terrified, most of them have been young here lately. As I pass them, I hear a faint whisper of my name. All the new inmates with face tattoos have heard of me. I am a topic on the other side of the prison. The East Haven Reformatory only has one mess hall; therefore, they stick both the "crazies" and the other inmates together for feasting. The guards follow me everywhere, making sure I don't kill someone with a half-eaten rotten sandwich. They walk with me through the line and when I sit down with my food; they stand near me. The "normal" inmates watch me intensively. I don't know why they are considered "not insane" they all committed a crime too. So, in other words they are as insane as I am, hell, you could argue they are crazier. They just killed someone because they wanted to and not because the voices in their head told them to.

"I heard that he has a death sentence," I hear someone whisper.

I look up at the guard who is grinning at me and the flash of the guards beating me in my first year in juvie snapped in my mind. When I was little, I just huddled into a ball whenever they would start at me. I snap back to reality to see the guard has his Taser at the ready. I look around at everyone who is staring at me with a shocked look on their faces. I realize I flinched and accidently flipped my tray.

"Having a seizer again, bitch?" says the guard in front of me.

The guards start laughing along with some of the inmates. The other inmates have terrified looks on their faces. My face gets hot as fire tingles throughout my body. I dive across the mess table and launch myself at the guard. I put my hands around his neck and begin squeezing as hard as I can.

"You fucking bastard!" I yell in his face.

I watch his face gets red with a guilty grin on my face and crazed eyes. All I see now is the blurry silhouette of the man as if my mind is trying to blind me from the reality of what I am doing. I feel an excruciating electric shock run through me with the sound of the Taser. I black out and fall on top of the mess table. What a sight that would have been.

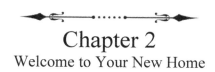

Chapter 2
Welcome to Your New Home

I wake up in a dark room, my face is in pain as the blood coming from my forehead trickles into my eye. My throat is dry and sore as I sit there with a rag tapped in my mouth. I can barely open my eye and my sides are sore. I try to move a little but remain trapped in a straitjacket that should very well have my name on it. I try to swallow but it is almost impossible.

I close my eyes and I flashback to when I was let out of juvenile jail. During that time, I was let out, but I never understood why. Maybe good behavior or they thought I was "cured." Of course, I was just good at acting like I was.

It was 1995 and I was seventeen. I had dark brown hair and green eyes. My jawline was slightly defined and clenched most of the time and I desperately needed a haircut. I was not allowed to leave the state of Connecticut and I didn't want to leave and live in a different city. I was given random clothes because it wasn't like they could give me what I came in. I signed papers and was walked out by a couple of guards. When they let me out the sun stung my eyes so bad that they watered. No one was there to pick me up, so, I walked to the nearest bus stop. I decided to go back to my old house.

My old house had a dark blue color to it with yellow trims outlining the porch and doorway. Its style was old fashioned, and the porch was big enough to fit a couch. It has been abandoned for eleven years because no one wants to live where a murderer lived. I walked in my parent's room to see my mother's dresses hung in the closet and her jewelry on their dresser. She liked her Sunday dresses and pearls. Some old makeup was stained to her dresser. Shades of red and tan smeared on the wood. Tears ran down my face as I remembered her smile. Her light shoulder lengthened brown hair and hazel eyes. I remember she always kept her hair curled. I wiped my face, walked out of the door and slammed it behind me. I stormed into my room which still had my toy trains spread out on the floor. I opened my closet to see the drawings remained. The blue walls were dull and some of the paint started peeling off from the last time my mother painted it. The room gave me chills and I put my hands on my head and ran them through my hair. I dropped my arms and slammed the closet door shut. I sighed and ran back down the stairs. My living room was dusty and had black couches and a brick fireplace. I looked up at the fireplace to see my father's picture staring down back at me. My father was one of those pretentious pricks who needed a mural of himself in the living room as if to remind us he was "the man of the house." My mind forced me to see his smirk as he killed my mother and the look he gave me when I shot him. I ripped the picture off the wall and threw it across the room. My rage increased as I smashed and knocked down everything that reminded me of him.

I remembered that my father never lived a moment without an alcoholic beverage in his hand, so, I ransacked his alcohol cabinets. I figured that if I drank enough hard liquor, I could kill what was inside me. It was numbing and every time I finished a bottle, I would smash it into the wall. The breaking of each bottle was music to my ears. I could feel myself getting bad as I began to laugh at my own pain and at the fact that my life was a shit show. I drank and drank until I passed out on the dirty kitchen floor.

"Jessie, hurry up we need to be on the road if we want to catch that sunset," said my father.

"I'm coming dad," I said as I picked up my blue camping bag.

We started packing up the car and I handed my bag to my mother. She smiled at me and put my bag into the trunk of our car.

"You ready for your first camping trip?" She got to my level and kissed my cheek.

"Yes," I giggled.

"It's time for you to learn how to be a man," my father said.

He put a cooler in the car and popped a cigarette in his mouth. My father was a tall and toned man. He had his dark hair in a short buzz cut and was relatively tan. His attitude was constantly angry with the occasionally random acts of kindness. I figured this camping trip was one of them. My mother was so happy that he decided to do something nice for us and we headed for the camp site.

When I woke up my head was throbbing, and my eyes were red and foggy. The tears were dried to my face and for some odd reason my shirt was off. I looked down to see cuts on my hands and arms from the glass I smashed. They weren't too deep but still very noticeable. My muscles were sore, and I groaned as I pulled myself up. The phone began to ring which sounded ten times louder than I remember. I struggled to reach over and pick up the phone. I supported myself up with the counter and put the phone up to my ear.

"Hello Mr. Reids. My name is Mrs. Jones; I am your guide," said the lady.

"You mean a probation officer," I mumbled.

"It is more like a guide Mr. Reids. I am here to help you, not scold you. Anyways I apologize for not being able to make it to your release. I figured you went back to your old house and I can be there in about thirty minutes to talk about your schooling and work."

I looked around the destroyed house and at myself in the kitchen mirror. I looked completely trashed.

"Shit," I mumbled.

"Excuse me?" said the lady.

"Uh… I mean shit, I'm starving. Can we meet at a restaurant or something?" I asked.

"There is a café by your old house. I will meet you there. Work on your language," she answered.

"Yes ma'am."

I hung up and stood still for a couple seconds before I rushed upstairs to clean myself up. There is no water at the house except a jug that was left in the fridge. I throw some of it on my face and go on a scavenger hunt for my shirt. I finally found the shirt with an embarrassing "Welcome to Connecticut" on it. I slipped on an old pair of my dad's sneakers that was lined up against the wall in the hallway. I looked down at my shirt to see it had a blood stain on it, but it was currently all I had that fit me. I rinsed one of the rags and tried rubbing out the blood stain, but it only faded it a little. I rushed out of the door with my hair still damp from the water. I quickly shook my hair and kept running. My father's shoes kept sliding off my feet because they were a little too big. I ran down the porch stairs and stopped for a second and realized I was in the sun again. Instead of it burning me, its warmth took over me, tingling my face. I smiled and put my arms up. I have forgotten what it felt like to have warmth. In jail, everything is cold and damp. They didn't let me out often because they were too busy with treatments and the "special" room A.K.A padded room.

A lady I assumed was the "guide" was staring at me from the restaurant with her head titled to the side and a "what are you doing?" look on her face. I looked at her, quickly put my arms down and gave an awkward smile and wave. She waved back, shook her head and walked in the café.

"This is going to be great," I said to myself.

For a second, I forgot about my throbbing headache, but I was quickly reminded as I walked in the café and noticed a lot of eyes were on me. The lady was sitting at the table; she was a short woman with dark skin and brown eyes. She looked like she was in her 40s but also had amazing skin. Her hair was cut short, in fact, it was shorter than mine at the time. My hair was at chin length because I haven't done anything to it for a while. Since my hair was still damp it kept sticking to my face and I could tell that I still looked like a wreck. I walked over to her and sat down in front of her.

She looked up at me and said, "Honey, you need a haircut." She looked at my outfit and laughed. "And new clothes."

I looked down at my outfit and back at her.

"What's going on with your eyes? Are you high?" she said a little loud.

"No," I answered and quickly looked around to see if anyone else heard her question.

"Today we get you cleaned up and tomorrow you go to school. You already have a spot, and you can thank the classes they allowed you to take in juvie for that," she said.

Yeah, I took a couple classes in between beatings I thought to myself.

"What so I can get more glares and become the poster child of this year's prison release?" I snapped.

"You need to stay strong. First step is getting something in your stomach," she said.

To be honest, right away I knew I'd kind of like her because she wasn't the fake nice type and didn't seem like she hated my guts either. Her voice was oddly monotone and even every time she talked. She seemed more realistic than any other person that was telling me they were "helping me."

She got me some pancakes and coffee which helped soothe the throbbing pain in my head a little bit. The pancakes were fluffy, and the maple syrup reminded me of the "homemade" kind my mom would buy. We mostly sat in silence while we ate until Mrs. Jones broke the silence when she asked for the check.

After that, we got in her Station Wagon and drove downtown. She first took me to a barber, and it seemed like she knew everyone there. My barber's name was Isiah and Mrs. Jones explained to him that I needed a haircut, so I don't look "homeless." They all laughed and started giving me ideas. The only one I liked was a standard haircut that is short but shaggy at the top. I liked this barber shop because no one judged me or maybe they just didn't know. They discussed politics and entertainment. I had no clue about what they were talking about because it was hard to keep up to date while you are behind bars.

She also took me to a couple of stores and got me new clothes and sneakers. Most of the clothes consisted of blue jeans and different solid-colored t-shirts. That was fine because I didn't have much of a style and a lot of clothes, I was seeing people wear were wild. We walked into a coat store and she let me pick the leather jacket if I got a denim one too.

"Why a denim jacket?" I asked.

"Everyone is wearing one and it looks nice on you. Your leather jacket makes it look like you should be riding a motorcycle," she said.

"Motorcycles are cool," I answered.

She rolled her eyes and motioned to the cash register. As she paid with cash I just stared at the worker. She had poufy hair and munched on her gum extremely loud. Her eyelids were blue which looked strange. I felt a punch in my gut from Mrs. Jones when she realized I was staring at the worker for a while.

"What?" I whispered.

"Stop staring," she whispered back.

I laughed and we walked out to her car. When we got in her car her face grew serious.

"Alright here's the rules and you might not like them, but they are rules, and you need to follow them."

"So, they aren't guidelines," I interrupted.

She just glared at me and seemed very unamused.

I cleared my throat. "Continue."

"Anyways, as of now you would be in your junior year of high school. Unfortunately, they will not allow you to skip the grades and you will start as a freshman. That means go to school and get all your classes in. No skipping. You can't live in your old house. I know it is your home but there is no one there for you. So, I am putting you in a home with kids who are sort of like you. It might be good for you and will give you a new perspective," said Mrs. Jones.

"Isn't that what jail did?" I asked.

"Let's go get your stuff," said Mrs. Jones, ignoring my remark.

"Right now?"

"Yes, right now. They are waiting for your smart ass," she said.

I sighed and looked out of the window. Mrs. Jones put on the radio. It was all static as she switched through the channels. I looked over at her as she still switched around the radio and coughed to get her attention. I tried not to smile when she looked at me with a dead straight face and continued to switch through the stations without looking at the radio. Finally, she landed on a song that kept saying "rocket man" and she seemed pretty content with it.

We arrived at my house and I stared at it. It literally looked like one of those haunted houses kids would dare each other to go by. I followed her inside to get my stuff which wasn't a lot. I grabbed my old suitcase and packed the stuff I recently got while hiding a bottle of vodka in the bottom of the suitcase.

"What happened?" yelled Mrs. Jones.

I came downstairs to see her standing in the kitchen with her hands on her hips. I forgot what my morning was like.

"Yeah, I came back, and it was like this. I guess that means someone broke into it while it was abandoned," I explained.

"Teenagers," Mrs. Jones mumbled.

I just nodded. "Teenagers."

I walked out of the house and Mrs. Jones followed me out to her car. I looked back at the house. I don't know why I felt sad to leave it. It wasn't like I had many good memories there. I guess because what was left of my mom was there. I packed a couple of her necklaces and an old polaroid of us but other than that I decided to keep it light.

"It'll always be your home," said Mrs. Jones.

"That's the thing," I said, "it never really was."

We drove for a while, past the high school and into a woodsy area that was practically in the middle of nowhere. The driveway to it was long and lined up with trees. It looked as if Mrs. Jones was driving me to my doom.

The house looked almost like a shack. It looked like they sloppily painted gray paint over wood. The house was huge, and it gave me a chill down my spine. I thought my house looked haunted. A man and a woman walked out onto the porch.

"Come on, honey," said Mrs. Jones.

I remained quiet and got out slowly. I felt shaky.

"Hello Mr. and Mrs. Weaver my name is Mrs. Jones." She shook their hands.

They had a kind look to their faces. The woman had a warm smile and the man seemed laid back as he stood there with his arm around his wife.

"This here is Jessie," said Mrs. Jones.

I walked up to them, shaking their hands while my heart was pounding. The woman had light gray hair that was pulled up. Her eyes were brown, and she had wrinkles by them that showed when she smiled. The man had a beard that was gray, and his eyes were a little darker than hers. He was a tall and bigger man, but he also didn't look threatening.

"Welcome to your new home, Jessie," said the woman.

"Thank you," I said shyly.

"Thank you, Mrs. Jones. Come on in Jessie," said the woman.

Mrs. Jones nodded at her and turned to me.

"Jessie, here is my number whenever you need me, call. Here is your bag."

I nodded and took the piece of paper and my bag.

"Thank you," I said.

I felt bummed that it wasn't her I was staying with because I just started to really like her. I haven't met decent people in a long time.

I walked in the house and straight into the kitchen where four kids were standing. Every single one of them were staring at me and standing in a clump next to the wooden kitchen counter. Inside the house was more brown than gray and you could tell it had aged. The table was in the middle of the kitchen and it matched the kitchen walls perfectly. Everything was the same old wood except the kitchen floor which were rusty blue and white tiles.

"Alright Jessie. My name is Sara, and this is my husband Mark. Then these kids are somewhat around your age. Declan is seventeen and Adeline is sixteen. Then we have Brady and Annmarie who are both 12. Everyone this is Jessie Reids," said the woman.

"Welcome" said her husband with a faint warm smile.

Everyone else just stared at me. Adeline stared at me in a way that made me uncomfortable. She kept on repeatedly looking me up and down with her head tilted to the side. She was tan and had a defined, curvy figure and her hair was dirty blonde. Her eyes were a more hazel color, and her eyebrows were thin.

Annmarie was quieter and looked as if she was constantly refraining from something. She was wearing a couple rubber bands around her wrist like they were bracelets. She had dark hair that was almost black, and her eyes were blue. She was very small and pale.

Declan was a muscular guy with black hair. His eyes were a dark brown and his hair was super short. His skin tone was dark like a golden brown. He looked at me as if he wanted to kill me.

Brady looked nervous and a lot like Annmarie. He had blackish hair and was also small and pale. Brady had spiked up hair and his eyes were a grayish blue.

Sara took me upstairs while the two boys followed. It all seemed awkward and almost like I was in a strange dream.

"This will by your room. You are sharing with Declan and Brady," she said.

I nodded and put my suitcase by the bunk bed. The room had a bunk bed and a pull-out couch. It had old wood walls and a wood flooring with a gray carpet in the middle of the room. There were landscape pictures hung up around it and a small window next to the bunk bed. The bunk bed was metal which reminded me of a prison bed except the mattress looked much comfier. The couch and the bunk bed were on one side of the room while the other side had a lot of boxes. It looked like they just moved.

"We are having a late dinner tonight, you hungry?" she asked.

I nodded.

I followed her into the kitchen and Declan and Brady also followed, still watching me wearily. We all sat at the kitchen table, eating steak, mashed potatoes and cooked carrots. I ate quietly occasionally looking up at Adeline who continued to stare at me. I began to eat quicker, hoping I could go upstairs as quick as I can.

"Can I go upstairs and unpack?" I asked.

"Yes of course," said Sara.

I nodded and quickly went upstairs. I unpacked my stuff but left the bottle of vodka in the suitcase. I looked down at my suitcase and at the boxes. I wasn't sure where to put it, so, I just tossed it with the boxes.

"The top bunk is yours," said Declan, walking in.

"Fine with me," I said.

"Good," he said, falling into the pull-out bed on the other side of the gray carpet.

It was around 9:00. I didn't realize how long they waited for me to have dinner. I crawled up to the top bunk and lay on my back. Brady rushed in and practically dived into the bottom bunk without saying a word. Declan acted as if it was normal or maybe he was just used to it. Sara came in to say goodnight. So, I said goodnight back, but Declan looked at me as if I wasn't supposed to say it back. I don't know, maybe it was lame? Sara smiled and flipped off the lights.

As I closed my eyes my mind was still moving. I went back to a faint memory. I was planting flowers with my mom and we were throwing soil at each other. My mind raced to my father hurting her throughout the years. Visions of her crying kept going through my mind.

I woke up for a second and snuck down to grab the bottle of vodka out of my suitcase and quietly got up to my bed and drank some of it. It didn't ease the pain as much by just sipping it, so I started taking big gulps, enjoying the sting it brought to my throat. I thought of me killing my father and how he deserved that bullet. My mind started to blur until I was no longer thinking of anything and I was just staring at the ceiling. Eventually, I drank myself to sleep.

Chapter 3
Isabella

"Jessie, Wake up! You're going to miss the bus!" yelled Declan.

I got up so fast that it made my head spin. I threw a sweatshirt over my head and slipped on my blue jeans and a pair of Chuck Taylors that Mrs. Jones bought me. I quickly washed my face and brushed my teeth. I ran downstairs, almost tripping on the last step and rushed out the door.

"Nice job newbie," said Declan as we were both running for the bus.

When we got there the bus driver rolled his eyes. He was a tall and thin man with gray hair. Declan went in first and I followed. I was stuck sitting by myself across from Adeline, so, I stared out the window to avoid her stare. The bus stopped at East Haven High first and once we got off, it would head to the middle school. Brady and Annmarie just stared at us through the window when the bus started to leave. I followed Declan and Adeline into the school, and we walked together like a troublemaker trio. It was a moment that could have been in slow motion if we were in some cheesy young adult film. All the students were swarming the school in mini groups and as I walked towards the office, they would look over at me one by one. Some of them were whispering and some stood there frozen as if I had a bomb strapped to my chest. The further I walked, the smaller I felt. I finally got in the office and a wave of relief washed over me when I saw a familiar face.

"Hi Jessie," said Mrs. Jones.

The office lady smiled in an uncomfortable way and handed me my schedule which looked foreign to me. Mrs. Jones looked at my facial expression and decided to explain, "That is your class schedule and locker combination."

"Is there a map on here?" I asked, flipping it over two times as if it would magically appear.

"Can we get someone to help this poor child," Mrs. Jones asked.

Right on cue, a girl walked in. She had light brown skin with almost black hair and her eyes were hazel brown. Her smile was perfectly white, and her hair had messy waves with the length at mid back. She was a bit shorter than me but not by much.

The office lady waved at her and she put her hand up and half smiled. The girl looked up at me but looked away quickly and looked again from the corner of her eye. I realized that I was completely staring straight at her and that I probably freaked her out. So, I tried to casually look up at the light which made my eyes twitch because it was probably the brightest light I have ever seen. Not sure why they needed the lights in the office to be so bright.

"Isabella, could you help Mr. Reids find his classes?" asked the office lady.

"Why do I have to do it?" she asked, her accent was beautiful.

"You were new recently," said the lady, "you know how it feels."

Isabella glanced over at me and I realized I was accidentally staring at her again.

"Fine. Was this the reason I was sent down here?" she asked.

"No dear, here is your new schedule. We added the art class you wanted."

"Thanks."

Isabella turned to me and nodded for me to follow her. I started to follow but looked back at Mrs. Jones who was smiling at me and giving me a "thumbs up." I turned back around to follow the girl. The hallway was tan with marble flooring and all the lockers matched the wall. It looked very uniformed and somewhat new. We walked side by side in silence as a couple of people brushed past us. I finally decided to break the silence.

"Isabella, right?" I asked.

"Izzy."

"What?" I asked.

She turned towards me which made me step back a little bit because I realized how close I was to her.

"You can call me Izzy," she said.

"Jess," I said, holding out my hand.

She shook my hand and nodded, half smiling.

"Well, Jess, this is your locker, and your class is right beside it. Meet you after class," she said, turned and walked away.

"Thanks!" I yelled after her.

She threw a piece sign up in the air while holding her black medium purse in the other. She wore a graphic t-shirt that was tucked into a jean skirt and long boots. I smiled as I got my stuff in my locker. The fact that I smiled shocked me. A rush of warmth ran through me, giving me some sort of fascination that was drawing me towards her. I went to class with a strange feeling in my gut. To start out the day was a social studies class with a teacher whose voice puts the whole class to sleep. I kept drifting off thinking about Izzy. I sat there watching the class clock intensively watching it tick. The classroom had a little TV that was on wheels and each desk was tan like the lockers in the hallway. I guess this school wanted to match.

The bell rang and it was almost like I dove for the door. As I waited in the hallway people were looking at me and some of them even moved to the other side of the hallway. It was a little over dramatic if you asked me. I mean damn, you kill one person and all of a sudden you are the devil walking among the earth. Izzy came up to me, interrupting my thoughts.

"Eager to get to your next class, Jess?" she asked.

"Yes," I said quickly.

What I wanted was to get out of the hallway. Izzy gave me a weird look and pointed me to follow her.

"Your next class is with me. English, very interesting, right?" she laughed.

"I can't write very well," I said.

I felt like I was just spitting out words when I talked to her and never fully thought about what I was saying before I said it.

"It's not for everyone but you've got to do it," she said.

I was watching her as she talked, her words flowed perfectly with the light accent she had, it completed her. She turned to look at me.

"Why are you staring at me like that?" she asked, stepping back a little.

I froze, looked at my feet and the words "I don't know" escaped my mouth.

"Okay," she paused. "You're strange. Anyway, here is our class," she mumbled.

I nodded and walked in behind her.

"Oh class! We have a new student," said the teacher when I walked in.

It surprised me considering the other teacher just pointed at my seat. I stared at him, shocked and frozen. The teacher waved me over to stand by him, so I walked over slowly. Izzy went to sit down by a guy with a haircut that had shaved sides and a little hair on the top. His hair was blonde, and he was muscular with a square shaped face. His eyebrows were thick and brooding. Muscles were visible under his letter man jacket that made it clear he was a football player. When Izzy sat down, he pulled her into him and kissed her. He glared over at me as he let go of her. Although, I only knew this girl for maybe an hour, anger ran through me. I wanted to strangle him. I clenched my jaw and stood there like I was nailed to the floor. I could feel my heart heat up as if it broke right then.

"Everyone meet Jessie Reids," said the teacher.

For a moment you could probably hear a feather hit the ground until the blonde guy laughed.

"Keep quiet Kyle," said the teacher pointing at him.

Kyle wrapped his arm around Izzy's chair. The way the room was set up, there were two people at a desk, and all lined in four rows.

"You sit in the back, Jessie." He pointed towards the back. Of course, the one desk that had no one but I preferred that anyways.

Izzy and Kyle were in the desk in front of me. I got a front row seat to my nightmare. I sat in my spot and starred out of the window. I could feel myself breathing heavily as I tried to control my anger. Izzy turned to me and her boyfriend looked back at me too. I just looked back at them as I leaned back in my chair and crossed my arms.

"Do you not like being called Jessie?" asked Izzy.

"It's fine. I just prefer Jess," I answered.

"Jessie sounds like a girl's name," remarked the asshole.

"Shut up. It can go both ways," Izzy said to him and turned to me, "but yeah it is the same thing with my name too." Izzy smiled.

"Yeah," I replied, looking down.

They both turned around, but Izzy glanced back at me again with a confused look on her face. The teacher began to talk, and class finally started but I could not get myself to pay attention. Thoughts of breaking Kyle's neck brought slight smirks to my face, but I knew I couldn't. I occasionally heard comments about Shakespeare come from my teacher's mouth, specifically Julius Cesar. When the bell finally rang, I rushed out of that classroom as fast as I could.

"Jess!" Izzy yelled after me.

I stopped and turned to face her with a sigh.

"Are you okay?" she asked, looking confused.

"I'm fine," I shrugged.

"Is it because of Kyle? I am sorry he was being an ass."

"No shit. I need to get to class," I said, walking away.

"Do you even know where that is?" she asked.

"I'll find it," I snapped.

I paused to look at my schedule and sighed.

"Where is room 263?" I asked without turning to look at her.

"Downstairs, directly underneath this hallway," she said.

"Thank you," I said still not turning towards her.

My classes were a drag after that. I couldn't help but fall asleep during most of them. My last period I fell on the floor in the middle of my sleep and became the laughingstock of the class full of freshman. I guess Math class is a little hard to make a couple jumps within the grade system. Science class was another one that was full of freshman. They all had their cliques and I just remained sitting in the back of the class. I didn't even have a science partner and was the oddball that will need to start joining a group whenever needed. It was like all the teachers banded together to make my year a living hell.

However, it is amazing what you will notice when you pay attention. I could tell this girl was flirting with her science partner while the man behind them stared in anger. I related to the angry teen but of course it could be a different story than mine. There were some band kids that sat next to me talking about the instruments they play and "how dare Jessica get first chair." Not sure what that means, I didn't know there were ranks in band. How could the teacher tell what students were good amongst all the band kids playing? Do they just make them play one by one if the song sounds like shit? My mind raced way too much in that class. I didn't even remember what we went over in Science.

After the class, I got to my locker and opened it. I looked over to see Kyle kissing Izzy's neck. I grabbed my book bag and began stuffing my homework in it, not even paying attention to the fact that I was crumbling up every single page.

"Why don't you just pluck my eyes out with a knife and feed it to a raven," I mumbled, turning to see Izzy right in front of me which made me jump.

"Well, that would be painful, don't you think?" She was standing there with her arms crossed.

"It sounds delightful right about now," I answered, starting to walk away.

Izzy stopped me and turned me towards her.

"What is that supposed to mean?"

"Just really into Edgar Allan Poe." I half smiled and continued to walk out of the school without looking back.

I don't know why I was taking it out on her. We knew each other for less than a day and yet I acted like she betrayed me by already having a boyfriend. I was nuts and I knew it.

I walked to my bus and got in once the driver swung open the doors. I sat in the first seat I saw. My mind was filled with so much. I didn't know how long I would be able to handle it before I started breaking again. I just close my eyes and let my head fall back.

After a while, the bus gets to the creepy house in the woods. It stops at the beginning of the driveway and drops me off. I walked down the driveway and looked up at the trees that align it. There was something both beautiful and eerie about the trees here. Beautiful because the sun shined through them perfectly to the point where it seemed like it was creating spotlights. Eerie because the old wood and leafless trees created just enough wind to bring a chill down your spine and make you feel like you were being followed. When I walked in the house Mr. and Mrs. Weaver were already in the kitchen with the two younger kids.

"Hello Jessie. How was your day sweetheart?" asked Mrs. Weaver.

"It was okay," I answered.

The rest of the kids filed in which made me realize that I might have just been actually followed instead of the trees creating the feeling. It surprised me how much I was not paying attention to my surroundings. Adeline went over to help Mrs. Weaver cut up some vegetables right away like it was a tradition.

"Did you make any friends?" she asked.

"Yeah, one, sort of," I answered, standing awkwardly in the kitchen with my hands in my pocket.

Adeline waved me over and I walked towards her.

"Cut this up," she said, handing me a potato.

Adeline's voice was kind of raspy and she wore her make up like she was about to be in a show. Adeline was beautiful and reminded me of Marilyn Monroe, just tanner. When you are closer to her you can see the powder on her face and the slight blue eye shadow on her eyes. It looked like a professional did her make up. I grabbed a knife and started cutting the potato, trying to follow what her and AnnMarie were doing. They both were effortlessly cutting the potato and vegetables perfectly even. Brady quietly and quickly pulled out a chair and sat on it but continued to keep his head focused on his feet.

"I met a friend too," Adeline whispered to me.

Adeline had this huge grin on her face that again creeped me out and I wasn't about to question what she meant by that. I stopped cutting and went to sit by Brady who just kept looking at me from the corner of his eye. The entire situation was completely awkward and made me so uncomfortable.

"Your English teacher." She winked.

My face scrunched up at the thought of Adeline and my 40-year-old teacher who always seemed too happy all the time. I looked over to see Brady just shaking his head. For how little he talked, he was oddly the most relatable so far.

"So, newbie, how many weird looks did you get? I bet you beat all our scores," said Declan who was leaning up against the door.

"A lot," I answered.

He started laughing. Declan's voice was extremely deep and made my voice sound incredibly wimpy.

"You mean you didn't count? Come on, that takes the fun out of it," said Declan.

"Sorry?" I asked.

I began to understand Brady even more. It must be so much easier to just remain speechless.

"Next time count," Declan demanded.

"Now honey, he doesn't have to if he doesn't want to," said Mrs. Weaver in her extremely light voice.

"Can I be excused to my room?" I asked.

"Of course, Jessie. We will call you down when it is dinner time." Mrs. Weaver gave a warm smile.

I nodded and went upstairs. As I was walking up, I heard Declan say, "Hey how come he doesn't need to help?"

I didn't bother to get out any homework and instead just lay there. I thought about school, this place and Izzy. I was so tired these past days and felt like I haven't slept at all throughout the nights. I ended up falling asleep and woke up to hear the Weavers talking about me. They were probably debating on waking me up for dinner, but I wasn't hungry, so I just pretended I was still asleep.

"Is he dead?" I heard AnnMarie's light voice say.

"Wouldn't be the worst thing," said Declan followed by an, "ow."

"Let's let him sleep," said Mrs. Weaver.

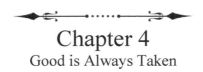

Chapter 4
Good is Always Taken

"**D**ude!" I heard Declan yell.

I quickly woke up and practically flopped off my bed.

"You need to set an alarm and put it by your face. I am not going to be the one waking you up and saving your ass all the time," said Declan, following me and mumbling as I grab my clothes.

I got in the shower and did a quick wash in the rusty blue shower and threw on my clothes with my hair still soaking wet. I looked in the old-fashioned mirror the Weavers hung above the sink and threw on a black t-shirt and a pair of sweatpants. I walked out of the bathroom with my feet still wet. The cold floor made my feet feel like I was walking on snow.

"Socks, socks, socks," I mumbled to myself, still trying to rush.

"Just throw on your shoes dumbass; you don't have time," said Declan.

"Why are you still here?" I yelled out of frustration.

Declan scoffed but his facial expression became confused, probably questioning why he was still there himself and he headed downstairs. I gave up and shoved my wet feet in my sneakers with a disgusted face. I remembered that I haven't brushed my teeth and ran into the bathroom to brush them. After that, I finally ran down the stairs and passed Declan.

"Come on we are going to be late. What's taking you so long," I said as I passed by him.

"Asshole," I heard him mutter.

Declan and I sprinted down the driveway in a race which was difficult because he was faster than me. The bus driver was about to close the door, but I yelled "Hey!" so he would open it back up and let us in.

"Thanks," I said out of breath.

"Uh huh," said the bus driver with a dead straight face.

I sat down on the first seat I saw empty and focused on catching my breath. Declan brushed past me mumbling angrily to himself. I breathed slowly and looked over to see Adeline staring at me from the seat across from me which made me slightly jump.

"Nice sweats," she said.

I just nodded at her and looked forward for the rest of the bus ride to avoid her stare. I felt like she stared at me throughout the entire ride to school which made it feel ten times longer. I knew she was doing it because it made me so uncomfortable. It was like she just liked watching me get squirmy. I stared out the window and watched the trees fly by and looking as if they were all connected some way. The trees were lined up by the road on each side as if they were about to battle each other. I started picturing them yelling "charge" at each other.

I thought about how Mrs. Jones said the Weaver's foster kids were like me and that it must mean they all had an illness. I could tell because they were all peculiar, but I couldn't tell what they each have. I had no idea what Adeline and AnnMarie had but I wanted to say that Adeline's "illness" had something to do with how provocative she is. Was that even an illness or just a strange personality trait? Brady is different because I saw myself in him. I guess the way he acted and the awkwardness of it reminded me of myself. Declan had something to do with anger that was for certain.

The bus finally stopped at the school and we all filed out, mostly organized, besides Declan who pushed himself through the crowd and ended up in front within two seconds. I walked out of the bus with my head down and tried to shake some of the dampness out of my hair. The water must have hit some people because I heard a couple of "ewes" and "heys." I tried to walk away and act like I didn't do anything, but I could feel all the pissed off stares. I looked up at the school forgetting how big and monstrous it was. It looked like one of those old universities except it was just a high school.

I got into the school and went up to my locker. When I got there Izzy was already by it. She was leaning against it with rolled up dark gray sweats, black chucks and a black cut off turtleneck. It is an outfit I would usually wear if I were running late except it looked like a fashion trend on her and yet, when I wear sweats I look like a homeless person.

"Hi," I said.

"Hey, I just wanted to make sure you are going to be alright getting to your classes," Izzy said.

I felt myself staring at her, watching her speak and looking straight into her eyes. I don't know what I was looking for or if I was attempting to read her mind but either way, I'm sure I looked strange staring like that.

"Yep, I'm fine." I still had my eyes fixed on her.

"Why do you keep looking at me like that?"

I snapped out of my daze. "Like what?"

"Like you are in love with me or something," Izzy said, laughing.

I froze and had to think if I was or not. I also had to think if I knew exactly how that would feel. During my eternal confliction, Izzy was waiting for an answer and watching my facial expression with one eyebrow raised.

"Jess?" Izzy seemed worried.

I looked around me, not sure what to say and finally looked back at her and the words "I am tired" came out of my mouth. Izzy just looked at me weirdly.

"See you in class." I half smiled and quickly walked away from her and into my first classroom.

Smooth, I thought to myself.

History class took forever it seemed. The teacher was going on about the Presidents and what each one did. I will admit some of our history is interesting but when it comes to politics and the Presidents; it bored me to death. Plus, half of the things we learned didn't seem as accurate. If Christopher Columbus 'discovered' America, how come there were already people there? I think they discovered America and he just walked or sorry sailed there, acting like he just found it. It is like when you are looking for something and ask someone to help you and they find it and you're like "I found it!" Anyways, I was looking forward to English class. Not necessarily seeing Kyle with Izzy but seeing Izzy in general.

When I went to English class Izzy's boyfriend Kyle was sitting there waiting, his eyes were on me as I walked to my desk and I was half expecting his head to turn all the way around like an owl.

"Bumming today, Jessie?" he mocked.

I wanted to pick up my chair and smack it right across the side of his head. Instead, I leaned over close to the side of his face.

"Trying too hard Kyle? Do you need to insult other men because you are afraid Izzy will leave your ass once she finds someone better,"

I said with a grin on my face.

"What did you say?" Kyle yelled, standing up.

I backed up just in time for his fist to miss my face.

"Kyle!" yelled Izzy.

"You didn't hear what he said to me Izzy. This asshole needs to be taught a lesson!" yelled Kyle.

Everybody in the classroom stood up as if they were eager to watch a fight break out. Izzy ran in front of him, but Kyle was in the mist of charging at me and he pushed her out of the way. That rose a whole new anger through me that boiled through my body. As he charged at me, I quickly punched him in the face and Kyle fell to the ground, holding his nose. Kyle looked up at me with rage as he held his bleeding nose.

"Jessie Reids, office now!" yelled the teacher.

My immediate reaction was to yell that maybe he should go to the office and report himself for sleeping with a student, but I surprisingly held my tongue. I could feel Izzy's stare, but I didn't look at her. I didn't look at anybody. I just walked out of the door and into the office. I barely noticed that I punched him until my eyes cleared and saw him holding his nose. It was so instant and thoughtless that it scared me a bit. I walked through the hallway and into the office in a trance. The hallway looked like the lockers were spinning in a circle. Like I was a hamster in a wheel and everything around me was spinning on an axis.

They put me in a room by myself so I could reflect on what I did like a preschooler. I knew I egged Kyle on, but he didn't have to push Izzy. I put my head in my hands and tried not to let the thoughts come in but of course they came at the most unbearable times...

The images forced themselves into my mind like they were charging the gates of my brain and prying open the door to my thoughts.

"Go to sleep little Jess. Everything is going to be alright. Daddy was just angry; he didn't mean those things. I love you sweetie," whispered my mom.

"I love you mommy," I whispered.

I was back in my bedroom. It had my drawings everywhere of trees and stick figures stuck on the walls with tape. The blue paint was fresh, and my blankets had zoo animals on it. My mom squeezed my hand, gave me a kiss on the forehead and started for the door. Once she closed the door behind her, the yelling began.

"You were planning on leaving me!" I heard the muffled sound of my father yelling.

I heard my mom pleading for him to stop yelling because I was sleeping. After that, all I heard was her being slammed against my bedroom door. She was slammed so hard that my door cracked a little.

The image was interrupted when Mrs. Jones closed the door behind her. I jumped and looked up at her with tears in my eyes.

"Jess? What happened?" asked Mrs. Jones, closing the door behind her.

This room was off the principal's office. It was small and had one metal desk with two chairs. To me, it looked like an interrogation room you saw on those black and white mysteries.

"Why do people hurt other people who have done nothing to them?" I asked.

I could tell what I said left Mrs. Jones puzzled. She froze and looked for the words to say but just said "not all people are like that."

"Where?" my voice shook.

Mrs. Jones sighed and pulled out the chair in front of me and sat down.

"There is no good in this world," I continued, "you're fooling yourself if you think there is."

Mrs. Jones studied my face and said, "Your foster parents are good. My husband was always good to me. Your mother was good. I know you didn't hurt her Jessie. She loves you and you love her."

Her words shocked me. No one has ever thought I was innocent when it came to my mother. I knew I should have said thank you for saying such nice things about my mother, but I could not get myself there.

"Your husband WAS good to you?" I emphasized, "Let me guess… he is gone now. My mom WAS good, but she is dead. That good was taken," I said.

"You're right. He is gone. He died in combat, but he is still in my heart and your mother is still in yours. Believe it or not she is still looking out for you."

I looked at her confused, so, she continued.

"The reason you got out at 17 wasn't because your time was served or even good behavior." She chuckled but her face grew serious.

"They were thinking about keeping you there because they didn't think you were cured. They let you out because they found the police records stating your mother kept calling about the abuse taking place."

"Then why didn't they do something then? All those times my mother called, why didn't they bring that up in court when I went to juvie?" I asked.

"I don't know. I'm guessing during the time of the abuse your father did something to cover that up or bribed an officer. But after it was discovered I offered to watch over you." Mrs. Jones smiled.

I managed to crack a smile. "So, you're good."

Mrs. Jones smiled and nodded.

"Which means you'll eventually be taken away from me somehow," I said coldly.

I could tell that sentence phased her a bit because she looked at me like she understood exactly why I said it. She was someone who suffered and understood the paranoia of suffering more.

"Jess, listen to me. I am not going anywhere." She looked at me in a way that almost made that sentence look convincing.

I gave her a half smile and just looked down. I didn't believe her but for now I decided to just let it go.

"Let's get you home," said Mrs. Jones.

"I don't want to go to the Weavers." I looked up at her.

Mrs. Jones shook her head. "You have to."

"I don't want to. I want to go home, my home," I said frustrated.

"Jessie, there is nothing there for you."

She was right, there was absolutely nothing there for me but for some reason that comforted me more than a room full of people. The Weavers walked into the room with warm smiles which at the time sickened me. How could people be so warm and happy all the time?

"Can't I stay with you?" I whispered.

Mrs. Jones face grew sad. "I can't do that."

"Come on Jessie, let's go home," said Mrs. Weaver.

I looked at Mrs. Jones who still looked hurt to tell me I couldn't live with her. My guess was she has already tried to fight for that. The courts had a funny way of setting things up and treating it like it's their way or the highway. I quietly walked with the Weavers out of the office and toward the school doors.

"Jess!" I heard Izzy yell.

I looked back to see her running towards me.

"You okay?" she asked.

I nodded. "I'm sorry," I said as my hands were in my pockets.

"It's okay." Izzy looked confused at my apology.

"Come on Jessie," said Mrs. Weaver.

Izzy looked at the Weavers and at me. I turned around and walked out with them without saying anything else to Izzy. We walked out to their old mini-van quietly and I sat in the back seat. The Weavers filed in quietly while glancing at each other. Mrs. Weaver turned around and looked back at me and elbowed Mr. Weaver.

Mr. Weaver coughed and preceded to ask, "Jessie, is there anything you would like to talk about?"

"No," I answered.

Mr. Weaver shrugged his shoulders in a 'well I tried' manner and Mrs. Weaver glared in return.

"You sure?" Mr. Weaver added.

"Yeah," I answered.

The Weavers gave up and were silent throughout the rest of the ride home. I sat there with my arms crossed and looked through the window. I felt like a little kid who was told he couldn't get candy at the grocery store.

We finally got to the house and I walked in and went straight to my room. I did it so quickly that the Weavers couldn't attempt to stop me. I got to my window and decided to jump out of it. I climbed the roof which had different levels to it that allowed me to scale the house. I finally got close enough to the ground to jump off but landed rather hardly. I groaned and looked up to see I was in front of the dreaded woods, but I felt like they were calling me. It was like they were whispering my name.

"Jessie!" I heard Mrs. Weaver yell and so I ran as fast as I could into the woods.

I wasn't sure on where I was planning to go until I thought about my house. It took a while to run through the woods which gave me a bad feeling. I kept on hearing my name except the voice was close. I could almost feel someone's breath saying it next to my ear. I paused during my run to look around, but the woods were eerily empty. I shuttered and quickly ran and did not stop until I got to my house. I didn't want to stop, nor did I want to know who or what was whispering my name.

I burst out of the woods to see my old street. Wicker Street the sign read. I ran into my old house which was all too easy because the door was completely open. I walked in slowly and cautiously. The house looked the same as I left it which was a mess. I closed the door behind me, and it caused a whole bunch of dust to fly. I sat down on one of the dusty couches. I sat there wondering what would happen when I got caught or even worse if someone else was in here. I went to my father's cabinet and grabbed a whisky bottle and did a sweep around the house. I occasionally did the dumb thing horror movie characters do and that is say "hello" in every room just in case the bad guy who is trying to kill me says "hello" back. After I decided the coast was clear, I sat down and started to drink the whisky bottle in my hand.

My mind was thinking too much and images of children screaming in the padded rooms, the screeches of the electric current running through your body and the doctors calling it treatments was running through my mind. I sat there as my vision got blurry. I could only see the blurred shape of the fireplace in front of me. I chuckled at my current situation, but my laugh sounded muffled to me. I chugged the whisky bottle and threw it against the fireplace banister. I began to laugh hysterically at the sound of bottles clashing into the picture frames. I could feel myself slipping away from reality.

The idea that I needed to be fixed or cured confused me. Why do we need to be fixed? It makes us think we are broken, and it gets drilled in our heads. It comes with societies ideal citizen. That us humans must be normal. A shred of differences must be hidden away. They use the words "insane" or "crazy" to convince you that you should be ashamed of your madness. Perhaps the only way to survive it, is to embrace your madness and learn to love yourself for it.

I got up and stumbled my way into the kitchen and grabbed one of the knives. The knife looked as if it was melted and laid limb in my hand. There was a hazy glow around it. I grabbed another half empty bottle and chugged what was left and dropped it. The shatter of the bottle was faint. My insides felt like they were poisoned and stopped working. My gut felt like I was stabbed in the side and the pain burst through the rest of my body. I collapsed to the ground and saw nothing but a blur of the ceiling fan. There was a faint chill where my back was as I lay on the kitchen floor. As I watched the ceiling fan dance around that should have been still, the corners of my vision began to blacken and eventually I saw nothing.

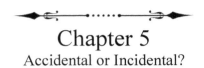

Chapter 5
Accidental or Incidental?

I woke up seeing a white ceiling and the blur of people in doctor masks. A huge striking pain shot through my arm and I looked over to see that a knife was stuck into it. I yelled in agony of the sting. Blood was all over my arm while a white gauze bandage was covering some of the wound.

"He's conscience," said one of the doctors.

My insides hurt like hell and I felt like I could barf at any minute. They turned me to a door which made me face the hallway. There in the hallway was this little girl with brown hair standing there. She shies over close to the wall as she stared at me.

"Whose girl is that?" I tried to say but my voice was raspy.

"What girl, sweetheart?" said one of the doctors.

"The one right there." I nodded towards her, half asleep.

I could feel myself slipping away.

"He's hallucinating!" yelled the doctor.

I chuckled at that. Haven't heard that a billion times. They pushed my bed into a room, and I got a glimpse of the little girl again. She was waving goodbye to me in a shy manner. I watched her wave at me while biting at her nail until she started to become a blurred silhouette. Everything was so blurry, but I still felt conscience. I started feeling numb as the doctor's drugs started working harder but could still feel the occasional piercing pain in my arm. I slowly looked over to my arm to see them pulling out the knife and a lot of blood poured out which made me want to gag. It looked like a fucking red water fountain.

I thought of the little girl to preoccupy myself. I knew she wasn't a hallucination, she couldn't have been, she looked too real. Usually, I wasn't too bad at telling if my hallucinations were real or not. They often didn't look like real people. There was always something about them that would allow myself to think *if they were real, they wouldn't look like this.* Probably the only beneficial thing I learned in juvie.

I could feel myself falling asleep and it was a scary feeling. I was afraid to close my eyes because I thought it would mean I would be officially dead, but the scarier feeling was the thought that I wouldn't be fully against dying now.

My mind flashed me back to when I was around 10 years old, waiting for one of my "treatments." I was sitting on a hard and cold bench in the middle of one of the hallways. There was a guard sitting at his desk behind glass while others roamed the hallways. I sat there looking at the walls and watching the peels of the paint slowly move. I was dreading for it to be my turn. They sat me right in front of the rooms so I could hear the electric current and what sounded like a young girl screaming in pain. The guard stood there to make sure I didn't budge. I jumped every time I heard a shock. At that time, I was always staring into space but never fully catatonic. I decided to not speak to anyone and remain in my own head. I created whole worlds to escape to where I was its hero or rather an anti-hero, saving the world.

The sound of the shock treatment fell silent and was replaced by the murmuring of the doctors. The voices became loud and angrier and finally the doctor came out yelling. He was yelling at the guards who were pulling out a bed with a little girl with almost white hair laying on it.

"I think she should have gotten more time!" yelled the doctor.

The warden walked out behind him.

"That's not your decision doctor. We looked at your data and saw there isn't anything else we could've done," he said.

I was always confused on what they did to her, but the girl has been stuck in my head forever. She was the girl who scratched up a guard's face because he called her crazy and said, "She was just like her mother."

The girl threw herself at him so quickly and scratched the shit out of his face. I remember thinking how brave she was and how I envied her even though I didn't know her. Right then I realized I would never get to buck up the courage to ask her name. I found her beautiful, she was technically my first crush I'd say. The inmates just called her Snow because of her hair and the guards just called her crazy like they did everyone else. I started thinking they should have at least called people "crazy 1" or "crazy 2" because it started to get confusing. The guards would yell "hey crazy" and everybody's head would pop up.

I stared as they walked away with the girl and saw how ghostly pale she was. The way that girl smiled flashed in my mind and how the only conversations I have ever had with her made zero sense. She would talk about the world like it was a fantasy novel. She would say one day she is going to fly out of here or that in another life she was a mermaid and she'd eat people like the guards for breakfast. She always made me smile but seeing her on that bed; it looked like all that sunshine was brutally sucked out of her.

I looked up at the warden who was looking at me with a smile. The warden's smile was worse than the face he made when he was angry because he would only smile when we were in pain. He was this tall bald man who looked like a harmless old man until you met him and realized how twisted the guy was. He doesn't seem so warm after you see him smile and say, "Welcome to your new home, we are going to make you feel better."

The guards rolled Snow away while the warden followed them out of the room. The doctor looked at me after watching the warden walk away with a concerned face. He had a very circular head with grey hair on top of it and large glasses. He always wore the stereotypical lap coat doctors use to show off their credentials.

"Jessie Reids," he said.

I nodded at him and followed him into the room. The doctor and a couple of nurses started strapping me to the bed.

"We are performing ECT, this will put electric currents through your brain," said the doctor.

The rest of the explanation became muffled to me because tears started running down my cheeks as they put some type of cold metal helmet on my head and shoved a mouth guard in my mouth. They stuck my arm with a needle and told me it would "relax my muscles."

The doctor left my sight, and I could hear him hooking up more stuff. I started crying loudly when he switched on the electric current. The feeling was excruciating. I felt as if my brain was frying and the buzzing of the electric current was ringing in my ears. The treatment was supposed to rid the pain of our troubles but instead it brought new ones. New nightmares were formed instead of deleted. The feeling and thought always haunts me.

EAST HAVEN HOSPITAL

I wake up back in the hospital with the bandage on my arm. I opened my eyes to see Mrs. Jones, The Weavers and all the kids sitting there like they were bored out of their minds.

"He's awake," said Mrs. Weaver smiling.

Seeing all of them there made me want to play it off like I was still sleeping but I knew it was too late for that. They all surrounded my bed, asking me how I was feeling. Everyone but Mrs. Jones who stayed back, she had the most saddened and painful expression on her face. Once she realized I was looking at her, she quickly changed her expression into a smile, but I knew it was just for my sake. I tried to convince the Weavers that I was fine, and I wanted to go home but it took even more convincing to the doctors that it was all just an accident. In reality, I am not sure it was nor do I remember how I got the knife in my arm. They decided to let me go and just took the Weavers in another room to discuss the possibilities that it was self-inflicted and how to handle me.

After some paperwork, we were on our way heading back to the Weavers. Mrs. Jones followed us there because the Weavers invited her to stay for dinner. All the Weavers went inside but Mrs. Jones pulled me aside to talk to her on the porch.

"Sit on the steps with me," she said.

I sat down by her and her face still looked painful. I didn't like that I made her feel that way.

"I loved my mother and father. They taught me everything I know. Pops taught me how to fight and my mom taught me how to take care of myself. My father went to the army and never came home; he was killed. It tore my mother apart, but we took care of each other. She cooked dinner and I would help. I'd be there for her every time she'd break down and every time she wouldn't get out of bed. Once I went off to college with a scholarship, I still visited her regularly, but she got sick and died before I graduated."

My heart dropped as I listened to her and she continued, "Bad things happen to many people, Jessie. What you went through; no child should have to go through. After I lost my parents, I devoted my life to helping people get back on their feet after loss. I know you have a strong heart, but you also have a lot of hate and anger. One day you'll find the good in this world because it's there. It won't come easily but you just have to look for it," said Mrs. Jones.

Every time Mrs. Jones spoke it was like an inspirational speech that left me speechless. She understood things about life that no one did. It was almost like she was wiser than the entire world. To me, it seemed like she was almost above the world. All I could say in return was, "Thank you for everything."

"You're welcome Jess," she said with a smile.

We both walked into the house while the Weavers made dinner. All the kids sat in the living room. We all sat there quietly and awkwardly as we ate our dinner. Sometimes, someone would try to come up with small talk, but I never cared to join in. It was like everyone felt like they were walking on eggshells. I think most of them didn't believe my incident was an accident. I only knew one thing; I must have known what I was doing. I must have wanted to stab myself and maybe I was so drunk that I missed, and I couldn't tell if I was thankful for that or not.

Chapter 6
My good

I slowly got up and realized this time I was the first one up. I got down from my bed and was shocked by the cold floor. I went to the bathroom and washed my face in the sink and looked in the mirror. I remembered my doctor explaining to the Weavers that I needed to switch my bandages. I went to the room and got the bandages out of my book bag. This time I closed the door behind me and took the bandage off. There was practically a hole that was just sewn shut with stitches. It looked like a damn football on my arm. I sighed when I realized to take a shower, I had to find a way to cover the stitches.

I went downstairs and jumped almost a foot in the air when I saw Brady sitting on the couch. I leaned against the wall to catch my breath while Brady didn't say a word. I just cleared my throat and asked, "do we have grocery bags and tape?"

"Under the sink," he said with a blank face.

"Thank you," I said.

I walked into the kitchen and looked back at him over the countertop. He was just sitting on the couch and staring at the wall. It would make sense if the TV was on, but it wasn't. I got out a couple of plastic bags from under the sink and put my arm in them. I reached for the tape and heard Brady say, "you should use a garbage bag" which made me jump because I didn't see him walk in the kitchen.

I just looked at him and grabbed a garbage bag and put my arm in it. I motioned the tape to him and said, "will you do the honors?"

Brady smiled like he was proud to be elected and started taping up my arm.

"Thank you," I said.

"Don't slip in the bathtub," he said.

I raised my eyebrow, "I'll try not to."

Brady nodded and sat back down on the couch in the exact same position. I walked back upstairs and looked back at Brady who still didn't turn the TV on. I shook my head and got in the shower. I quickly washed my hair and body. Meanwhile, images were coming in at a rapid pace… I started thinking about the little girl I saw in the hospital. I almost forgot about that whole ordeal and whether she was an illusion. Maybe she was a patient at the hospital. The image of her shying away near the wall and waving at me circled in my brain.

I got out of the shower and put some clothes on which was a bit difficult because I didn't fully dry myself off. I brushed my teeth as I did a weird lunge to stretch out the feeling of my legs being still damp in my jeans. I freed my arm from Brady's impressive rap up and suddenly Declan burst into the bathroom. I looked at him confused thinking I locked the door, but Declan didn't give a shit that I was in there and started taking off his clothes, so, I quickly rushed out of the bathroom before he took off his pants. I forgot I haven't put my shirt on yet and Adeline was standing right by the bathroom with a grin on her face. I quickly covered myself up by pressing my t-shirt to my chest, sideways walked away from her and put on my t-shirt. I got all my stuff together which mainly consisted of shoving the already crinkled papers in my book bag and went downstairs.

I walked downstairs and the Weavers looked over at me.

"Look who woke up early today," said Mrs. Weaver.

"It is a miracle," I smiled.

"You want something to eat?" asked Mrs. Weaver.

I shrugged, "I'm okay."

"You should eat something sweetie," said Mrs. Weaver.

"I'm not hungry," I said.

I sat at the table and all at once the kids started running to the table to join Brady who was already sitting. They all sat down, and Mrs. Weaver started putting eggs and toast in front of them. Everything smelt amazing which convinced me to eat this time. I started saying "on second thought" and before finishing my sentence Mrs. Weaver gave me a plate. I didn't realize they did this in the morning but then again, I never got up in time. We all ate our breakfast silently and finally the silence was broken when AnnMarie looked at the time and began to dart out the door.

"Come on, man!" yelled Declan.

I stuffed my face with the last bit of eggs, grabbed my book bag and started running after them. The bus was there at the end of the driveway and to think this time I woke up early and am still running after the damn bus. We all got on and headed for our seats. We were all breathing heavily. The bus driver did his usual shake of his head at us.

The kids in their seats stared at me which made me wonder if my incident would be public or not. Also, the gauze I didn't think to cover up that well was showing. An even worse thought was what if it got to Izzy and if she is going to question the gauze. To be honest, I am surprised she doesn't know about my past by now. I mean she couldn't have known because she wasn't terrified of me. The thought of her knowing anything about me honestly made my stomach hurt.

The bus ride felt shorter than usual, probably because this is the first time, I have hoped for a longer bus ride. When I got off the bus my stomach was turning. I kept on looking around to see if the rumor has spread by studying everyone's face. This just caused for me to get a lot of weird looks as if I didn't get enough of that already.

I got to my locker and couldn't see Izzy. I forgot that I told her I didn't need her help anymore. I put my stuff away in my locker and grabbed my books while occasionally looking around to see if I could see her. She was nowhere to be found and I headed to History. Again, History was boring but right when I walked in some kid just nodded at me and went "battle scars." I looked down at my arm and looked up at him.

"Yep," I nodded.

I went to my seat and pulled out my notebook. I tried to pretend I was writing notes, but I was mainly scribbling random things. I learned a way to easily draw 3D blocks which now covered my notebook. I decided to add to the blocks and wrote in "Christopher Columbus is a dick" amongst the linear decoration.

In English class, Izzy was sitting next to Kyle with a black and blue nose. Her arms were crossed and the two of them were not talking to each other which brought me more joy than it should have. She looked at me with a worried face. *Did she know?* I asked myself. I quickly went to my seat, making it too noticeable that something was wrong. I sat there hoping she wouldn't look back at me. She looked as if she was about to turn around but thankfully the teacher started talking so she quickly straightened back around and stayed looking straight.

The class went slow, and I felt like the entire time I was staring at the back of Izzy's head. Whenever I snapped back to reality, I heard him talking about this messed up guy named Oedipus... something about screwing his mom. It surprised me this is covered in a classroom full of high school students. I waited impatiently for the bell to ring, tapping my pencil and moving my toes within my shoe. Once the bell sounded, I started for the door and got to my locker. Before I could even close my locker, Izzy was right beside me.

"What happened to your arm?" asked Izzy.

"Um… I," I forgot to come up with a good makeup story.

"I'm clumsy," I finished saying.

"Clumsy," Izzy paused, "What did you do, fall through a window?"

"Um… well not really. I just had a clumsy accident while cooking," I said.

"Is it bad?" she asked, looking at my bandaged arm.

"Not too bad. It's healing."

She went to grab my arm softly and I let her, but she went to feel around my arm. Although her touch sent chills down my spine; I didn't want her to have any idea about what the wound was.

"When you put pressure on it, it hurts," I said quickly, pulling my arm away.

Her eyes were fixed on me like she was trying to read my mind and all of a sudden I felt very transparent. I swallowed my words, feeling like she was noticing every lie and every nervous twitch. I panicked and quickly walked away without saying a word which probably looked more suspicious. I went to all my classes and avoided Izzy. Then again it didn't seem like she was looking for me either and I couldn't tell if that made me relieved or bothered.

At lunch, I sat by myself and I kept my head down and just ate the lunch they had for today. This consisted of gross looking ham and very chunky mashed potatoes. I looked around the lunchroom to see that Adeline and Declan had a group of friends. I don't know why this surprised me because it wasn't like they had to be exactly like me. Declan was in with the jocks which made sense. Adeline was in with the cheerleaders with all their hairs up in curls. Some of the cheerleaders were flirting with the jocks. One kept twirling her hair between her fingers as she talked to a man who seemed preoccupied by a different teenager. It made me think about how high school always seemed like a cheesy movie.

Today in Science, I broke a beaker which drew a lot of attention. This beaker fell and every single student's head turned towards me while I was in a stance of trying to catch it. The Science teacher Mr.

Gordon just shook his head and got out a broom. I stayed in my seat with my hand pressed up to my face as I watched him sweep up my mess. He just looked at me after it was cleaned up and said, "be careful." The two people I was partnered with was the couple that constantly flirted with each other. I felt like me dropping the beaker was the first time they realized I was there. I wasn't necessarily older looking but for some reason I could tell that I was visibly older than these freshmen and I think they could tell too.

Finally, once school was over, I went to my locker. I kept on looking around to see if I could find Izzy because I wanted to say something instead of leaving the day with me practically running away from her. I stand at my locker a little bit longer than usual and I could tell I was missing my bus. I didn't know why I was waiting for her because there wasn't anything I could say. It wasn't like there was a very good excuse for having a hole in my arm. I closed my locker and just stood there for a little bit.

"Jess?" asked Izzy.

I looked over to see her standing there.

"Oh hi," I said.

"What are you doing?" asked Izzy, "you usually leave right away."

I shrugged and laughed nervously but her facial expression still looked concerned.

"I don't know," I said.

"Jess?"

"What?" I asked.

Izzy held out her hand, "come with me somewhere?"

I looked at her and she had a smile on her face. I smiled back and grabbed her hand and she pulled me. We ran out of the school. She kept on running so I ran with her. I didn't ask where we are going because I didn't care as long as I was with her. Until I realized we were going towards the woods which made me freeze.

"Jess, what's wrong?" said Izzy.

Images of the camping trip came to my head and I couldn't remember if it happened here or at a different trail. I had a feeling it was the trail near the Weavers since I could walk the distance to my house, but I still wasn't sure. It was too long ago to tell.

"It's just the trails, Jess."

My heart started beating. I didn't want to tell her no or tell my story. I didn't want to explain that every time I seem to enter the woods, I start seeing people and hearing voices. That would be an awkward first date. I wasn't even sure if this was considered a date or not.

"Sorry," I laughed and started walking with her.

We walked side by side, looking at the trees and enjoyed the view of the sun soaking through them. I tried to ignore the random shadows from the corners of my eyes and refused to let my body twitch.

"This place is very beautiful," said Izzy.

"It's trees," I answered.

She paused and looked at me.

"It's more than that," she chuckled, "it's mother nature, beautiful and full of colors. The woods are the closest we get to being in a painting," said Izzy.

"So, it's good" I said with a smile.

"Yeah, I think so," Izzy smiled.

"But bad things happen in the woods," I mumbled.

"What?"

"I mean in movies this is usually where people get kidnapped." I quickly somewhat saved myself.

"Bad things happen a lot of places. That doesn't necessarily mean the place is evil," she said.

"So, when something is good, evil comes to destroy it. Is that what you are saying?" I asked.

Izzy glanced at my arm and looked back at my face and smiled.

"Not always. When it all comes down to it the sun will rise through the darkness," said Izzy.

I nodded and managed a small smile.

"I think you're good," I said without thinking.

I realized how childish it sounded. Calling things good and evil like I was 6 years old again.

"I think you are too," Izzy smiled.

"Not yet," I mumbled.

"That's why there are second chances."

I looked quickly at her, thinking she did know but I couldn't see her trusting a murderer. She was kind but not stupid. But Izzy didn't ask why I seemed to have regrets, probably because she didn't want to pry or maybe she didn't care. That takes a lot of trust in somebody to not even want the slightest clue about what they regret so much. I guess everyone regrets something, but I highly doubt it is something as horrid as killing a man.

We got to this waterfall in the middle of these woods and it was small. It was mostly a couple of rocks with a little bit of water flowing down it.

"We don't have much, but I always thought this little waterfall was cute," Izzy said.

I nodded, "Yes, it is."

I looked at her as she stared at the waterfall.

"I need to come out and just paint this area. It's simple but I think it would make a good painting," she said.

I started noticing she saw things differently. To me, that was a rock with some water and to her...it was art.

We started walking back and she grabbed my hand again, this time not to lead me but to walk with me. Every time I would look over, she had a smile on her face. At that second, I did believe there was good in the world. Everyone has good in their lives and maybe, as ridiculous as it may sound, she was my good.

Chapter 7
Mood Swings

"Do you need a ride home?" Izzy asked.

"It's fine," I said, "you don't have to."

"No, it's okay! I can drive you."

"It's kind of far away," I said.

"Even more reason to give you a ride." Izzy smiled.

I thought to myself *she doesn't get hints very well*.

I tried one more excuse, "I live in a bad area."

"I'll be okay," Izzy smiled, "come on."

I followed her to her car and got in. I was picturing the Weavers smothering her and the rest of the kids glaring at her like she was the only human amongst the monsters. Izzy's car was a small red Volkswagen Beetle that smelled like lemons. It was very clean in the front but had books and papers everywhere in the back. Her air freshener was shaped like a ladybug to match her car which made me giggle. Izzy looked over at me confused, "what?"

"Ladybug," I said, pointing at her freshener.

She looked at me confused and I realized that didn't explain much. So, I tried to save myself and continued with "because your car also looks like a ladybug."

"Oh yeah. That's why I got it," she laughed.

I just laughed nervously and looked down at my hands. I had them folded awkwardly in my lap like I was waiting for a bus. You know that awkward moment when you sit on a bench next to a stranger while you wait for the next bus… that is what I looked like.

"Alright, where is your house at?" Izzy asked.

"Turn left," I answered.

She looked at me weirdly but shrugged and turned left. Izzy followed my directions and we sat there quietly listening to the radio as she drove. The song was some weird piano music that didn't have any lyrics. It sounded very peaceful and relaxing, but it was also kind of weird, sitting in a ladybug car while listening to Mozart or some other old dude playing a piano. Finally, I saw us pulling up to my driveway.

"Left at this driveway," I said.

She pulled into the driveway slowly and the Weaver's house comes into view.

"This isn't a bad spot. It looks peaceful actually," said Izzy.

"I was talking about the house itself," I answered.

"What is it haunted or something?" she said in a spooky voice.

"Yeah, it's haunted with crazy people," I laughed.

"Are you talking about your family?"

"They aren't my family," I mumbled.

Izzy looked confused, "what do you mean?"

"Foster kid," I chuckled.

"Oh, I'm sorry Jess. I didn't know. So, were those two people you left with the other day your foster parents? Or is that one lady you were with your first day your foster parent?" she continued to ask.

I laughed nervously, "you ask a lot of questions."

"I'm sorry," she said.

"It's okay. The couple are my foster parents and the lady who was with me on my first day is just someone who is helping me," I answered.

Izzy nodded but her facial expression still looked confused. I could tell she wanted to ask more questions, but I didn't want to answer any more questions. I am guessing a random woman helping you sounds like a sobriety sponsor.

"Well, thank you for the ride," I said.

I looked up to see Declan on the porch glaring back at us which made me feel uneasy. He looked like he was pissed about something, but I couldn't tell what I recently did to piss him off.

"You're welcome," said Izzy.

Izzy also seemed preoccupied by Declan who was now glaring right at her.

"Do you want to do something tomorrow?" I said before I got out of the car.

"Yeah, sure. We can go get some breakfast or something," said Izzy.

I smiled, "I know this one place. I forget what it's called but I could get Mrs. Jones, the lady from the first day, to take us since she's the one who showed me it," I said.

Izzy nodded. "Sounds good."

"Pick you up at 10? Where do you live?" I asked.

"Elm Street 282," she answered.

I smiled and shut her door and started walking up to the house. I heard her car starting to drive down the driveway as I got on the porch.

"Could you be any less creepy?" I asked Declan.

"Psycho gets a girlfriend now?" he mocked.

"What's your problem?"

I tried to get past him, but he blocked the doorway. I heard Izzy's car break and went to look back, but Declan took my shoulder, spun me around and slammed me against the door. I grunted at the striking pain that went up my back.

"I wonder if she knows you are a prison junkie," he said.

I grabbed his face with my free arm and shoved him off the porch so quickly it caught me by surprise. I stormed through the kitchen to see everyone there all staring at me.

"Where have you been?" said Mr. Weaver.

I ignored him and started upstairs.

"Jessie!" yelled Mrs. Weaver.

I heard Declan barge through the front door.

"That asshole just threw me to the ground!" he yelled.

I quickly ran upstairs and picked up the phone. I dialed and took it with me to the bathroom because it was the farthest the cord would go.

"Hello," she answered.

I could feel tears of frustration crawl out of my eyes, but I held them back.

"Mrs. Jones" I choked out.

"Jess?" she said worried, "what's wrong?"

"Nothing. I'm okay. Could you do me a favor?" I asked.

"Yes of course. What is it?"

"I met this girl. Her name is Izzy and she is good. I wanted to have breakfast with her at that one place you took me. Do you think you could take us there in the morning?" I asked.

"Sure honey, but you have to be careful when it comes to getting a girlfriend during this time," said Mrs. Jones.

"I know, I know. Listen I said we'd pick her up at 10."

"Okay, see you at 9:30 then," said Mrs. Jones.

"Okay, thank you."

"You're welcome, Jess."

I hung up and remained in the bathroom with the phone dangling by my side. I didn't want to be in the same room as that kid. I paced around the bathroom for a bit, practically pulling at my hair to try to calm down. I went over to our rusty sink and rinsed my face. I looked up to see myself in the strange mirror that deformed my face. The blue walls in the bathroom and the white tile floor seemed almost florescent to me. I leaned against the sink and put my head into my hands. After a while, I finally got myself to walk out of the bathroom to see Declan coming upstairs. I was waiting for the yelling and fist throwing but instead Declan looked at me and said "hey man" so casually.

"What?" I asked.

Declan looked at me confused "hey?"

I stood there confused and only managed to get out the word "hi."

I just walked over to my bed and got in it. Before I lay down, I looked over at Declan who was calmly laying in his bed. I lay back and stared at the ceiling. That mood change was so quick.

"Dinner!" yelled Mr. Weaver.

Declan and I both jumped up and headed downstairs. When we got downstairs, we both grabbed plates. I was studying Declan's face still confused.

"Dude, what?" Declan looked at me, "quit staring at me."

I just shrugged my shoulders, "sorry."

I sat down with my dinner. It was steak and cooked vegetables which tasted amazing. As much as I didn't like living with the Weavers, they did make amazing food. Again, we ate in silence. I found myself studying everyone's face. I guess Declan must have mood swings like that a lot because everyone was acting incredibly normal. After everyone was finished, they said "thank you" and headed up to their rooms. Mr. Weaver kissed Mrs. Weaver on the cheek and went outside to his little office in the backyard.

"Here, I'll help you with the dishes," I said.

"Oh, thank you Jessie," Mrs. Weaver smiled, "here you can dry while I wash."

I grabbed the towel out of her hand and started drying the dishes she was handing me.

"So, I have a question," I said.

"Ask away."

"Declan was just really mad at me and was getting in my face and then maybe a minute later he completely calmed down. He acted like nothing happened. What is that?" I asked.

"Declan has a bit of an anger management problem and the doctors think he is bipolar. Kind of like how they think you are schizophrenic," said Mrs. Weaver.

"Huh," I said, "is everyone here like me? Did their parents die or did they spend time in juvie like me?"

Mrs. Weaver shook her head and smiled, "I think those are questions to ask them. It might help you kids connect. You'd be surprised by how much you all have in common."

I shook my head and continued to help Mrs. Weaver dry the dishes. I always wondered why the Weavers took an interest in taking in kids who were insane or troublemakers. Out of all kids, why would those be the ones you let in your home?

"Mrs. Weaver"

"Yes?" she said.

"Why do you take in the troublemakers?" I asked.

"The troublemakers?" she laughed.

"Well yeah, you know, the ones who are strange or did something wrong. People like us," I asked.

For a moment, Mrs. Weaver's face grew sad and she set down the dish she was washing and gestured for me to sit down.

We both sat down at the table. "I grew up in a very strict place. Our parents were set in their ways. They were very traditional and wanted us to act accordingly. The men worked and the woman stayed home and cooked. I was thirteen and my older sister was sixteen. At the time, she was very into human rights. I remember her so well; she had this gorgeous long blonde hair and boys would swoon over her but of course she was above them. She had something abnormal about her that came with her beauty and that was this increasing sadness and the inability to see her beauty. Our parents didn't understand it and in fact told her to stop looking for attention. Anytime she had mood swings, our father would smack her and tell her to knock it off. They figured it was her just being a teenager but sometimes she wouldn't get out of bed. I tried my best to be around whenever she needed me, but she needed more. She needed her parents to understand that she wasn't okay, and she needed someone to help her get back on her feet. Elizabeth was her name. She loved these woods that was next to our house and eventually disappeared in them. When she went missing, I kept telling myself that she was happy living in the woods. That was until the police found her body in a lake. She jumped off a cliff."

My heart dropped and I watched Mrs. Weaver's tears fall slowly.

"Ever since then my goal was to help those who needed it but were too afraid to say it. It is the only thing I can do to make up for what happened to my dear Elizabeth. You kids aren't hopeless just like Elizabeth wasn't hopeless. You just need someone to care and help you."

I looked down at my lap and back up at her. The tears were forming around the wrinkles near her eyes.

"I'm sorry about your sister," I said.

"I'm sorry about your mom," she said.

I kept noticing people like her and Mrs. Jones would always apologize for my mom which made me feel relief that more people were getting the correct story. In this case, Mrs. Weaver could relate to the shitty father club. I wondered if she mainly blames him for Elizabeth's death like I blamed my father for my mom's. Our fathers were both murderers just in different ways.

After that, I headed upstairs to see Declan and Brady passed out in their beds. I was curious about their stories, but they were about the last people I wanted to ask.

Mrs. Weaver's story got me thinking; how come the most beautiful people in the world, inside and out, fall so far? Why are they the ones who are treated the worst? How come the good die young and the faithful are cheated? Is it possible, that perhaps there aren't any rewards for being a good person? Does this mean that the best people are the ones who have to go through obstacles to find peace? Do all the beautiful minds have to become warriors to survive the inevitable? The ones who have suffered the most are usually humble in the end because they found their peace in whatever form it came. Like how Mrs. Weaver and Mrs. Jones suffered but found peace in helping people. Perhaps being the best you can be, can only come with the price of a broken heart. However, in my opinion, the soul and mind of those who suffered will always be better than those who have suffered none.

Chapter 8
And I Was Free

It was Saturday but I woke up to silence. Everyone seemed to have left already with friends or work. Mr. Weaver worked in a factory and I think Mrs. Weaver just spent her time volunteering to various places. I got up and could feel the butterflies in my stomach. The feeling heated up my whole body. I couldn't wait to see Izzy again, but I was so nervous for it. I enjoyed the feeling because it was on a good note even though it made me feel sick. I got up and picked out a nice plaid shirt that buttoned up with a collar and my good pair of dark blue jeans.

I took my time in the shower and enjoyed the feeling of the water trickling down my entire body. I couldn't help but think about Izzy and relate the feeling of the shower to standing in front of her. Every time I saw her my heart heated and the heat would trickle down my body like the warm water did. I found myself breathing heavily just thinking about it. My feelings for her both excited and scared me. I wasn't sure how I should've felt but I was completely mesmerized by her. I finally got out of the shower and dried myself off with a towel.

I slipped on my clothes and realized the light blue shirt made my eyes stand out so much that it creeped me out. I mean my eyes looked bright green with this shirt, but I just went with it. I combed my hair but still allowed it to be messy, although it is not like I could help it much. I brushed my teeth and stared at my deformed reflection and wondered if she found me attractive or felt the same way about me as I did her. All I knew is how desperately I wanted her to.

I heard a knock on the door and rushed downstairs to open it. Mrs. Jones stood there with a big smile on her face. She wore this jean dress and curled her hair a bit.

"Hello Jess, you look nice," she said.

"Thanks, do you think she'll like it?" I asked.

Mrs. Jones laughed, "I'm sure she will."

I smiled and walked to her car with her. As I walked to her car, I heard a snap within the woods. I froze and looked around but all I saw was a faint sight of brown hair that disappeared amid the haunting trees. My stomach turned and I felt my heart skip a beat.

"Jess?" said Mrs. Jones.

I snapped out of my stare and answered "damn...bunnies" I quickly thought of an animal. Mrs. Jones started laughing and I just laughed with her. It started getting easy to act like nothing was wrong with me. On the inside my mind was still bad and all I wanted to do was scream and hope that it shuts my mind up. However, on the outside I looked like someone who was "cured." We got in the car and started to drive to Izzy's house. We remained silent until I had to tell her the directions.

Finally, we arrive at a white house. It had a white porch with flowerpots dangling and her front door was dark brown with a golden knocker on it. You could tell it was one story but still a very nice size. Izzy opened the door and walked down her sidewalk. She was in a little black dress that was slim fitted and showed every curve on her body. She had a jean jacket draped over it and her hair all pulled back in a ponytail. I was leaning against the car like I was in a movie while Mrs. Jones sat in her car with her window down.

"I think I just ruined my pants," I mumbled.

"Jessie!" Mrs. Jones scowled.

"Sorry," I jumped, not realizing she would hear it.

"Hey," Izzy said.

I stared for a little bit but I noticed her giving me an unsure look, so I quickly said "hi," but my voice went high which made my eyes widen.

She laughed and asked, "should we go?"

I nodded and opened the car door for her and got in myself. We were all in the car and again it was filled with silence. I sat right next to her in the back seat which made me wonder if I should have sat in the front with Mrs. Jones. I couldn't tell which would have been more awkward; leaving Izzy in the backseat by herself or making Mrs. Jones look like our cab driver.

Izzy breaks the silence by saying, "thank you for driving us."

"Oh no problem sweetie," said Mrs. Jones waving her hand.

Izzy looked at me and smiled. I started to get nervous and could feel my palms getting sweaty. I opened my mouth to say something, but I couldn't manage to say anything, so I kept quiet and quickly looked forward. We got to the restaurant and I tried to give myself a recovery by holding the car door open for her. I looked up at the grey sky, the clouds swirled around each other and it looked like a storm would come soon.

"Looks like it's going to rain," whispered Izzy.

I looked over and realized she was close to my face. I automatically looked at her cherry red lips and I could feel myself biting mine. I looked up at her eyes intensively, "yes it does," I said awkwardly and swallowed in a noticeable manner.

She just smiled and walked in and I followed her. Behind me I heard Mrs. Jones begin to chuckle and I looked back and glared at her.

"Win her over, Romeo," she whispered.

"Shut up," I answered rather loudly.

Izzy looked back at me confused "excuse me?"

My eyes got wide "Oh! No, her," I pointed to Mrs. Jones, "I wasn't talking about you. You're per...look seat," I stumbled.

"Um...Alright," she said giggling.

I desperately hoped she was finding this awkwardness cute and not creepy. We all slid in the booth. I sat by Izzy and Mrs. Jones sat across from us.

"This place is adorable," said Izzy.

"Thank you," I said. I don't know why I said thank you; it wasn't my restaurant.

"I agree Izzy. That's probably why Jess wanted to take you here." I could tell Mrs. Jones was trying to save me from embarrassment.

It gave me some courage to finally try to have a decent conversation. "Yeah, it is my favorite place in the world. So, I thought I'd share it with you," I said.

The East Haven Diner being my favorite place was decided right then because I've never had a favorite place. It made me feel at home. The waitresses wore button dresses with aprons and the waiters also had button downs. It had tile flooring and light wood walls. There were plain white tables and red cushion seats. The food took me back to the good times of my past when my mom used to cook me dinner. This was also the place I met Mrs. Jones, who was the first person in a long time to look at me and smile. She smiled instead of glared and was welcoming instead of darting away from me.

"I'm honored," said Izzy with a big smile on her face.

Mrs. Jones got up from her seat. "Excuse me, I am going to the restroom," she mumbled.

"Why is it your favorite place?" asked Izzy.

"It's where I met Mrs. Jones and it reminds me of my mom because their food reminds me of her cooking. It's a place my mom would've loved," I said, hesitantly.

"Wait, your real mom?"

I knew this would bring questions. "Yeah," I said.

"What happened to your mom?" Izzy asked curiously.

The scene quickly flashed through my mind and her faint cry filled my ears which made me noticeably flinch.

"Jess?"

"She was murdered," I answered.

"Oh, I'm sorry. I didn't mean to pry," said Izzy.

"It's okay. It's just hard still," I said.

"How old were you?"

"Six," I shortly answered.

I looked up to see the little girl walking out with her brown hair covering her face. She was looking down but when she looked up at me, I saw a tear running down her face. It made my heart pound and I felt uneasy when no one else noticed her.

"Jess?"

I looked over at Izzy and looked back but the girl was gone. I tried to cover up what just happened and looked back at Izzy.

"You look beautiful, Izzy," I said.

Izzy smiled. "Thank you."

"You're welcome."

The waitress came right as Mrs. Jones came in and I ordered breakfast and everyone else followed what I got. I couldn't help but notice a white man who was glaring at Mrs. Jones. Mrs. Jones looked straight at him but didn't seem bothered. She continued smiling at us. At the time, I didn't think much of it but later it made me realize something. I knew Mrs. Jones did not have an easy past but it didn't occur to me that she also had problems in the present. When you are so focused on your own problems, you are too blind to see other's problems. The fact that she didn't let it bother her proved how strong she was. I wasn't the only one who gets nasty stares. Although of course there was a reason behind the glares I got, I was convicted of murder, she simply just had different skin.

We all talked about school. We joked about the teachers and my eyes were fixed on Izzy most of the time. I felt in some way completely connected to her which I knew was also completely stupid. I tried to stay within the conversation and focus on talking to them, but my mind would stray to its abyss of confusion. It felt like a rollercoaster because for a second I would be smiling and the next my heart would ache. All I could do was hang onto this little happiness I had. These two people were it; it wasn't a lot, but it was enough.

When Mrs. Jones dropped us off, she gave me some time to walk Izzy up to her door.

"Hey Jess," said Izzy.

"Yeah."

"You weren't there when…" she asked.

"Yeah," I answered before she could finish her sentence.

"I'm so sorry," she murmured.

I shook my head, "not your fault."

"And your dad?"

"Dead," I blurted out, coldly.

"Murdered too?" she asked.

I swallowed hard, "again with the questions."

"I'm just interested to know about you," she answered.

I stopped walking and turned to her.

"Tell me about your parents then."

"They are divorced, and I live with my mom. We get along well, I mean, she is like my best friend. My dad, however, wants nothing to do with us," she answered.

"I'm sorry," I said, looking down.

"Don't be," she smiled, "I'm not. I don't need him."

That made me smile a bit.

I felt a sprinkle hit my cheek and looked up to see the darker sky. When I looked back at her I realized she was much closer to me again and I jumped a little.

"Sorry…no not sorry… I just," she whispered.

She pressed her lips to mine and it felt like an electric shock ran through my body except this one wasn't painful. She released and looked at me with a smile. I looked at her in shock, but I knew I wanted more of that feeling so I slowly walked closer to her and gently grabbed her face and pressed my lips against her firmly. Izzy threw her arms around my neck, so our bodies were pressed up against each other. We parted our lips and kissed slowly. The rain started to fall gently occasionally touching our faces. I ran my fingers through her hair as she did the same with one hand on my shoulder. The feeling of kissing her was a certain sensation that I couldn't explain. It felt like I was addicted to her and have been deprived of her. My heart was beating quickly, and I was warm. For the moment, I forgot about all the bad things in my life and my mind didn't wander. The visions stayed away from this moment and nothing was ruined by horrid thoughts; I was free.

Chapter 9
"You Killed Me"

Prison 2012

I lie here in the padded room with my face covered in blood and there is a huge weight on my chest. I look down at my straight jacket and try to situate myself to a more comfortable position. My body aches as my limbs lie on the hard floor. I try to scooch myself up on to the wall and prop myself up. You would think I would get used to the hard floors and the feeling of being trapped in a magician's box.

I look over to see a little girl hovered in the corner of the padded room. Her brown singed hair is lying in front of her face and her white dress is torn. The little girl is hiding her face, sobbing into her arms with her knees pulled up to her chest. Her presence gives me an uneasy feeling.

"Hello?" I say, my voice croaking.

"Why?" she answers.

"Why what? Are you okay?" I ask her.

"What did I ever do to you?" she wails with a shaky voice.

"What do you mean?"

"Mommy's crying. I try to tell her it's okay, but she can't hear me or see me," she sobs.

Her voice has an echo to it that rings throughout the room.

"What are you talking about, sweetie?"

"I miss my mommy. I miss my life and I can't have it because of you," she mumbles.

"Because of me?"

The little girl looks up at me and I notice her face is all burned. All the little girl's young skin is practically gone. Patches of pink and brown travel from her face to her neck. She looks at me with such empty green eyes.

"You killed me," she whispers.

She starts coughing up blood and it spurts all over her. Deep red starts to cover the padded walls with a splash.

"Somebody help!" I cry, trying to get out of my straight jacket.

She falls to the ground, limp and pale. All the life looks like it has been brutally sucked out of her. The guards open the door and start dragging me out.

"No! Help her!" I shriek.

"No one is in there, you fucking idiot," they laugh.

"Yes, there is!"

I look at the girl lying there in a pool full of thick, red blood.

"I'm sorry! I didn't mean to! I'm so sorry!" I continue to yell and cry out as the guards drag me to my cell.

The guards toss me in my cell and my body slams onto the ground. A guard comes at me violently taking off the straight jacket.

"The little girl," I groan, my voice all raspy.

"You're done, Reids," whispers the guard.

I look up at him confused and I see a blur of him drawing his fist back and punching me in the face. The pain stings and I swear one of these days they are going to blind me. I lie there on the cold hard floor as the guards file out and close the gate behind them. I don't want to move so I just lie there looking at the ceiling. The blur of it creates a void circling around and making me dizzy. I start thinking to myself:

Is it possible to die while you are still alive? Like the world moves but you remain standing still. You move and talk but you don't feel yourself moving or talking. You are numb to your actions and feel like your mind is somewhere else. Is it possible? That your body is something completely different from your soul and your soul can die while your body is still moving.

All my life, I have felt like I was never really there or that someone else was controlling me. It made it hard for me to understand consequences. It makes me wonder if your soul can be revived or will you remain soulless until your body catches up with death and meets your soul in the afterlife?

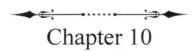

Chapter 10
"You are the one with the blood on your hands."

When I got home, I was soaked but I didn't care because I was so happy. I haven't felt like this in a long time.

"You look happy," exclaimed Mrs. Weaver.

"Did you get laid?" sneered Declan.

"Declan!" yelled AnnMarie and Mrs. Weaver.

"No, but did you?" said Adeline, intrigued.

"No," I answered.

"So, you are still a virgin?" Adeline said with a grin.

Declan laughed and coughed out the word "loser."

"Manners," snapped Mr. Weaver sternly.

I just glared at them. I wanted to start lashing out on them, but I refrained myself.

"Lunch time," said Mrs. Weaver.

"Not hungry but thanks," I murmured, walking away.

Adeline shoved her way in between me and the steps.

"Who is she?" she asked.

"None of your business," I grumbled.

"I could give you better. You know for your first," she said looking me up and down.

"I highly doubt that," I objected, trying to shove past her.

She puts her arm on the ledge to stop me.

"Just ask the people I've been with. I'm experienced," she said proudly.

Adeline started walking away and I started up the stairs mumbling to myself, "you probably got a shit ton of STDs too." Adeline turned around with a disgusted look on her face.

"Fuck you Jess!" she screamed.

"Fuck you too!" I yelled back.

I went into the bathroom and slammed the door behind me. I violently tore my shirt off and the rest of my clothes and threw them against the ground. I turned the shower on hot and stepped in. I let the water fall on me as it trickled down my body. I automatically thought of Izzy and that kiss. I wished I could feel like that for the rest of my life. I tilt my head back and let the water fall on my face. My breathing slowed down, and I started to feel my muscles relax. I thought of Izzy's smile which made me smile.

After my second shower of the day, I wrapped myself up in a towel and shook my head, throwing the water droplets everywhere. I looked at my reflection and my hairs were sticking out everywhere. I looked towards the doorway to see a little girl standing there. I jump causing me to knock over the products on the counter. I quickly looked back through the mirror to see she was no longer there. My breath released and I held my chest. My hands covered my face and I screamed in frustration.

I wanted to know who this little girl was and why I kept seeing her. I slowly sunk down, so, I was sitting on the ground and leaning against the cabinet under the sink. I sat there for a little bit with my face in my hands and breathing so heavily it made my chest ache. The sound of someone banging on the bathroom door makes me jump.

"Some people need to use the restroom too, asshole!" yelled Declan.

I got up, grabbed my stuff and walked out the door to see Declan standing right there with his arms crossed. I just slid past him without saying a word. I got in our room and saw Brady sitting on the floor, drawing something in a book.

"Hey buddy, I got to get dressed," I murmured, "do you mind stepping out for a second?"

He just looked at me with a blank face and slammed his book closed and walked out of the room.

"Thank you!" I yelled after him.

I put on a white t-shirt and some sweatpants and opened the door to let Brady know he could come back in. Brady walked back in and sat right in the same place. I sat by him on the ground.

"What are you drawing?" I asked.

He looked at me and just held up his book. A chill went down my spine. They looked like the shadows I see sometimes. Three shadows hovered over a stick figure who I was guessing was him. The sketching was amazing with dark alien-like circled heads and extreme shading.

"Where'd you come up with that?" I asked.

Brady just shrugged.

Declan stormed into our room with a towel wrapped around his waist.

"I'm going to kill you," he snarled.

I quickly got up and ran, "bye Brady!" I exclaimed.

I could hear a chuckle come from Brady with a "you took all the hot water!" scream from Declan.

I ran downstairs and decided to get out of there.

"Jess!" yelled Mrs. Weaver.

I kept running until I got into the woods. Luckily, it stopped raining, but the floor was muddy. It was pitch black in there. I wanted to know if I would see the little girl again. I thought maybe I had to look for her instead of her finding me. I stumbled through the woods as my mind kept spinning and things started getting worse. The woods would've been beautiful if I weren't so afraid of them. The trees looked as if they were hovering over me and staring at me. From the corner of my eye, I kept seeing dark shadows creep through the trees, which started terrifying me so much I had tears in my eyes. A ball was forming in my throat and I knew it was a bad idea to be in here. Every time I saw a shadow, I would try to dodge away but they wouldn't leave me alone. The little girl passed through my twisted mind to the point where I was so gone from myself. I dropped to the cold, wet ground. I began to scrape the mud up and slam it against my face as if it would wake me up. I pushed my fists into the ground, creating deep imprints and I screamed to drown out the sound of a young girl crying. I covered my ears with my muddy hands and screamed on the top of my lungs. Tears began to involuntarily fall from my face as my throat burned from the screech. I lay there on the muddy ground and closed my eyes, but the torture didn't stop there.

I opened my eyes to a pitch-black room. It was strange because the walls and floor were pitch black. It looked like a dream, but I couldn't remember falling asleep. The woods were gone. Amidst the darkness, Izzy stands there with tears falling down her face. She was in the little black dress I last saw her in. All I could hear were whispers and they were filling her ears. They whispered words of hatred but not about her; the whispers were about me. The shadows were telling her my dirty secrets and there was nothing I could yell out to drown their haunting whispers. Izzy's face grew sadder and more broken. She looked at me with such pain and grabs her heart. Her gaze started focusing on something behind me and I looked back to see a little boy who was crying and looking at me. He was in a similar tux I wore to my court hearing with his green eyes standing out. Izzy dropped to the floor in screaming pain.

"Stop! You're hurting her!" I screeched to the shadows.

"No daddy, you are," murmured the boy.

"What?" I whispered.

The boy disappeared from the room and I looked at Izzy who was no longer moving.

"Izzy!" I screamed.

I ran towards her and dropped down beside her. I shook her but she didn't wake up. She lays there with shut eyes and red, thick blood coming out of her mouth.

"Psycho!" I heard her yell in the distance.

I looked around to see Izzy again standing before me and I looked down at her dead body and back at Izzy. There were two of them.

"Izzy, I can explain," I said.

I held my hand out to her and realized there was blood on my hands. I stared at my hand as my vision started to shake like there was an earthquake forming.

"What's there to explain? I'm dead because of you!" she yelled pointing at herself, dead on the floor.

"No Izzy, the shadows killed you," I stammered.

"Then how come you're the one with the blood on your hands?" shrieked Izzy.

I looked at the blood on my hands; they were covered with it.

"No!" I yelled.

I looked up to see Izzy was gone. I stood up to see pools of blood on the floor and no body. The blood was so thick, and it was up to my ankles. I yelled out in agony and dropped to the floor, causing the blood to splash all over me. It was warm and wet as it clung to my skin. The smell was an awful metallic scent. I wanted to either puke or die.

I woke up in the woods to a man's voice. I saw the glowing of a flashlight and looked up at the part of his face being illuminated by the light.

"Where's Izzy?" I whispered.

"Where you should be. In your own bed," said Mr. Weaver.

"Declan will beat my ass," I mumbled.

"So, you decided to roll around in the mud as an ultimatum?" Mr. Weaver chuckled.

I looked around to see that I was laying in the mud and was covered in it. It literally looked like I decided to roll around in mud in the middle of the woods.

"It seemed good at the time," I tried to fake a smile.

"I'll deal with Declan, now come on back. You've got the wife all worried." Mr. Weaver held out his hand.

I let him help me up and walked with him. I couldn't help but look back but this time there was nothing there. It just looked like woods. The weirdest part was there may have not been something there, but I could still feel something there. The cold air of the shadow lingered near my neck making me want to try and shake it off me.

We finally get back to the house and I quietly go upstairs. I hoped Declan wouldn't be waiting for me and luckily, he was passed out on his pull-out bed. I creped in and grabbed a t-shirt and sweats to change into. I was off to take my third shower of the day. I stepped in still shaking from the images remaining in my head. The feeling of the blood still lingered on my skin and I couldn't help but let the tears fall. I let my head fall back and allowed the water to fall directly on my face but an instant feeling like it was acid stung my face. I backed out of the line of the stream and looked back at the water. The faucet just continued spewing out water and I held my hand out to feel it. It went back to normal at first, but it started to turn red. I was breathing heavily and just shook my head. I decided not to trust what I was seeing and just let myself bathe in the blood as fast as I could. My eyes became sore with how tightly I was squeezing them, not daring to open my eyes.

When I got out, I was washed off and there was no blood in sight. I wrapped myself up with a towel and sat on the toilet seat for a second. I couldn't understand what was happening to me. I know I have never been normal, but everything was happening so frequent, it made me wonder if something was triggering it.

I got out of the bathroom and silently lay in bed trying to clear my mind so I could have at least the slightest chance of getting some sleep tonight. I closed my eyes but never fell asleep. My body was still shaking, and I tried to ease my mind by thinking about Izzy. Unfortunately, that led to me thinking of her laying there dead with her blood on my hands. I felt like the little girl was a sign of some sort.

The fact that the dream of Izzy dead might be a sign made my stomach turn. I wanted to scream to let out my frustration, but I held it in which added to the difficulty of falling asleep. I wondered if maybe the shadows were telling me to stay away from Izzy. I felt like it would be impossible for me to even try to stay away from Izzy because something was drawing me to her constantly.

Chapter 11
The Weaver Misfits

I opened my eyes to see Declan standing beside my bed with his arms crossed.

"Can I help you?" I asked.

He just stared up at my bunk, grunted and walked away.

"Nice talk," I whispered.

I slowly got up with a little bit of a headache and headed downstairs. It was Sunday and I wasn't sure what to do with the rest of the day. I came downstairs to see Mrs. Weaver making breakfast. Brady and AnnMarie were sitting next to each other playing some sort of card game. I sat down beside them on the floor. I decided to take Mrs. Weaver's advice and ask them about their past. Might as well embrace the fact that I am stuck in this foster family.

"What are you guys playing?" I asked.

"War," answered AnnMarie.

"Huh," I took a long pause, thinking of what I was going to say next, "So, you two kind of know my story, right? Like how I got here, my past and all of that."

AnnMarie started counting on her fingers while saying "you killed your dad, ended up in jail, got diagnosed with schizophrenia, got out of jail and now you are here living like a normal boy."

I paused. "Well then. I think you summed up my life pretty well," I said, "what are your stories?"

I found out that AnnMarie and Brady are twins who grew up in a foster home. They explained, or really AnnMarie explained that they were born from a young lady who had kids at 16 and their father had run out. The two never got to meet their parents and were stuffed into a foster home that had many children. The foster parents didn't pay much attention to the children and many roamed free. Brady got picked on for his strange and quiet demeanor and AnnMarie would be the one to stand up for him. One day, the foster children were gaining up on Brady after he started screaming that the "monsters were coming" and AnnMarie started to defend him. The entire time she lived there her interest in the fireplace was mesmerizing, she explained, it was as if the fireplace was taunting her. So, AnnMarie decided to use it to defend Brady. She grabbed a log and started swinging it at the foster children, burning several of them. The ambulance was called and many of the children got third-degree burns. Automatically, the foster care agency called the Weavers and they agreed to take the two twins in. The two were new and have only been there a year.

"Wow, burning children huh?" I scoffed.

"Burning things is my specialty but I won't do it to the Weavers because I like them."

"Thank you AnnMarie, we like you too," smiled Mrs. Weaver.

AnnMarie did a little dance and drew out her card which ended up winning the game somehow. I am guessing because it was the higher number. Brady just rolled his eyes and gave her his cards.

"So, what's everyone else's story?" I asked.

It turns out AnnMarie knew just about everything about everybody…

Declan's strange temper was discovered at his old school at about 11-years-old. It was during recess when kids are supposed to be playing tag while all the lunch monitors watch them. Well, there was this kid who punched Declan's so-called girlfriend which at 11 that meant holding hands occasionally at lunchtime. Anyways, Declan's anger arose and punched the kid in the face, as he should, but it didn't stop there. Declan beat the kid so bad he ended up in the hospital and was in a coma for weeks. Declan lived with his father because his mother left them when he was young. Declan got called into court and got out of going to juvie if he went to a mental hospital. He was in the mental hospital for 2 years and once he got out his father moved away without telling him, therefore, he was moved to a foster home at age 13. Of course, Declan didn't get along with any of the kids or adults and it didn't help that his foster parents were incredibly racist. The Weavers found out about him after witnessing Declan being treated ten times worse than the rest of the foster kids at a restaurant. They offered to take him in, and his foster family seemed all too happy to get rid of him.

Adeline lived in a small town and was known throughout it and not in a good way. She was 14 at the time and had many suitors already at a young age. She called herself the *Lolita* of the town but some of those suitors had families and wives at home. The word spread out and instead of accusing the older men of screwing a 14-year-old, she was accused of promiscuity. Her parents disowned her calling her every word in the book and saying she should wear an "A" on her clothes as if they were trying to sound smart by quoting *The Scarlet Letter*. Adeline ran away with a small duffel bag that had rainbows and unicorns on it. She stole cash from her wealthy father to take a cab after hearing the story of Declan, a mental patient, who was taken in by a couple who were dedicated to helping 'troubled youth.' Mrs. Weaver opened the door to see a sad girl in a pink dress on her porch, asking for a home. Immediately Mrs. Weaver let in the girl to have a cup of tea and became her foster parent which wasn't hard considering her parents didn't care. In fact, when the parents met the Weavers, they told her "good luck with the harlot," I seriously think they thought they were from a different time-period.

"And that is the story of the Weaver misfits," said AnnMarie proudly.

I laughed and it got Brady to at least half-smile.

"Glad to be a part of it," I smiled.

Although my story may be a bit different, it made me feel a bit more comfortable that I wasn't the only fuck up in the house. I was not the only one who had a shitty parent. Instead, I was just joining the band of misfits. Perhaps, being with the Weavers wasn't as bad as I thought.

As AnnMarie was telling me the Weavers' stories, I noticed I was missing something that seemed like a big deal. Mrs. Weaver was on the phone looking distraught. She signaled for Adeline when Adeline came downstairs. Brady and AnnMarie started another game and I almost didn't realize AnnMarie was asking me if I wanted to play.

"No, I'm okay, thanks," I mumbled.

I stared at what was forming in front of me. Mrs. Weaver was telling Adeline something that was causing her to get upset. Declan came downstairs and witnessed it to. I wanted to ease drop, but I was sitting in the living room while they were in the kitchen. Adeline started to explain to Declan what they were so worried about and it caused Declan's anger to rise. He backed away from them and ran upstairs with rage. Brady's eyes got big and followed Declan upstairs. I decided I wasn't staying out of it anymore and followed Brady upstairs.

Upstairs I heard Declan stomping around and tossing things left and right. His whole body was tensed up that made his muscles look twice as big. The look of him was intimidating and it made me want to turn around and mind my own business.

"What the hell is going on?" I said, hesitantly.

Declan paused and muttered, "Nothing."

From downstairs, I could hear Adeline crying. Declan started kicking around the boxes with frustration.

"Brady! Where the hell is my bat?" Declan shouted.

"How am I supposed to know?" Brady said quietly.

I just smiled at Brady and continued with "Declan, why do you need a bat?"

Declan found the bat he was looking for and patted it against his hand. "There you are."

I looked at him wide eyed. He looked completely pissed and slightly in love with his bat.

"What happened?" I repeated.

"She got expelled," Declan finally said.

"Why the hell would they expel her?" I asked.

"That English teacher," Declan said through his teeth, "they found out they were sleeping together and instead of firing the kid fucker, guess who is being expelled?"

"What!" I yelled.

"Exactly Reids. Which is where this bat comes in," Declan grinned. He started to head downstairs.

"Wait, Declan," I said, "are you just going to show up at his door and start swinging?"

"Nope, the school. He hangs out there Sundays to get his papers graded which is sometimes when he would meet with Adeline," he said as he almost missed a step.

Adeline was standing at the end of the stairs with tears in her eyes. I don't know why I was surprised she cried, everyone cries, she just seemed like someone who wouldn't.

"Declan, what are you doing?" she whined.

"Declan, no," I said.

I snatched the bat out of his hands and immediately regretted it after I saw his facial reaction to it. Let's just say if the bat was still in his hand; it might've cracked my skull.

"Since when are you against a bashing?" Declan snapped.

"I'm not but if you are going to do this, you should be smarter about it," I said.

"Or not do it all," said Mrs. Weaver, shrugging.

Declan and I both looked at her with confused expressions.

"Just don't kill him," said Mr. Weaver who must have been in his shop.

"Mark!" Mrs. Weaver exclaimed.

"What?" he shrugged.

Declan looked back at me and crossed his arms, "Fine. What's your plan?"

We decided we are just going to scare the shit out of the teacher and possibly try to get Adeline back in school. We borrowed a car from Mr. Weaver who I was surprised let us and drove to the store. I waited in the car while Declan got "supplies." I wasn't sure what all he was going to get. We figured it would be better if he went in considering my criminal record. I could imagine the look of the cashier as a former convict is buying shit like rope and duct tape at his store.

He got back in the car with a couple of bags and a cigarette in his mouth.

"Did you get snacks?" I asked.

He looked at me confused. "What?" he muttered under his cigarette.

"In case we get hungry," I shrugged.

Declan looked at me unamused, "I don't get you."

"Not much to get," I mumbled.

Declan nodded and I started driving towards the school. We still haven't found a connection, so it was hard to have a conversation. I kept looking over to see Declan cutting into fabric and creating something.

When we finally got to the school, Declan handed me a ski mask that had poorly cut out eye sockets.

"What the hell is this?" I asked.

"A mask, what does it look like," Declan snapped as he stomped on his cigarette.

Declan put on his which looked properly cut.

"Why is yours better?" I whispered.

Declan just looked at me, I couldn't see his face but I'm sure it wasn't a nice expression.

I realized I have never been in the school when it wasn't in session. Something about the dark halls made it extra apparent that we shouldn't be there. Baxter's door was ajar which made it easy to open. Declan slowly opened the door and we walked in to see a shocked English teacher. He was sitting at his desk with a couple of papers.

"Which girls got A's?" Declan asked.

"Who the hell are you?" Mr. Baxter asked.

Declan sat on one of the desks and I locked the door behind me and sat with him. It looked like we had no clue what we were doing. The scene looked like a bad soap opera.

"Is it worth it? Screwing your students?" Declan asked.

"And ruining their lives when you stand just fine?" I added.

Mr. Baxter looked shocked, but he also seemed like he understood what we were talking about.

"Look, she came on to me, okay? What was I supposed to do?" Mr. Baxter gritted.

Declan snapped, shot up and slammed the bat right over his head so it hit the chalkboard behind him.

"You don't sleep with your student, that's what!" Declan yelled.

I got in his face, "you think you are so clever. You think you got away with everything, but you didn't."

After I said that, Declan knocked him out with the end of the bat. Mr. Baxter lays limp on his desk with the papers sticking to his face.

"Let's go," I said.

Declan threw the teacher over his shoulders.

"Double check if the coast is clear," Declan said.

I looked out of the door and into the dark hallway to see a dark silhouette at the end.

"Hold on," I said and walked down the hallway.

It was just standing there in the middle of the hallway. It was small like a young child, but the hallway was too dark to tell who it was. I went to walk closer but stopped when I heard Declan say, "Are we good or not?"

The figure ran off at the sound of his voice. My heart was beating fast and I had a feeling I knew it was the young girl. Who knew she could look even creepier than usual?

"Come on out," I said.

Declan walked in the hall and motioned for me to walk out with him. We threw him in the trunk and drove off into the woods. Everything knocked around as the car drove into the woods but luckily the pathway was just big enough. It would've sucked for Declan to carry the English teacher that long. I grabbed the rope while Declan grabbed Mr. Baxter and put him near the tree. I wrapped the robe around the teacher to keep him trapped against the tree. Declan took out a bottle of vodka and put it under Mr. Baxter's nose to wake him up.

Mr. Baxter jerked awake and in panic, "what did you kids do? Where am I?"

"Kids," I laughed, "now we are kids."

"You didn't think Adeline was a kid? Or is that something you like?" Declan asked as he took off his mask.

I took off my mask as well. There was something about him knowing who we were that made it exciting. It felt like justice was served even more.

"Adeline is a whore. She was a whore before me! The girl lost her virginity at what 12?" Mr. Baxter yelled.

"14," Declan and I said at the same time.

"Exactly," Mr. Baxter said.

Anger arose in me and I couldn't feel restraint. I punched him in the face and kicked him in the gut. I looked up to see two shadow figures lingering. One on each side of the tree. I looked up at them with raging eyes.

"Fuck you, Jessie. I was nice to you because I figured everyone would hate your guts. But you are so twisted; there is no hope for you," Mr. Baxter laughed, "you might as well do the world a favor and jump off a bridge!"

I took out a knife and went to stab him, but Declan's hand stopped me.

"Jess," he yelled.

I froze and realized I didn't feel like I was in my body all of a sudden. My breathing was uncontrollable. Declan calmly took the knife out of my hand and put it in his back pocket. He continued with our plans as I sat there frozen on my knees.

"Listen up Baxter," he said as he poured vodka on him, "you are going to leave East Haven High but before you do, you are going to make sure that Adeline can come back to school."

"Why would I do that?" Mr. Baxter said after he spit some blood.

"Well, I have this problem," Declan said as he dug into his pockets, "I have a nicotine addiction and I can't seem to break it. So, I need to carry a lighter with me 24/7."

Declan lit the lighter close to Mr. Baxter. His breathing got heavy as he stared at the flame. Mr. Baxter looked from the flame to Declan.

"You won't do it," he laughed, "you just stopped the psycho from stabbing me."

Declan smirked, "only because I wanted a change for Adeline first but don't think I won't set your ass on fire. Perhaps Reids will be nice enough to end your suffering quicker with his knife."

I looked at Mr. Baxter with pure hatred and his face changed to terror. My whole body was shaking but I knew I needed to keep this façade of seeming threatening.

"Declan," Mr. Baxter said.

That just made Declan put the lighter closer to the vodka.

"Okay deal! Deal!" Mr. Baxter screeched.

Declan looked at me and smiled.

"Excellent. It's settled then," he said.

He got up and motioned me to follow and I gathered the rest of my stuff.

"Wait, are you going to untie me?" Mr. Baxter said.

"Get yourself out!" Declan yelled.

We got in the truck and Declan drove because I think he could tell I was still in shock. I looked in the rearview mirrors to see Mr. Baxter trying to grab his cellphone out of his pocket. The shadows were still hovering over him. Apart of me wondered if they were getting ready to finish him off.

"What the fuck was that?" Declan grumbled, breaking my concentration.

"I was just threatening him," I muttered.

"No, you weren't. You were ready to kill him. Our deal was to threaten him, not leave a dead body in the middle of the woods," Declan said angrily.

"I don't know what happened. What he was saying about me jumping off a bridge," I stuttered.

"People have been saying that shit our entire life. Are you really going to murder everyone who does?" Declan said, "I may be twisted but I'm not a murderer, Jess."

"I know. I'm sorry," I said.

Declan shook his head, but his face grew soft. Something I haven't seen his face do. It changed from anger to sadness.

"I just think you are letting them get to you, man," Declan

continued, "I know I'm not a good example of self-control, but we can't become the monsters they say we are."

"Don't you get tired of trying to prove that you aren't?" I asked.

"Oh, hell yeah but If I give in; they win and I'm a sore loser," Declan smirked.

I scoffed. Declan was right but a part of me was still wanting to give up on being a decent person. Perhaps that just meant Declan was a better person than I was. It is funny, who we see as a villain sometimes is a better person than we are deep down.

We pulled up to the Weaver's house. Mr. Weaver was waiting on the porch with his arms crossed.

"You didn't go too far did you?" he asked us.

Declan and I looked at each other but Declan answered, "no we didn't. Adeline should be back in school soon."

Mr. Weaver just nodded, and we walked inside. Everyone was eating in silence. They all knew we were scaring the shit out of a teacher. You could tell it made them uneasy but at the same time silently okay with it. Besides AnnMarie...

"Did he pee his pants?" she asked.

Declan laughed, "yeah, your fire idea was a good one."

Adeline looked up at both of us, "thank you."

"You're welcome," we both answered.

Declan sat down to eat but I felt too shaken up to eat.

"I'm going upstairs," I said.

"Okay, Jess" said Mrs. Weaver.

I walked up slowly upstairs. I tried to run the moment through my head and figure out when I got fuzzy. Declan, someone who was clinically diagnosed with an anger issue had more control than I did. I thought of how fast I grabbed that knife and went for his body. The fact that if Declan didn't stop me, who knows how many times I would've stabbed him. My stomach grew upset and I could feel a build-up in my stomach until I finally blew chunks into the toilet upstairs.

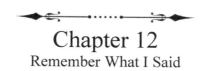

Chapter 12
Remember What I Said

I got up completely tired but this time I couldn't wait till school. I got in the shower and quickly got dressed in some cuffed jeans and a black shirt. I went downstairs with my sneakers in my hand. Everyone was eating breakfast and I quietly sat down to join them. The whole time I was eating the oatmeal they made, Declan was staring at me and Adeline was grinning. The other two kids just silently ate while occasionally glancing at me. The whole weirdness of the dinner gave me an uneasy feeling. It was like all the kids have just planned to kill me the day before and were scoping out their victim. Declan and I haven't talked since the moment with the teacher. I think we were both still processing it. I am sure it just gave Declan another reason not to trust me and I don't blame him.

Finally, it was time to get to the bus and we all got up and headed for the driveway. I glanced at the woods but tried to shake them out of my mind. I sat in my seat silently as the bus took us to school. Part of me wondered if Izzy would even be at school based on the whole vision I had in the woods. As I thought about her lying there dead and the blood on my hands; I started to feel anxious. I wanted to see her as soon as I could for some reassurance.

Once the bus stopped at the school I rushed off and ran towards her locker. I panicked a bit when I didn't see her there, but I heard a "BOO."

I looked behind me and saw her standing there smiling with another little black dress on. This one flared out at the end and she had on this soft looking blue sweater over it. Her hair was in a bun with strands falling out, I have never seen that hairstyle on her, but it looked cute. I let out a big sigh of relief and quickly hugged her.

"Oh hello," she said.

I stepped back after I gave her a long hug.

"Hi," I said.

"You okay?" she asked.

"Yeah, I am now," I stammered very awkwardly.

Izzy gave a big smile.

I realized again I was staring at her like I was mesmerized. I quickly snapped out of it, so I didn't freak her out.

"I like your dress," I managed to say.

"Thank you. It's one of my favorites," she said while nodding.

"Mine too," I said, realized what I said and revealed a confused facial expression.

Izzy laughed which was comforting. At least she got a kick out of my awkwardness around her. It would be embarrassing if she didn't. When it was time for English Izzy met me at my locker. I was wondering if Mr. Baxter left right away. I'm sure he did since Adeline was able to go to school today.

"Shall we learn about educational books?" I asked.

She laughed, "yes we shall."

We both walked into English together and I forgot her assigned seat was right next to Kyle. I clenched my jaw at the thought and Izzy noticed.

"It's okay, I will be fine," she told me.

I just nodded and pulled off a smile.

She sat by Kyle and I sat behind them. Again, I wanted to just rip his head off but instead I remained glued to my seat. There was a student teacher today. A woman with circle glasses and short hair. She signed the chalkboard Mrs. Bennett. She explained her reasoning for being there was that Mr. Baxter transferred schools due to a "better opportunity" and they are working on replacing him. I wondered how many people knew that it was because he screwed a student. As long as no one knows how he got fired.

During the class Kyle slipped a note to Izzy but she just passed it back to him without reading it which made me smile. I was curious to know what it said. Kyle tried passing it again which made Izzy upset so she crumbled it up and threw it on the floor. Luckily, the paper rolled over to me which made Kyle's muscles tense up. I picked up the note and started to unravel it. Izzy looked back at me and watched me open it. It took a lot in me to not change my expression once I read...

"Stay away from Jess. He's a psycho. He murdered his parents." Short and to the point.

I violently crumbled up the paper and put it in my pocket which made Kyle jump a bit. I locked eyes with Izzy, shrugged my shoulders and acted like it was nothing important. Class went on and my mind was thinking of different ways I could confront Kyle to make it so he didn't try to tell Izzy anything.

After class, I brushed past Izzy who didn't say anything. I knew exactly where Kyle would be and I knew I had to confront him and make sure he kept his mouth shut. It was already a shocker that Izzy wasn't caught up in the news of my jail time and I wanted to keep it that way. I will admit Kyle and I had something in common; we both fell under bad habits which made it easy to approach him during his smoke break. It was always just before lunch.

"Kyle," I said in a firm enough voice to make his friends disperse. It was kind of comical the way they quickly staggered at the sound of conflict. Leaving Kyle to fend for himself.

"What's up Jess?" Kyle said calmly while he crushed his cigarette under his foot.

"You know exactly what's up." I went closer to him.

"Look, I just figured Izzy had a right to know who she is getting involved with," Kyle put up his hands as if he were being held at gunpoint.

"You don't get to make that choice," I tried to maintain my anger.

"Then who does? You? How am I supposed to sit back and trust you with her? Who's going to take care of her?" Kyle started pointing towards the school.

"She doesn't need to be taken care of and if you took the time to get to know her you would know that," I got in his face. Up close Kyle's eyes had this mixture of blue and green. His pupils showed he was in shock and yet his eyes never wavered. Like he was fighting himself to not look afraid.

"Right, like you know her? You are probably waiting for the right time to murder her like you did your parents," Kyle said in a cold tone.

Before I could mindfully respond; my hand was already around his neck and my other hand covered his mouth. At this point, I could have easily taken the hand that covered his mouth and snapped his neck. It was agonizing how much I wanted to because a big part of me felt like someone was telling me to. It was like my brain had its own voice telling me to kill him. Kyle's feet were trying to keep him standing up as I held him up against the side of the building. He kept struggling and trying to use his hands to free himself from my grip, but I wasn't letting go. I swallowed hard and looked at him wide eyed as his eyes began to droop.

"Stay away," I muttered.

It took a lot of power in me to let him go but I did. My eyes were beginning to blur as tears were forming in my eyes. The tears were hot like I rubbed my eyes while eating something with hot sauce. Kyle dropped to the ground and desperately gasped for air. Kyle's body dragged before him as he crawled away. The sound of his struggle gave me both pleasure and pain. I wanted to start crying at the confliction.

I started to walk away when Kyle choked out.

"Where's our English teacher, Jess?"

"How the hell am I supposed to know," I grumbled and walked back into the school.

I felt completely drained and tired. I started to believe the words and that a psycho killer is inside me; dying to come out. First the teacher and now Kyle. How could I get that close to killing two people within two days? I knew my father's death had a big reason behind it. I would have been killed, and he killed my mother. Sure, there was a decent reason behind wanting to kill Mr. Baxter but it still wasn't something I should be able to do easily. Kyle? Killing Kyle for loving the same girl as me and wanting to protect her? I knew it was ridiculous.

"There you are!" I heard Izzy say.

My heart dropped and I turned around to see her bright smile which made me feel a lot better.

"Sorry, I was in the restroom," I said.

"That's okay, ready for lunch?" Izzy asked.

I nodded and held her hand as we walked in the lunchroom. Once we got our food, we sat together at a separate lunch table and for a while we ate quietly until Izzy broke the silence once she saw Kyle walk in. His eyes were a little red and his neck still had redness to it but not enough to draw attention.

"What did it say?" she asked.

"What did what say?" I asked after giving Kyle a glare.

"The note," Izzy added.

"Oh. That you're beautiful," I quickly made up.

"Oh, well you know it is over right?"

"Yes of course," I smiled.

Izzy smiled back and continued to eat her food.

During my last class, all I could think about was the incident with Kyle. I hated to admit it but something he said stuck. Izzy should know who she is associating with but at the same time I didn't want her to ever know. Kyle was right by saying Izzy deserved to know the truth, but I knew that when she found out, she would be gone. I was being completely selfish. After school, I went straight to my locker where Izzy was waiting.

"Hey Izzy," I said a little more down that I planned.

"What's wrong?" Izzy cocked her head.

"Nothing," I responded quickly, "I'm just tired."

"Too tired to hang out?" she asked.

"Never too tired for that."

Izzy smiled and grabbed my hand. She dragged me outside of the school and over to her car. I was almost tripping over myself, trying to maintain my balance as she walked quickly.

"Get in!" she said.

I went over to the passenger side and got in. Once I did, I glanced at the review mirror to see the little girl's reflection with her hair in her face. I jumped and hit my knee on the dashboard which made me hiss a bit.

"Jess, are you okay?" asked Izzy as she got in the car.

My heart was racing and all I could manage was a nod. I looked in the rearview mirror to see the girl was gone.

"A bug went by the windshield," I said.

"Jess, the window is shut. It can't get you," Izzy laughed.

I managed to get out a laugh which sounded like an awkward chuckle. Izzy started driving with an excited look on her face.

"Where are we going?" I asked.

"My house," Izzy said happily.

"What? Is your mom there?" I panicked.

I wasn't ready to meet her mom especially after I just choked out her ex and almost killed her teacher. I felt so transparent like the word murderer was written on my forehead.

"Yes, but she's leaving tonight to go on a date and said you can come over. She wants to meet you," said Izzy.

"Izzy, I wish you would've warned me," I said.

"Why?" Izzy asked.

Because I would've ran the other way, I thought to myself.

"Because… I would've dressed a lot better and practice talking to them in the mirror," I muttered.

"Calm down. You look fine and you'll do just fine," Izzy smiled.

"This is how I die," I whispered.

Izzy laughed and rolled her eyes. She continued to drive and talk about her day. Izzy started talking highly about 'contemporary art.' I wasn't entirely sure what she was talking about, but I loved how her face lit up when she talked about it. Describing the meaning behind the art that didn't make sense to everyone else. She always seemed to find beauty in things people thought were chaotic or "controversial."

We got in the driveway of her house. The way the white picket fence had flowers growing over it made it look like a fairytale.

"Why is this house cuter than my face?" I said quietly.

Izzy giggled and said, "nothing can be cuter than that."

I smiled and got out of the car with her. We slowly walked towards the porch and I kept my hands in my pockets as we walked up. As we walked on the porch, I looked around to see a nice yard with next door neighbors whose houses looked bland compared to Izzy's house. Izzy opened the door and before I walked in, I looked over to see a porch swing which made me smile. My mom used to always say her dream home was a place with a porch swing. Out of all things, that is all she asked for, a damn porch swing.

"Mom!" Izzy yelled.

Inside the house, it was wooden everything with metals and tannish paint added to the walls. There were family pictures and plants everywhere. For the first time in my life, I saw an actual home. It was small and cozy and the whole place looked comfortable. Izzy's mom came downstairs all dressed up. Izzy looked a lot like her mom.

"Hello Mrs.…" I looked at Izzy for help. I probably should have learned her last name.

"Dantuono," Izzy said rather quickly.

So, I tried to quickly repeat her words and hoped I pronounced it as nicely.

"Hello, Jess," said her mother in a stronger Latina accent than Izzy's.

"I've heard so much about you," her mother smiled.

"You as well," I smiled.

I shook her hand, hoping my hands weren't too sweaty.

"You hungry?" asked Mrs. Dantuono.

I nodded and smiled.

"Alright, I made you two some pasta. It is on the stove," she said with a smile on her face.

A knock on the door sounded and a tall man who had tan skin and short dark hair was welcomed in. He had a flower in his hand and looked at Mrs. Dantuono with such a smile. She introduced the man to Izzy and me as Cameron Smith who was a banker. I watched as Mrs. Dantuono and Izzy gave each other a secret thumbs-up while Mr. Smith was looking around the room.

My heart hurt with envy to see that there was a possibility that someone could have a relatively normal family. Even though technically Izzy's family was broken; it looked whole and happy.

"Thank you, ma'am, for the invite. I hope you both have a goodnight," I said.

I tried to hide the overwhelming sadness I was already feeling but I was positive I showed it. I walked away into their kitchen and left Izzy's mom and her date in confusion.

"Is he okay?" I heard Izzy's mom whisper.

"I'm not sure but I'll figure it out. Have a good night mom. Take care of her mister," said Izzy.

I sat down at their kitchen table and looked through the glass door that led out to their peaceful backyard. The sunlight shined down on me and shined through the white cupboards in her kitchen.

"Are you okay?" Izzy asked.

"Sorry, I didn't mean to rude," I said.

"You weren't."

She sat down beside me and held my hand. I looked down at her hand and back outside.

"What's it like?" I asked.

"What's what like?" she asked.

"Having a family" I said.

"It's good… not perfect but my mom means the world to me," she smiled to herself.

"What was your dad like? You talk about your mom but not about your dad," she added.

"My dad was an asshole to my mother," I said bluntly.

"I'm sorry, Jess. My dad cheated on my mother back in Brazil and we decided to live a new life. So, we moved here," Izzy explained.

"I'm sorry your dad did that to you and your mother," I said.

"Sometimes it hurts but my mother is all I need," Izzy smiled but frowned. "Who murdered your mother? Was it a robber?"

The image popped in my head which made me twitch a little. It was time to be at least a little bit honest with Izzy.

"My dad killed her," I muttered, swallowing hard.

Izzy knelt in front of me and hugged me, "I'm sorry."

"I'm bad for you. If you knew my past…" I continued to say but she interrupted me by saying, "Jess, stop. The past is in the past for a reason."

"I can't put it behind me."

"You can let it go. You will always remember it but that doesn't mean it has to weigh on you," Izzy whispered.

I wondered if Izzy had things she regretted. That would explain the reason behind her being so understanding. Her hands were on my face and she was looking in my eyes. I both disliked and liked the look in her eyes. They had sadness in them which made me feel like she was pitying me, but her eyes still gave off a warm feeling. The feeling that maybe I wasn't alone in the world of complete regret. I could tell I wasn't alone when it came to pain because Izzy felt pain too. My biggest question was: how the hell did she remain so strong?

I quickly grabbed her and pressed my lips against hers in one quick motion. My heart began to pound and my whole body became warm. I ran my fingers through her hair and pressed her close to me so that she was on my lap. While making out with Izzy I had this unsettling feeling like I was going to lose her. The feeling crawled down my spine and I could almost feel her slipping through my arms even though she was still glued to me. I pressed her even closer to me, so her chest was pressed to mine.

"Jess," whispered Izzy.

"Yeah?"

"You're holding me really tightly," she chuckled.

"Sorry," I let go instantly, realizing how much I was squeezing her.

Izzy just smiled at me and remained on my lap. She began kissing me again and I rested my hands around her waist. The fact that she wanted to continue settled my nerves. I could focus on the very thing I fantasized about happening more times than I would like to admit. Our mouths opened at every kiss, and I enjoyed the taste of her lips. The texture was soft, and I kept feeling like there was a spark stinging my tongue every time it touched hers. I wrapped her legs around me and carried her upstairs, almost tripping over the first step. I led us to her room after asking multiple times if that room was indeed hers. I struggled opening her door which made her laugh and we finally got into her room. I threw her onto the bed and took off my shirt. After I got a face full of fabric, I noticed Izzy already had hers off which made me freeze long enough to make it awkward. Luckily, it made her smile, and I got on top of her. My head was spinning, and my heart was pounding. Every touch gave chills and I never wanted to stop.

We both took turns taking each other's clothes off and I couldn't help but sling shot the panties across the room. Izzy rolled her eyes at me and let out a giggle. I laughed and froze again as I was looking at her naked body. She was the kind of beauty that deserves to be painted and put in a museum.

"You're beautiful," I muttered.

"Thank you," she whispered.

She grabbed me and pulled me close to her and we made love for the first time and yes it was my first time. It was the best feeling I ever experienced, and I knew I loved her. Part of me wondered if I loved her too much or if that was even possible. We fell asleep together, which was peaceful.

"Jess," she whispered.

I opened my eyes to see her beautiful face which made me smile.

"My parents just opened the front door," Izzy whispered.

My smile immediately dropped, and I got up extremely fast and quickly got dressed. Izzy got dressed in her leggings and tank top while occasionally glancing at me while I did the same. We both stood straight up and looked at each other.

"You should probably brush your hair," I laughed.

"Shit," she said as she looked in the mirror, "Jess, we have sex hair!"

"Sex hair?" I laughed.

Izzy grabbed a brush and quickly untangled her hair.

"Izzy!" her mother yelled for her.

Izzy tossed me the brush which I failed to catch. I picked up the brush off the floor and tried to flatten my hair.

"We're upstairs!" Izzy yelled.

I fixed the covers and straightened myself out in time for Mrs. Dantuono to open the door. She had a worried face but relaxed once she saw us in a decent state.

"Izzy has a very clean room, you taught her well," I said as I was looking at her pictures on her desk. That was probably the dumbest thing I could have said. Luckily, I was facing away from her because my face winced at the cringy remark I just made.

"Why thank you Jess," said Mrs. Dantuono, awkwardly.

"You're welcome," I said.

"You wanted to see the cleanliness of her room?" asked Mr. Smith who came up from behind her.

"Well, to see her room in general," I said, turning to them.

Mr. Smith nodded and looked at Mrs. Dantuono who said, "well you should probably get home, Jess."

"Yes ma'am," I nodded and followed all of them downstairs.

"Nice meeting you!" said Mrs. Dantuono as Izzy and I walked outside.

We both got in the car and Izzy drove me home. It was an awkwardly silent ride home. The nerves in my body were going crazy and I kept going over the moment in my head. We pulled up to my house and both stared straight ahead.

"Izzy," I finally broke the silence.

"Yes?" she was still looking straight.

"You were okay with what happened, right?" I asked.

"Yes, why weren't you?" Izzy got quickly worried.

"Yes of course but I wanted to make sure you were," I said.

"I am," Izzy smiled.

I smiled back "good."

I hugged her and got out of the car. I looked up at the porch and there was Declan with a smirk on his face.

"Bye Jess, see you later!" Izzy yelled out of her window.

I waved goodbye and walked up to the porch.

"Why are you smiling like that?" asked Declan.

"Sorry for enjoying myself," I said.

"You screw her?" Declan laughed.

I rolled my eyes and opened the front door.

"Hey Izzy! Answer a question for me sweetheart!" Declan yelled after her.

Izzy rolled down her window.

"Declan leave her alone," I said, firmly.

"Did you use protection Izzy? Wouldn't want your baby to end up like its father!" Declan laughed.

"I'm sorry Izzy, get out of here!" I yelled.

I grabbed Declan's shoulder and dragged him away.

"What does it feel like to fuck a psycho!" Declan yelled.

I slammed him against the side of the house and covered his mouth. "Shut up," I whispered.

Mr. Weaver came out and pried my hands off him.

"Jess, I got him," said Mr. Weaver.

"Didn't mean to piss you off," Declan laughed.

"Get a fucking life instead of messing with mine!" I yelled.

Mrs. Weaver came out with her hands in front of her.

"Jess, I'm sorry that was very wrong of him. Talk to Izzy and make sure she knows we are sorry," said Mrs. Weaver.

I nodded at her and backed away. I turned around to see Izzy still in her car staring right at me. I walked towards her and stood in front of her window. Izzy looked up at me.

"I'm sorry. He's an ass," I said.

"It's okay, it's not your fault," Izzy said, "are you going to be okay?"

"No, I'm not. You are a good person, and you deserve more than me," I snapped, sounding more annoyed than I meant to.

"Jess, stop saying that. You are a good person too."

"But I'm not. I love you Izzy and me keeping you is being selfish," I said, softly this time.

"I want you and no one else. So, I guess just deal with being selfish, Jess," said Izzy a little coldly.

She quickly rolled up her window and drove off. I watched her leave a little shocked at her snapping back at me but slightly proud of what she said. I look back to see Mrs. Weaver looking back at me, which pissed me off a little. What the hell was up with his family?

"I'm going to go on a walk," I said, walking away.

"Jess come back," Mrs. Weaver said.

"I'll come back this time," I said.

I could not understand Declan. I could tell that deep down he was a decent person. It seemed like he was the opposite of me. I seem decent on the outside and terrible within. Declan seemed cruel on the outside but on the inside, he had a better moral compass than I did. I could hear in the background Mr. Weaver calming him down.

"I'm fucking fine, Mark," I heard Declan's voice say.

I looked down the driveway and could still see Izzy's car which either meant she was driving slowly or stopped. I disregarded it and went into the woods. Even though the woods gave me a bad feeling and often delusions; it felt more like home than anywhere else. A part of me hated the delusions and part of me was searching for them. It was like I had a thing for facing my fear. I was searching my mind for answers, and it only responded when I was in these woods. The floor looked like someone was dragged across it. My stomach turned at the strange stench in the air.

"Jess!" I heard a woman squeal.

I ran towards the squeal until I saw two figures before me. My mother and father stood there. My father had my mother in a head lock facing me.

"Mom? Dad?" I stammered.

They didn't say anything to me, but my father held up a gun towards me and pointed it at my mom's head.

"Drop it. You don't want to do this," I said.

"How would you like it? If Izzy was in love with Kyle and not you?" he asked, hot tears in his eyes.

"She's not," I said.

Izzy showed up holding Kyle's hand in a wedding dress.

"Yes, I am Jess. We never stopped loving each other," said Izzy while Kyle had a smirk on his face.

My heart felt like it tore apart. I sucked in my anger when all I wanted was to murder Kyle as slowly as possible.

"That's what your mother did," said my father.

"My mother never cheated," I muttered.

"How would you know? But you know him now, don't you? Mark Weaver," he said with a smirk.

My breathing stopped for a second at the sound of the name.

"Whores must pay," my father chuckled.

"They aren't whores!" I yelled.

My father started laughing and pulled the trigger. It burst into my mother's brain as she fell out of his arms. Blood was everywhere and was coming from her mouth. I screamed in agony as tears streamed down my face. I ran after my father and strangled him.

"You will destroy her like I did your mother. You are a killer just like your father," he said laughing.

His laugh echoed within the trees. Black ink began to leak out of his mouth as I desperately chocked him to death. I could feel a cold chill traveling up my spine and infecting my heart as I enjoyed the sight. Once he became still; I let go. I screamed and slammed my fists into the ground. I got up in a rage and continued to pull plants from the ground and throw them as far as I could.

"Jess!" I heard Izzy cry.

I looked behind me to see her wearing the outfit I last saw her in with a jean jacket draped over her. She was without Kyle and looked more like Izzy. I was breathing heavily as I held plants in my hands. I stared at her and wondered if she was real. I wondered what was real and what was in my mind.

"Jess, what's wrong? What's going on?" Izzy said with tears in her eyes.

"I need to go home," I cried.

I dropped the plants and walked past her.

"Jess, wait tell me what's going on," said Izzy.

"I can't," I muttered.

"Why not!" she yelled.

"Because it will scare you away!" I yelled looking back into her eyes.

"I'm not going anywhere," Izzy said calmly.

"I can't tell you right now. But I will."

"Why can't you right now?" Izzy asked.

"I have to talk to Mr. Weaver."

Chapter 13
Shadows

Izzy followed me through the woods and up to my house.

"Jess, talk to me," she pleaded.

I didn't say anything else, walked into my house and closed the door behind me. Izzy got into her car in a stomping manner and I heard her car drive off. In the kitchen was Mrs. Weaver doing the dishes.

"Welcome home stranger," said Adeline.

I felt a poke on my side, and it was Brady.

"Hey man," I said.

"You went in the forest?" he asked, staring at the dirt on my hands.

"Yeah, I took a walk," I hesitated to say.

"Did you see the shadows?" Brady tilted his head.

"The shadows?" I looked at him surprised.

I thought he was reading my mind for a second.

"I think so," I whispered.

Brady just looked at me, smiled and skipped off. I had so many questions about that conversation, but I was too focused on my father saying, "Mark Weaver."

"Where's Mark?" I asked.

"In his shop dear," said Mrs. Weaver.

I walked over to the back door and pushed it open a little hard; the slam of it hitting the house made me jump. Out back I saw a little shed which I have been told was his "shop." I heard him whistling as I got closer and stepped through the opening.

It was a small shed that looked like it was turned into his office. It was a mixture of an office and workshop.

"Hi there, Jess. I don't think you've seen my shop yet," said Mr. Weaver.

"Yeah, it's nice," I said as I looked around to see wood and tools.

There was a computer on his desk with a couple of office supplies. The shavings from the wood covered some of his office items. The smell was close to smelling like a paint can. I scrunched my nose as I walked through.

"What can I do for you?" asked Mr. Weaver.

"You knew my mom?" I asked.

Mr. Weaver paused to look at me and he gestured for me to sit. I sat down near his desk and faced him. He had a saw in his hand but instead of using it, he set it down.

"I was her friend and I tried to help her get away from your father," Mr. Weaver said.

"Did you have something with her?" I hesitated to say.

"No of course not. I've been with Mrs. Weaver ever since before you were a possibility. Both Mrs. Weaver and I tried to pull as many strings as we could to get her out of there. Your father found out and announced that you were going on a family vacation the very next day," Mr. Weaver sighed.

"Camping trip," I said. The image raced through my head which made me flinch.

"We searched the camps around but couldn't find you guys," Mr. Weaver said.

"Why didn't you call the police?" I asked.

"Your father was good friends with most of them," Mr. Weaver explained.

I nodded with tears in my eyes and noticed I wasn't the only one. Mr. Weaver had tears falling but he swallowed hard and continued "after hearing that you got out, we asked to have you," he said.

"Thanks," I muttered and got up and walked out of the shed.

I didn't know what else to ask him. All it told me is that nobody could have stopped what happened, no matter how hard they tried.

"Jess," he called out to me.

I walked into the house with a blank expression on my face.

"You hungry, Jess? I have leftovers," said Mrs. Weaver.

"No, I'm not hungry. But thank you for trying to help my mom, turns out no one could even if they tried," I said, tiredly.

I remained blank and walked upstairs.

"Jess," she called after me.

I looked over my shoulder at her.

"She really loved you with all of her heart," she said with blurry eyes.

I nodded and continued upstairs. I walked into my room to see Declan who looked at me weirdly.

"What's with the ghost face?" he asked.

I just sighed and sat on my bed. I studied my hands, unable to come up with any words to say. Declan just stood there awkwardly and sat on his bed.

"Declan, what did the doctors diagnose Brady with?" I asked.

"They couldn't figure him out. They just called him crazy and sent him here," said Declan.

Declan was sitting on his bed and throwing pieces of gum in his mouth. I just watched as he shoved three pieces of gum in his mouth.

"Just like all of us," said Adeline, breaking my concentration. I didn't even know she was in the room.

"No, they called you a slut. The rest of us crazies and this one is a psycho," said Declan, pointing at me.

"Why am I so different?" I asked.

"Because you killed someone. That is the difference between you and us. You earned your label," Declan snapped.

Everyone became quiet. I could tell Declan was still on nerve about the moment with the teacher. Declan's face was red, but his muscles loosened, and he sighed.

"I know you didn't do it without a reason. Who knows, maybe I would've taken someone's life if they killed someone I loved too," Declan added as he looked down at the floor.

"Thanks," I muttered.

"You're still a psycho though," Declan muttered back.

"That's fair," I said with a laugh.

Surprisingly, Declan cracked a smile at that.

"Do you guys think we are bad people?" Adeline asked.

"I don't know," said Brady who made us all jump. None of us realized he came into the room. He moved almost robotically to sit in the middle of the room.

"Everybody else thinks we are. That's why we try so damn hard to pretend that we are good," Declan said as he chomps on his gum which I was still confused about.

"But I'm not bad; my shadows are," said Brady sadly.

"You aren't bad Brady. We only become bad if we let our flaws define us," said Adeline smiling.

"That was deep," Declan teased.

Adeline shot him a glare and Declan put his hands up in surrender. I looked around and realized there was somebody missing in the house.

"Hey, where's AnnMarie?" I asked.

"Shit," said Adeline, running to the window like she saw something.

We all followed her to see AnnMarie was walking towards the woods with a lighter in her hand.

"How did she get that?" Declan asked.

"Well, you said you wanted to quit smoking, so, I hid your lighter and cigarettes in our room," Adeline explained.

"You're trying to quit?" I asked.

"Yeah, why do you think he's popping gum like they were his pills," Brady said still sitting in the middle of the room.

We all looked at Brady with shock at the vulgarity of his sentence.

"This isn't a time to talk about my damn habits," Declan said, running towards the stairs.

We all followed him and ran down the stairs quickly.

"What's wrong?" said Mrs. Weaver.

"AnnMarie is trying to start a forest fire!" yelled Declan as we all ran outside.

We all file outside in a hurry to see AnnMarie gazing in awe at the fire she created. You could almost see the reflection of the fire in her eyes. She had the biggest smile on her face like she was in a candy store. The closer I got I could feel the burning heat grazing my skin. Declan grabbed AnnMarie away from the fire and I quickly ran to Mr. Weaver's shop.

"Mr. Weaver!" I yelled.

"What's wrong?" he asked.

"AnnMarie set the woods on fire!"

"Shit," he mumbled.

Mr. Weaver grabbed a fire extinguisher and we both ran towards the family. AnnMarie was trying to kick her way out of Declan's arms and was screaming on the top of her lungs... "No! I want it to burn! Let it burn!"

Mr. Weaver put out as much as he could and ran to his shed and came back with a second one and put the rest of it out. I am guessing once a pyromaniac enters the home, you need as many extinguishers as you can get. AnnMarie was screaming and crying as the flames were being put out. The chaos of the scene made me freeze. All I could do was stare at the girl as she tried to get out of Declan's arms. He was holding her as tightly as he could without hurting her and shushing her like he was trying to put her to sleep.

AnnMarie immediately calmed down once all the flames were out of sight. Declan let go of her and she just looked at all of us and went into the house without saying a word. We all looked at each other confused. Declan sighed and plopped on the grass. Mrs. Weaver's facial expression changed into panic and said "stove" and quickly ran inside after her.

"Maybe we are crazy," said Brady, who was standing there just watching the whole scene.

We all laughed, and Declan just smirked and shook his head. He lays on the grass and just stared at the sky, exhausted.

"Huh?" said Mr. Weaver, which made us all laugh more.

For a second, I felt like we were a family. Which was a feeling I haven't felt for a long time. When we all went in the house everyone sat down exhausted from the night. Mrs. Weaver filled AnnMarie a bath to calm her down. For a second, I figured I was the only truly crazy one in the house but turns out I wasn't alone. I got up and excused myself outside. I leaned up against the entrance to the porch and started dialing Mrs. Jones number.

"Hello?" I heard her say.

"Thank you," I said.

"Jess? You're welcome honey," said Mrs. Jones, her voice soft on the other line.

I went back inside and saw that the kitchen was empty and that everyone was going upstairs. I went upstairs and saw everyone getting ready for bed. I climbed up to my bed and lay on my back. I thought about AnnMarie's insane impulse to light up the woods. A part of me wished she did because maybe the voices from them would stop. The lights were turned off and everyone started getting to bed. Something made me want to look out the window at them, but I had this bad feeling I shouldn't. I could hear Declan snoring and Brady's light snore filled in the gap. I slowly and quietly got down from my bunk and looked out the window. The woods were still standing as if it was mocking me. I went to turn away but paused once I heard a little girl whisper "Jess."

My stomach dropped and I whipped back around to see a little girl in a white dress standing in front of the woods. Her head was tilted as she stared back at me with a sad look on her face. I smacked the window to see if it would scare her off, but it didn't; she just stood there and stared. I rested on the windowsill to stare her down until she disappeared like she usually would but this time she was staying. I gave up and grabbed my jacket and headed downstairs to quickly sneak out the door.

"This is a bad idea," I whispered to myself.

I truly was that idiot in horror movies. *Go in the woods, Jess. Follow the ghost girl who is haunting you.*

"I'm such an idiot," I whispered.

I walked along the side of the house until I stood in front of her. This pale, brown haired little girl just studied me with the saddest eyes.

"You're third victim," she said in the most angelic voice, yet the words were haunting.

I looked at her confused, "I never killed a little girl."

"Yet," she whispered.

I looked at her confused and backed up a little bit. She turned and began to run away from me. I couldn't let her disappear now; not after saying what she did. I ran after her.

"Wait!" I yelled.

I ran through the woods, following the white glow of her dress.

"Wait! What do you mean by third! I only have one victim. I never killed my mother!" I yelled after pausing my chase.

The rustling leaves became quiet meaning she stopped running.

"I know," I heard her say.

The woods echoed her voice and left an eerie ring in my ear. The woods were foggy and silent. I spun around in a circle to see if I could see her. A ball started forming in my throat. It caused my mouth to become dry as chills were causing goosebumps on my skin.

"So, how are you my third?" I asked.

I started feeling like I was talking to the air or maybe the woods itself.

"You'll have one before me."

"Who?"

"I can't tell you," she replied.

"Why are you my victim? You're a little girl, why would I hurt you?" I asked.

"There's something I know that you don't. Once you find out, you won't like it and I will be your third victim."

"How many victims?" I asked.

"Five" the echo pierced my ears.

I dropped to the ground.

"Five," I whispered to myself, "I don't want to kill five people."

Tears streamed down my cheeks, and I heard the rustle of the leaves again.

"I don't want to kill you!" I screamed.

The girl appeared from the leaves but as she was walking towards me her body started to crumble.

"It's your fate and you made it mine," she said.

My hands began to shake as I watched her body crumble and disintegrate before me.

"Stop!" I yelled in terror, "I'll stay away from you! I won't hurt you! Please!"

Her skin looked as if it was shaven off and her brittle bones started to show.

"It's too late," she said, and her jawbone fell.

The little girl's body was all bone that was crumbling to dust before me. Pieces of her skin tore off and fell on the ground before her.

"No!" I screamed.

Her whole body fell limp. I hovered over the little girl's body and sobbed at her corpse. My whole body was shaking as I rocked myself back and forth. I screamed in agony without caring if somebody heard me.

"Mom," I whispered.

I got up and stumbled through the woods. I felt numb and my vision was blurry. I wasn't fully there and instead in a trance.

"Mom, I don't want to be a killer," I mumbled.

I kept walking and tried to dodge the trees. I occasionally ran into the trees as I walked through them. Part of me didn't know where I was going but my body was following a path. Finally, an opening appeared and in front of me was my old house. It was now taped off. Half of the house was missing because they started knocking it down. It finally looked like the broken home it was. I walked through the entry and headed straight to the basement. In the basement, I gathered the booze and carried them like a baby. I sat in the living room and put them all on the floor. They were all lined up. I took my phone out of my pocket and found Izzy in my contacts. The phone rang for a while until she picked it up.

"Jess?"

"Izzy. Can you come over? I need help," and I told her the address.

Chapter 14
Love, Mary

As I waited for Izzy, I opened a bottle of wine and began drinking it. I sat there and stared into the entry way.

"I can't wait till this house is dust" I smiled.

I looked at the picture of my dad and quickly went into his work area. I looked through his old papers without being sure of what I was looking for. I opened a drawer to see a couple of letters. The one that stood out to me was a letter from a woman named Mary. I grabbed one of his old letter openers and peeled it open.

My dear,

I miss you dearly. I hope what you said about leaving your wife was true. Like I said I am pregnant, and I would love for our baby to have a father. When I go into labor in about 9 months, I hope to see you there at the hospital. I promise to provide you with a new life. I love you.

With Love,

Mary

Anger arose in me as I crumbled up the piece of paper and dropped it next to me. Hot tears formed in my eyes as I let the crumbled paper fall. I ran back into the living room and glared at his picture.

"Your fucking plan was to kill us so you could live with your mistress!" I yelled.

I tried to open the bottle of vodka but couldn't get the cap off. I smashed the bottle and busted the top open. The glass cut my hand; a quick striking pain hit my palm, but I couldn't care less. I drank out of the broken part of the glass. I could feel chips escaping and dragging down my throat. The taste of metal mixed in with the wine.

"Why didn't you just leave! You heartless bastard! Why didn't you just leave!" I screamed as I dropped to my knees.

"Jess!" I heard Izzy yell.

I looked over to see her running towards me.

"Jess! What happened to you!" she said with tears forming in her eyes.

I looked up at her with bloodshot eyes.

"Jess, you are drinking out of a broken bottle," she freaked, "Jess your hand!"

She tore off some of my already destroyed shirt and wrapped it around my bloody hand. My eyes were blurry, and my mind seemed fuzzy. I looked at her blankly and grabbed her face with my other hand and pushed my lips against hers. We lip locked for a while until it became French. I held her closely onto my lap and brushed my wrapped-up hand against her neck. I looked in her eyes and began kissing her neck.

"Jess," she whispered, "Are you okay?"

I looked up at her and she looked at me.

"I am now," I said calmly.

Izzy smiled and brushed my face.

"I'm sorry you're hurting," she said lightly.

"You numb the pain," I said.

I began kissing her again. I carried her and put her against the wall. The sparks flew every time she made the slightest noise. The pain was a beautiful one as she left scratch marks on my back. The drywall filled up my fingernails so I could keep a good control.

"You're going to hurt your hand," she whispered.

I took my hand off the drywall and brought her to the floor. It numbed every painful feeling I have ever felt; making me switch addictions. She was my perfect addiction and felt extremely better than chugging vodka. Sex with her was like nicotine because I swear it put me in a frenzy.

I woke up to see her beautiful face and body beside me. I grabbed an old polaroid camera and took a picture of her calm and sleepy face. The pain of my hand finally caught up with me and caused me to wince as I pushed myself up. I sat myself on the couch and watched her sleep. I didn't want to wake her because I was busy envying the peaceful aroma she was portraying. It was like one of those pretty scenes in a French Film. Her eyes opened to look up to me and laughed.

"Are you watching me sleep naked, Jessie Reids?" she asked.

"It's a better view than any movie I've seen."

She began to put on her clothes but stopped in her bra and underwear.

"You obviously haven't seen many movies," she smiled.

I grinned while looking her up and down.

"I've seen plenty," I answered.

She smiled and picked up my jacket, put it on and sat in my lap.

"Jess"

"Yes?"

Izzy looked around, "are you an alcoholic?"

I laughed "not anymore."

Izzy looked at me confused, "what do you mean?"

"You helped me out of it."

"How?" Izzy looked puzzled.

"You taste a lot better than alcohol does," I laughed.

She laughed and jokingly hit me in the stomach.

"Want breakfast?" I asked, still laughing.

"Sure, but that also means I have to get dressed," Izzy said teasingly.

"Never mind, I'm not hungry," I teased.

"Jess," she laughed.

She got up giving me a chance to quickly spank her. She laughed and continued to dress herself. Once I got my pants on, I walked over to her and helped her put on her shirt even though I knew she didn't need help. I kissed the back of her neck as I held her waist.

"I'm hungry," she said.

"Alright," I sighed.

We walked out to the diner to get some breakfast and as she walked away, I took a picture of her with the camera right as she looked back. The photo was perfect because it caught the flow of her hair as she looked back at me. We got in the diner and sat down in the first booth. I smiled at her as she got situated in her seat. She looked up and smiled at me, so I quickly took a picture.

"Did you just take a picture of me?" Izzy smiled.

I smiled, "Yeah I found this in the house."

"Izzy," I heard a guy say.

We both looked over to see Kyle who still had marks on his neck, but I hoped they were faded enough for Izzy not to notice.

"Kyle, what happened to your neck?" asked Izzy.

Never mind, I thought, she was very intuitive. Kyle side eyed me, and I stared him down to show warning.

"I wore a collared shirt that gave me a rash," said Kyle.

"Wow, was it the type of fabric?" asked Izzy.

"Either that or a psycho poisoned it," Kyle mumbled.

I let out an involuntarily laugh which made them both look at me.

"What's so funny?" asked Kyle.

"The chances of someone poisoning a shirt are quite slim. I am sure it was the fabric. Cotton or wool maybe? Or how about silk, was it, silk?" I asked him.

"Wool. I don't wear silk," Kyle answered.

"Good thing you know," said Izzy.

"That would really suck if you found out you were allergic by getting wool underwear...Ow," I said after Izzy kicked me under the table.

"Yeah, that would probably disappoint Izzy the most," Kyle snapped.

"Kyle," Izzy said angrily.

The anger rose and I went to jump at him, but Izzy beat me to it by slapping him in the face and storming off. Kyle looked at me still shocked while I grinned back at him. I walked away giggling to quickly stopping once I got out the door.

"Really Jess!" Izzy yelled.

"What?" I said confused.

"Is it really that hard to be civil?" she gritted through her teeth.

"In general, no. With him? Yes," I said pointing to the diner.

"Why is it so hard?" Izzy asked. She looked furious with me.

"Because he still likes you Izzy! It's a constant reminder that I could easily lose you to him someday!"

"Easily? So, you don't trust me? You know I love you and I have done everything I can to prove it to you! What more do you want?" Izzy yelled.

She shook her head and started to walk away.

"Wait Izzy!" I yelled.

She turned around and yelled "No! You know what, Jess. I shouldn't have to feel like I need to prove everything to you because it is exhausting."

Izzy started walking away again which put me into a panic.

"No wait. I trust you Izzy," I said grabbing her hand, "I love you. You are the only one I can trust."

Izzy got quiet and looked me in the eyes, "I love you too."

She studied my eyes as if she were trying to read me but then sighed. Izzy didn't let go of my hand and we walked side by side. I was kind of confused because she just did it without saying anything.

"So, eating something didn't go well. Can we eat at your house?" was the first thing she said after the long pause.

"No, that's not a good idea," I said, "Because my family is crazy; you've seen it."

"No, I haven't. You never invited me in," Izzy said.

I just shook my head at her.

"Jess, I don't care who they are. I want to meet who is taking care of you."

I sighed, "Fine."

I figured I should do something to make her happy considering I was a dick two seconds ago. Izzy smiled and started walking with me again.

"Here comes chaos," I mumbled.

Chapter 15
An Awkward Visit

W e got to my house and I was already shaking. Mr. and Mrs. Weaver were already heading to Izzy's car.

"Jessie Reids," Mrs. Weaver said.

"I'm sorry," I said, getting out of the car.

She put her hands on my face.

"Are you okay?" she whispered, looking down at my hand.

Izzy got out of the car and introduced herself to Mr. Weaver.

"Are you hurting again?" Mrs. Weaver whispered, which I could feel it made Izzy look over.

I sighed, "No, I'm okay."

"Okay sweetheart. Hello Izzy, I'm Mrs. Weaver," she said, shaking Izzy's hand.

"Hello, it's nice to meet you," Izzy smiled.

"Come on in," Mr. Weaver said.

"Um, who is all in there?" I asked.

"Everybody," Mrs. Weaver answered.

I glared at her.

"They'll behave," she said, reading my mind, "don't worry."

I shook my head and we all filed in.

"Hello everyone," Mrs. Weaver said as we walked in.

When I walked in Adeline was pressed up on the counter grinning at me while Declan was coming downstairs. AnnMarie pops up in front of Izzy.

"Hi," she said happily.

"Hi, who are you?" Izzy smiled.

"This one's AnnMarie," I said.

"I can introduce myself, Jess. I am AnnMarie," she shook Izzy's hand which made both of us laugh.

"This little guy is Brady," I gestured to Brady.

Brady just stared at Izzy, swaying his right leg tracing circles into the floor.

"Hi," Izzy said holding out her hand, but Brady just walked away shyly.

"He's shy," I mumbled.

"That's alright," Izzy smiled.

Adeline leaned away from the counter and stood in front of Izzy.

"So, you are Jess' lover?" Adeline asked.

I cleared my throat and gave an "*I'm sorry*" look to Izzy. Izzy looked at me and then at Adeline.

"Yes, I am. What's your name?" she asked.

"Adeline," she gave her a sinister smile.

"Nice to meet you," Izzy smiled.

"Aw. It's so nice to meet you too. It's rare to meet a normal person for once," Adeline said sarcastically.

Izzy half laughed, unsure how to react. She side-eyed me with a fake smile.

"Heal slut. Don't want to offend Jess' girlfriend," Declan scoffed.

"Family love, right?" Adeline rolled her eyes.

"And you are?" Izzy smiled.

Declan pulled out a cigarette and lit it.

"Wouldn't you like to know," Declan mumbled.

"Outside Declan," Mrs. Weaver snapped.

I looked over to see Brady giving AnnMarie a dollar. He rolls his eyes when AnnMarie kisses the dollar with such a smile. Declan sighed and brushed past me, bumping into my shoulder. Declan kicked open the door and stormed down the steps.

"I thought he quit," I mumbled.

"I'm sorry sweetie," said Mrs. Weaver.

"It's okay," Izzy smiled at her.

I took Izzy's hand and we sat in the living room. Adeline turned herself around to watch us. Adeline looked at me up and down and hoped off the counter to skip away upstairs.

"Did she just check you out?" Izzy whispered.

"She does it because she knows it creeps me out," I whispered back.

Izzy nodded with a confused look on her face still and just shrugged it off. We didn't feel like we were siblings but to the outsider that's how it looks. Which made the fact that Adeline flirts with me even stranger to Izzy.

AnnMarie marched up to Izzy. "Do you smoke?" she asked.

"No," Izzy replied.

"Do you have a lighter?" AnnMarie whispered.

"Hey AnnMarie, why don't you help Mrs. Weaver," I quickly said.

Izzy's face remained confused and shocked, but she just smiled at AnnMarie.

"Do I want to know?" she whispered.

I shook my head and laughed, "No."

For a bit, we watched another Brady and AnnMarie card game except this time it was slapjack which didn't seem fair because AnnMarie's reflexes far surpassed Brady's. The fact that he was shy around Izzy made him react even slower. I thought about striking up a conversation but for some reason I could only silently watch the card game.

"I won again!" AnnMarie shouted.

Brady just stared at her with a dead straight face, slapped both his hands on the table and pushed the cards off. The cards dart past her and onto the floor.

"Sore loser," AnnMarie teased.

Izzy stayed for dinner surprisingly, but it was very awkward because everyone stared at her intensively the entire time. Adeline kept staring at me to make things awkward for Izzy. Declan leaned in his chair and looked pissed off at the world. AnnMarie minded her business and kept slurping her spaghetti while Brady just stared at Izzy. Every nerve of my body was racked because this moment was by far the most awkward dinner I have had with the Weavers and I've had some awkward dinners with them. Shit, one time I almost committed suicide and this dinner was still more awkward than that one.

Outside started sounding wild. The wind was pushing on the Weaver's house like it was trying to break and enter. The rain sounded like hail. I imagined giant ice cubes just falling onto the house except it wasn't winter. Mr. Weaver came in soaked and mentioned there was a tornado watch. After we finished our dinner, we all sat in the living room to watch the weather channel. Mr. Weaver was right there was a tornado watch, and it didn't look good for us.

"Izzy dear, why don't you call your parents. There is a possibility that you might have to stay here tonight," Mrs. Weaver said.

Izzy and I looked at each other and she went to the kitchen to dial her parents' phone number. I looked at Mrs. Weaver and gave her a worried look.

"You two can sleep downstairs," she whispered to me.

"Thank you," I whispered back.

"Are you alright to stay here, dear?" Mrs. Weaver asked Izzy.

"My mom wants to talk to you first," Izzy said, handing her the phone.

While Mrs. Weaver sat up; Izzy sat next to me.

"Are you aloud?" I asked.

Izzy shrugged, "I'll have to be. She isn't very happy about it though."

Izzy sat down beside me and sighed.

"Alright dear, you are aloud. I'm sorry you can't go home," Mrs. Weaver said.

"It's okay, thank you," said Izzy, shyly.

"Of course," smiled Mr. Weaver.

All of a sudden the tornado sirens went off which made every one of our heads pop up.

"Declan and Jess grab blankets and pillows. Adeline and Izzy grab some snacks. Darling, get the little ones downstairs; I will be right back," said Mr. Weaver.

We all dispersed to grab the supplies. I was a bit worried about Izzy being stuck with Adeline, but I tried to focus on helping Declan.

"Just grab one pillow and one blanket off each bed. I will find extras," he said.

"Got it," I grabbed all the kids blankets and pillows. I met Declan in the hall to see him with a handful more.

"Has this happened before?" I asked.

"Yeah, you were behind bars," Declan chuckled.

"Oh yeah."

I remembered all the inmates being put in one area but still separate. We were all put in the bathrooms of the prison. It was terrible because they kept us huddled in sections which made even less room. A couple fights broke out because it was too tight of quarters for there not to be any drama. I remember closing my eyes and wished for a Wizard of Oz moment. That the prison would fly into some magical land and I could escape the guards. I created a whole fantasy world in my mind that I wanted to escape to that night. It's a pity I didn't name it, who knows it could've made a great fantasy novel. Then again, any fantasy novel I wrote would be depressing as hell.

I followed Declan downstairs and was relieved to see Adeline was being kind to Izzy.

"Yeah Mrs. Beil is definitely the best teacher. I didn't know you were into art," Adeline said to her.

"Majorly, I'm really into contemporary art right now," Izzy said to her.

Declan and I stared at them and they looked over at us with a handful of snacks in their arms. They were both smiling and had something in common; it was strange.

"Hello boys," Adeline teased.

Declan and I looked at each other and just motioned for them to follow us.

"Got the supplies," Declan announced.

"Good," said Mrs. Weaver.

Mr. Weaver came down, locking the door behind him. He was holding a box with him which he later revealed had cards and other entertainment in it. The walls were a collaboration of wood and stone. The ground was cold, and the basement had a spooky feel to it. It almost felt like there was something in the air. It would make a good location for a horror movie. I was half expecting to see some demonic creature huddled in the corner or at least one of my shadowy figures coming to visit.

"Jess," Izzy whispered.

I snapped out of a gaze.

"Yes?" I asked.

"Why did Adeline say watch you when you sleep?" Izzy whispered.

"Huh?" The thought of Adeline standing there watching me sleep gave me a shutter down my spine.

"She told me I needed to watch you sleep because you needed taken care of," Izzy explained.

"Nightmares," Brady said smiling at me like he was proud he guessed a question correctly.

I jumped and looked back at him. He always seemed to just appear.

"Brady, go play some board games," I said looking at Brady confused.

Brady shrugged and walked over to Mr. Weaver.

"Do you have nightmares often?" Izzy asked.

"Sometimes," I mumbled.

"What are they about?" Izzy asked.

"Just random things; it's no big deal," I shrugged.

"Okay," Izzy said, and she held my hand.

We all played monopoly with candles around the game board like we were summoning a ghost. AnnMarie ended up winning, which made her very happy. Declan accused her of cheating and Adeline came to her defense by saying "the only person that cheats during a game is you."

Declan glared at her and said, "Only sometimes."

That made everyone smile, which disputed the little argument.

The tornado lasted all night so eventually we decided to sleep down here for the night. Brady walked up to us as we were settling in.

"Jess," he whispered sitting by me.

I sat up. "Yeah, Brady?"

"The shadows are stronger here. How do you make them go away?" Brady whispers.

I could tell he was trying to be quiet, but I knew Izzy wasn't asleep. Being subtle was not this family's forte. Plus, I think Izzy's goal is to catch what Adeline was saying.

"You might not be able to make it go away but you can ignore them and think about things that make you happy," I whispered.

Brady nodded. "I like the Weavers."

"Then think of them," I smiled.

"Okay," Brady lit up, "I'll think of the whole family."

"That sounds like a brilliant plan," I said.

Brady nodded and went over to where he was sleeping. He snuggled himself into some blankets and closed his eyes with a smile on his face. It made my heart sink. The fact that he experiences similar things as me. It made me wonder what that kid is going through and how much of himself he hides. Although, for some reason, I could tell he would handle it better than I do. Even at such a young age, he seemed stronger and more intact.

"Shadows?" Izzy whispered.

"Shadows is what Brady calls his nightmares," I whispered back.

"Aw." Izzy smiled.

I was surprised at how quick I came up with that. It was clever considering we were just talking about nightmares. Plus, most kids are worried about nightmares and not hallucinations. Brady and I were just lucky, I guess.

"So, what do you think of?" Izzy asked.

"You..." Izzy smiled at the comment, "of course that occasionally becomes a problem in the morning," I whispered as I lay down.

"Jess!" Izzy gasped at the vulgar comment, but I just laughed.

She lays back down and turned to look at me and I looked back at her.

"No sex in here. I want to get some sleep!" Declan yelled.

"Declan, leave Jess alone," Mr. Weaver said.

"Who said I was talking about them?" Declan backfired.

"Declan!" Mrs. Weaver yelled.

The room filled with laughter from everybody in the room as we all lay on blankets and look up at the ceiling.

"Goodnight, everybody," Mr. Weaver said.

"Goodnight," everyone replied.

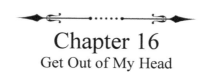

Chapter 16
Get Out of My Head

I am in the family's old basement absolutely terrified to the point where my body was shaking. My mother was on the stairs, her hair up in curls and her skin as white as snow. Her face was in her hands as she balled.

"Mommy, I want the sirens to stop," I whined.

I was 5 years old at the time.

"I'm sorry, honey. I can't control them," she sobbed.

"Why are you crying? Are you scared of the tornado too?" I asked.

"Yeah honey," she said, with a fake smile.

"I'll sit by you. We can be scared together," I said, getting up and sitting by her.

I curled up next to her side and lay my head on her shoulder. We sat there on the stairs and against the basement walls. It was a crummy basement that looked more like a boiler room. My mother didn't keep anything down there just in case things got moldy.

"That sounds wonderful," she smiled.

"Is dad going to be okay?" I asked.

She covered her mouth and swallowed her sob.

"I'm sure he is darling. He is strong," she smiled.

"So are you mommy," I smiled.

A big smile went across her face and she wiped her tears off her face. She always did that. As soon as a tear fell, she would wipe it quicker than it could fall. She was someone who hated people seeing her hurt even though she seemed to hurt the most. I wish I had her strength, but I think that is a gene that missed me.

"I love you darling," she said.

"I love you too," I answered.

I quickly woke up in shock.

"Jess," Izzy whispered.

I wiped the tears that were coming from my eyes and kept my hand on my mouth. I was trying to maintain the rage I was feeling and put my head in my hands.

"Jess, it's okay. It was just a nightmare," Izzy whispered.

"No, it wasn't," I mumbled.

"What do you mean?" Izzy asked.

"It was a memory of my mom," I said lying down.

I cuddled up to Izzy and she looked in my eyes.

"I'm sorry she isn't here with you but I'm sure she's keeping an eye on you," Izzy smiled.

I smiled and wondered if I wanted her to see the man I have become. I wanted to believe I was good, but I knew a part of me wasn't. Throughout the night I held Izzy closely, but I couldn't sleep. The thought of my mom watching over me just lingered in my brain.

The morning finally came, and we could go back upstairs. Once we got upstairs, I looked at Izzy and gestured to the porch.

"It was nice meeting you, Izzy," said Mrs. Weaver, "it looks like school is canceled so have a nice day with your parents."

"It was very nice meeting you too," said Izzy, "thank you for letting me stay."

"Of course, honey," Mrs. Weaver smiled while Mr. Weaver waved.

I walked Izzy outside, which looked awful.

"Izzy!" I yelled, grabbing her arm.

She just barely dodged the missing pieces that made up the porch. It was completely torn apart.

"Thank you," she whispered.

"You're welcome," I sighed.

"Jess, can we talk for a bit?" asked Izzy.

I swallowed hard, "Yeah sure."

"Want to walk a bit in the woods?" Izzy smiled.

"No," I said blankly.

"Oh," she paused, "alright."

"I mean with the tornado there is probably a lot of damage, and I would be pretty upset if a tree fell on you," I teased shakily.

"Where's your sense of adventure, Jess?" Izzy teased back.

"I left it in the basement," I quickly pointed back to the house.

Izzy laughed, "Come on Jess."

She grabbed my hand and hopped gracefully off the porch which caused me to fall off ungracefully. I stood up straight and let her lead me, but the shivers were already traveling up my spine. I could hear my name being called within the woods. We walked in and I was right about the damage. Trees were knocked down and were toppling all over each other. Branches were blocking passageways and trees were torn in half and hanging by threads. It looked like the trees finally had their battle and neither won.

"How about we chill here," I stop in the beginning of the woods.

"Jess," said Izzy disappointed.

"Izzy that tree looks like it's ready to snap. Look at this nice log," I lead her to it, "Let's sit there."

Izzy chuckled, "Fine."

We both sat down, and I looked around to see if we were alone. I couldn't see anybody, but I kept on hearing my name being whispered and it wasn't coming from Izzy.

"Jess, I love you," Izzy broke my concentration.

"I love you too," I answered.

"I know. I just... I am worried about you. Do you need help?" she asked.

"What?" I asked.

"I've heard that this sadness you always have in you can be dangerous. It could lead you to do things to yourself," Izzy's voice broke.

I got up quickly, "Izzy, I'm fine."

"Jess, it is okay if you aren't. It's okay not to be fine. I will always be here for you," Izzy stood up; tears were filling her eyes.

I knew she just cared and was worried about me but for some reason this conversation was angering me. I was getting tired of people wanting to get me "help."

"Well don't," I said beginning to walk into the woods. I was still intrigued by the voice I was hearing. This time it was a different tone of voice. It was a beautiful echo that just repeated, "Jess."

"What do you mean, don't?" Izzy asked, obviously shocked.

"I don't want you to worry about me. Don't ruin your life because you are worried about mine!" I yelled still not facing towards her.

"I don't understand," Izzy said quietly.

I realized I needed to calm down my tone and turned to her and said "I'm not okay but you aren't going to be the one to fix it. I won't let you pay for my mistakes."

Izzy looked at me confused. Tears were still in her eyes and she stood there with her hair in knots from sleeping in the basement. Her skin glowed in the sunlight and gave it this golden tone. I heard a crack which made me look behind me to see a tall shadow behind me. It hovered over us like it was about to attack.

"Jess!" Izzy screamed.

My head twisted over to her, and I followed her eyes up to see half of one of the trees let loose and was falling towards me. I quickly ran backwards.

"Duck Izzy!" I yelled, doing the same.

From that tree, it became a domino effect; the trees were clashing against each other making a loud numbing noise like avalanches collapsing. Izzy's scream became faint, but I could only hope she was clear. Everything was muffled as the ringing in my ears pierced them so much, I thought they were bleeding. I opened my eyes to make out the shadow which bubbled up a whole new feeling in my stomach.

"Pay back, you son of a bitch," said my father.

He grabbed my leg and dragged me through the woods. I screamed as he dragged me on the ground. I heard Izzy panicking but her calls for me became silent as I was dragged through the coarse floor of the woods. My nails stung as I dragged them into the ground. Mud shoved its way up my nails. I kicked my leg until he finally let go.

"You thought you could kill me and that would make me leave you alone?" he yelled, turning my body around to face me.

"You can't hurt me," I whispered. I tried to close my eyes and focus on reality.

"What did you fucking say?" he yelled.

"You're not real!" I yelled.

He laughed a cynical laugh that my ears still muffled. It still brought a chill down my spine.

"You are going to feel how real I am," he yelled.

I open my eyes to see his hand coming at me. He picked my head up and punched my face which busted my lip. I could already taste the blood. He picked me up by my collar and threw me against a tree which slammed my spine into the bark. I slid down and stood myself up. It felt like a million needles were just injected into my spine. I looked up at my father. His eyes were red, and his skin was glowing grey. A hole remained in his chest that looked like an ugly bloody blister.

"You're not real! You can't be real!" I said shakily.

"I'm real, Jessie. I am as real as your dead bitch of a mother. I am

108

as real as your victims. I am you and you are me," he grinned an evil grin.

"I'm not you," I mumbled.

"Are you sure?"

He ran at me and gripped my throat.

"You killed your mother, not me!" he yelled.

"No, I didn't. I saw you!" I screeched, my lungs pinching together.

"I am you!" he yelled.

"No, you're not," I began to cry.

I was beginning to lose my breath as my mind raced. It flew back to watching my mother being beaten by my father. A gun was pointed at her but behind it was me, "it's okay sweetie" she whispered. A few seconds later the gun shot, busting through her beautiful head.

"No!" I screamed, pushing him off, "Get out of my head! I know what I saw!"

"You saw what you wanted to see! You're psychotic just like me and your murders won't stop there," he grinned.

He disappeared, leaving me in the dark. I stumbled to the ground, coughed up the blood that was coming from my mouth and lay on the ground, wailing as my mind became infected with whole new images.

My mind raced back to when I was 6.

"Dad quit hurting her!" I yelled at him.

My father was standing over my mother and her body looked so beaten. My father pointed the gun at me.

"Kill her son or I will kill you," he said.

I backed up. "No."

"It's okay sweetie," cried my mother with a raspy voice as she struggled to breathe.

My father stepped over her body and grabbed me. He came up behind me and grabbed my arms and forced the gun to go in my hand. He backed away and yelled at me to do it. I cried to the point where I could only see a silhouette of my mother. My mother's hand reached out to mine and both our hands were on the gun.

"I love you baby," she whispered, and her hand pulled the trigger.

Every inch of my heart tore to shreds as I shrieked at the sight and fell to the ground.

"No mommy! Why did you do that!" I panicked.

I looked over to see a log laid by mother and I quickly picked it up and hit my father with it. Everything else was as clear as I remember...

I picked up the gun, raised it and pulled the trigger. The bullet busted through my father's chest as he clutches the wound, blood coming out of his mouth and falling limp to the ground.

After the new memory left my mind, I screamed and rocked myself back and forth. I attempted to erase the voices from my head. It pounded until I felt like my brain was liquefying through my ears. It was a terrifying thing; being afraid of your own mind.

"I'm so sorry," I whimpered.

I looked up to see the little girl.

"Did you lie to me? You said you knew I didn't kill my mother," I whispered.

"You didn't," she said with sad eyes.

"Then how come I had the gun?"

"You know Jess," she said, "your dad tried to make you, but you couldn't. So, your mom did it for you because she thought she was saving you."

I looked at her confused, "how do you know all of this?"

The little girl smiled, "I met her."

"You—" I mumbled.

"Jess!" I heard multiple voices say which caused the little girl to run off before I could finish my sentence.

I watched the little girl run but she started to blur as I started to pass out and everything went black.

Lying is hard for some people but hiding is one of the easiest things you can do. People can hide so much about themselves to the point where it bottles up and ends up destroying them. They hide it because letting out their true feelings or showing their true colors scares them to death. It makes them feel weak, weird or worse: it will hurt others they love. Even the most open person can have the most secrets. Even the kindest person can have a dark side. Sometimes people are even hiding from themselves. They are hiding under their beds; terrified that themselves will find them. The mind is a scary thing sometimes.

The mind is its own thing. It is a shadow that hovers over the bodies of humans, waiting. It is waiting for them to be at their weakest point so it can travel through their veins and into their hearts. You don't notice a human being infected until they drop to the floor in the agonizing pain you can't physically see. That is why these humans don't let anyone in. They don't want somebody to see the shadow and make it mad.

Every day they are terrified of this shadow. So, terrified that they numb themselves involuntarily. They start feeling like they aren't themselves. It is a numb, paralyzing feeling and it feels like they aren't really there. They are on the outside looking into a stranger who is living their life. They smile and laugh but it is all an act because when that same person is alone; they are sitting still, staring at a wall, as a tear falls down their cheek.

Someone can live through this. I'm sure it is possible but there comes a point where you can't fight anymore. When you fight all your life, the shadow gets stronger as you get older. Eventually the shadow will overcome you, unless you find your fight again.

Chapter 17
72-Hour Holding

I woke up in the hospital again with a terrible headache. My ears were ringing and every bone in my body ached. The first people I saw were Izzy and Mrs. Jones.

"Hi," I whispered; my voice sounded coarse.

"Hi sweetie," I heard Mrs. Weaver say.

I turned my head to see her and Mr. Weaver sitting on the couch beside my hospital bed.

"Missed seeing you Mrs. Jones," I said.

"Missed you too Jessie Reids," she smiled at me.

Mr. and Mrs. Weaver's face grew sad and Mrs. Jones noticed and began to walk out of the door. She turned to Izzy and motioned her to follow. They left the Weavers and I alone in the glass hospital room. I started noticing the smell of the hospital. It smelt like cleaning supplies and old people. I looked back over to Mrs. Weaver who had a tear fall down her cheek.

"Why did you do it?" she choked out.

"Do what?" I said confused.

"Why did you try so hard to hurt yourself, Jess? Why won't you let us just help you?" Tears were falling down her cheeks like waterfalls.

"What are you talking about?" I said a little more annoyed than I meant it to sound.

"Jess, the doctor said your injuries were self-inflicted. They weren't from the falling trees and nobody else was there," explained Mr. Weaver, coming to his wife's defense.

"No, they weren't," I whispered.

"Jess, look at your hands!" Mrs. Weaver yelled in sorrow.

I looked at the IVs and wires that lead to my hands. They were black and blue, and my knuckles were busted open. It made me realize that I didn't remember fighting back so how would my fists be so beat up? The thought of me punching and choking myself, made me shiver. It wasn't possible but then again, I knew it wasn't possible that my dead father did it either. My heart started racing and I could feel tears forming in my eyes. I looked at the Weavers with red eyes.

"I want to talk to Izzy," I said breathlessly.

Mrs. Weaver shook her head at Mr. Weaver but they both filed out and let Izzy in. She walked in slowly towards me, but I didn't look up; I just stared at my hands. I didn't even want to know what my face looked like.

"Why Jess? You told me not to worry," Izzy whispered.

"I know, I'm sorry," I said.

"I don't understand. You need to help me understand," Izzy said shakily.

I looked up into her tear-filled eyes and could see how much I was hurting her which killed me. I wished I could let her go but I was too selfish and needed her too much. She was the only person who made me feel the least bit sane.

"I don't understand myself," I said.

"You..." she paused and forced herself to say, "beat yourself up. How do I get past that? I know you had it rough but what about now? Aren't you happy now?"

"I love you," was all I could answer.

"That's not enough to live on, Jess," she whispered.

"Yes, it is," I answered.

I gestured for her to crawl into the hospital bed with me and she did. She curled up next to me and hugged me as she lays there.

"I'm sorry for being too selfish to let you go," I said.

"I don't want to go anywhere," she answered.

That made me smile but I also had a guilty feeling in the pit of my stomach.

The hospital came up with a 72- hour holding rule until I could go home. The Weavers signed paperwork as Izzy hugged me goodbye.

"I'll come visit you, okay," she whispered into my shoulder.

"I know you will, and I will be looking forward to it," I smiled.

She backed out of my embrace and nodded. Mrs. Jones came to her side and gave her a side squeeze. She walked up to me and put her hands on my shoulders. Her face looked kind and she had the same expression she usually gets when she is about to give me her speeches.

"This place isn't juvi, Jess. It will help you and not toss you aside. I know you don't believe in programs like this, but I believe it will help if you let it. Ultimately, it is up to you and I believe in you. If anyone can get through this, it is you," her voice calm and quiet.

"Thank you, Mrs. Jones," I smiled.

She nodded and gave me a hug. The Weavers followed after her giving me quick hugs and soon they were walking out of the hospital. I watched as Mrs. Jones consoled Izzy as they walked out together. It hurt but also brought a smile to my face because it told me she wouldn't be alone in this.

The nurses walked me to my room and explained I would be roomed with someone who had similar "problems" as me. I couldn't tell if that meant he saw things or tried to commit suicide. His name was Benjamin, but he preferred Benny. This guy had long, dark, shaggy hair that curled in spirals at the end and a little bit of scruff on his face. He was a tall and slim guy with crazy indented cheekbones. The man was wearing simple gray sweats and a black t-shirt but he cuffed the sweats, so it almost looked like a style. Again, me in sweatpants, I just look homeless. When I walked in the room, I saw that he decorated. It was a bunch of drawings that I guess where done by him. They were these strange looking cartoon characters.

"Nice drawings," I said.

"Thanks," he looked at me and back at the book he was reading.

I tried to look underneath to see what he was reading but he just gave me a weird look and quickly closed it. I sighed and started to go through what the Weavers decided to pack me. A couple of T-shirts, a pair of jeans and a book that I've never seen. I opened it up to see a piece of paper that said, "I thought this fit- Declan." I read the title *One Flew Over the Cuckoo's Nest*. I didn't get the joke until I started reading it. That is pretty much what I did the entire time. I went to the meetings with the therapist and the "group therapy."

The worst part was the groups. It was led by one of the nurses, his name was Tyler. This man was a bit shorter than I was and had a perfectly shaped dark beard that traveled from each earlobe and under his chin. He was wearing circle glasses that looked thick. Tyler paced around the room to look at all the strange people sitting in a circle.

I know for sure that I am not normal, but you wouldn't believe the other problems people have. Some of them were legit, I will admit. Benny seemed like he had a shitty life that he didn't want to talk about, and he just wanted to leave it. Apparently, he took a shit ton of pills and stole his parent's vodka. I didn't mind listening to him talk. It was honestly strange hearing about a kid who seemed like he had the world, struggle. Benny was rich, he lived in a big house and went to a private school. However, his parents were assholes and when he told them how he felt, they said to stop looking for attention. I guess he showed them by proving it wasn't just him looking for attention. Anyways, some of the other patients were just weird and some seemed like they were bragging about what was messed up about them. Congrats, your mind is the most fucked up; here is your trophy. I know that makes me sound like an asshole but there was one guy who bragged about how he beat up kids and how it made him feel better. There was one girl who always carried a baby doll. However, that one was kind of sad because I learned it was because she lost a child and believed that the doll was her child still alive. When we had to go in groups, I was stuck with her one time and I didn't know what to do, so, I talked to the baby doll. I'm not sure if I should have encouraged it or not but I did.

"Aren't you a cutie?" I said...to the baby doll.

She looked at me strange and said, "Babies can't answer you."

I looked at the woman and back at the baby doll.

"Right," I cleared my throat.

I could not believe I was the one that sounded like the dumbass in that situation. We both sat there silently as she rocked her pretend child.

"I didn't catch your name," I broke the silence.

"Rebecca," she smiled.

I nodded, "And your...child's name?"

"Rosa."

"Very pretty," I fake smiled.

That is about all I got out of her because she continued to rock the doll while I stared at my shoes which have gotten significantly dirtier. I looked over to see Benny just staring at the window, sat in front of the kid who liked to beat on people.

"Hey, Rich, can you speak?" said the kid.

I looked over, curious about the conversation.

Benny had his arms crossed and looked over. "Yes Mitch, I can speak. I just told my whole life story a second ago. There's nothing else for me to talk about."

Mitch scoffed, "If we were in school, I'd beat the living shit out of you."

"I'd like to see you try," scoffed Benny.

"That's enough!" yelled Tyler.

His shout made everyone jump and look at him. Tyler stood up and straightened his jacket. For some reason, he was wearing a full tux for this group session. Seems a bit overdressed to me but to each their own.

"Group session is over. You may return to your rooms," he said.

We all dispersed as quickly as kids who leave their classrooms at the sound of the bell. I nodded to Rebecca who shyly smiled at me. Benny and I walked out together.

"You okay?" I asked him.

"Just another asshole, right?" he sighed.

"Right," I said.

"Jessie Reids," I heard a nurse say.

I turned around to see this pretty nurse with blonde hair pulled back in a bun. Her eyes were green, and she had a doctor's coat that draped over her curvy body. She held a notebook on her hip and stared at me with a kind smile.

"Dr. Robinson would like to see you," she smiled.

"Thank you…" I waited for her name.

"Lacie," she smiled, "just down the hall and to your right."

I nodded and spun around to walk down the hall. I walked past Benny and I's room to see that Benny cracked open his drawing book. Also, Mitch seemed to be across the hall from us which seemed like a bad idea. I got to the door on the right to read "Dr. Robinson Therapist" on the door.

She was very tall, pale and had short brown hair. She had these glasses on that had the weird string that goes around her entire head. I'm not sure if there is a name for that or not…Anyways, she looked very young except the slight crow's feet around her eyes that seemed to be the only proof she aged.

Dr. Robinson was nice, but she always seemed like she was trying to dig deeper. I'd always give short answers on how I was feeling. They already had information about my time in juvie, so I didn't like repeating myself. She would ask things like "explain the shadows, Jess."

I would answer, "They look like shadows. They are silhouettes of people…like a shadow."

I tried to explain the moment with my dad in the woods, but it just got confusing to her. The thing that I don't think they get is with these illnesses you can get help, talk about it and even concuss it but it'll still be there. Even when you barely feel it so much that you think it's gone. It is still there buried deep inside you. It sits there waiting to come out when you are at your weakest. When it does hit; it hits hard to where it feels like a knife has been driven into your heart. We trick ourselves into thinking we found happiness when really, we have just got so good at pretending that we have started to believe our own lies.

"Have you thought about hurting other people?" the therapist asked.

What kind of question is that? If I say no, I am lying. I can't say yes because I'm afraid they will throw me in prison. I'm not sure if they can do that based on just saying I've thought about it, but I wasn't giving it a chance. Instead, I changed the subject.

"Why do you think we can kill this monster inside us?" I asked.

It startled her but she said something that I thought was actually decent.

"We may not be able to kill the monster inside us but we sure as hell can fight it."

It surprised me because first, she said, "hell," it brings the same shock as when a high school teacher cusses and second, she did more than the usual "and how does that make you feel." After she said that I decided to listen to her and give her a chance. I have never had someone make sense like that when they are talking about mental health.

The next day they allowed visitors, which made it a much better day. Benny stayed in our room drawing some character with bat wings.

"Do you want to join me with my family?" I asked, I felt bad that his family didn't visit him.

"I don't get close to temporary people," he mumbled.

I looked at him shocked, I mean, it made sense. I was only here for 72 hours and it seemed like he had to be here much longer. Why get close to someone only to never see them again?

"That's fair. Have fun drawing," I said.

"Always do," he muttered.

I walked out to what kind of looks like a living room. It's where they allow families to visit and for patients to hang out occasionally.

Since it was in a hospital, it looked more like a waiting room. The Weavers, Izzy and Mrs. Jones came.

Mrs. Weaver explained to me that everyone was doing decently. Adeline has been excelling at school ever since they let her back in. Declan had detention for starting a fight during his gym class. AnnMarie got a D on her test and she is very bummed about it and they are afraid they might want to hold Brady back since he doesn't talk in class much. Mrs. Weaver thinks she can get around that though because he is a brilliant kid.

Mrs. Jones told me about a date she might be going on which made me happy that she was living her life because here lately she seemed focused on me. It also made me happy that it was the man from the barber shop because that is probably the only man that might be deserving of Mrs. Jones. The way he made her smile and the genuine kindness that would radiate off him. Honestly, he and Mrs. Jones are very similar when it comes to being kind-hearted.

They all left to let me hang out with Izzy by ourselves. She brought me schoolwork that I was missing. They didn't allow PDA so that's pretty much all we did. She talked about her art class and how she missed seeing me at school. Every time she would try to ask me how it is going; I would just say I want to talk about her to get my mind off things. She seemed to understand that and would start talking about a film she had seen. I told her about the book Declan gave me and apparently Izzy loves the book. I hate to admit it because it was a joke from Declan, but I liked it too.

After a bit, I could see Izzy's face changing. Something was up but I couldn't tell if it was me being here or something else.

"Izzy, what's wrong?" I asked.

"I don't know. I was avoiding talking about it because I've been trying to keep my mind off it," Izzy sighed. A tear formed in her eye.

"Izzy?"

"My biological dad. My mom found out he died," Izzy said.

"Oh," I paused, "I'm sorry Izzy."

"I don't know why I'm sad because I don't really know him, and he left. Apparently, he was addicted to heroin or something," she shrugged, "and he overdosed on that. Turns out that's his reasoning for leaving too."

I put my arm around her. I don't why I couldn't think of anything to say. What could I say that would make her feel any better?

"What is it about addiction that makes people do things that are so cold?" she asked.

It stumped me. I didn't know too much about addiction other than being afraid of my alcoholic tendencies. I mean my father drank but he was never really a drunk. He was just an asshole who enjoyed his whiskey occasionally.

"That's a good question. I don't know," I sighed.

"A part of me wants to. Of course, not experience it myself, God no," Izzy chuckled, "but to understand what it does to people. You know?"

I chuckled.

"What?" she smiled.

"Nothing, you."

"Me?" she looked confused.

"Most people would say to hell with him. He chose what killed him over me. But you, I don't know, you want to understand people. Even the people that don't deserve your understanding," I said.

"Everyone has more to them," Izzy said.

"Maybe or you just think deeper than everyone," I smiled.

Izzy chuckled, "Is that good or bad?"

"Definitely good," I hugged her.

I pressed my lips against hers. A cough interrupts us, making us both look over to see Tyler, the group leader, standing there with his arms crossed.

"Visitation time is over," he said.

I nodded, "Yes sir."

Izzy smiled at him and looked at me, "Bye, see you again soon."

"Bye," I smiled.

She walked away, meeting up with Mrs. Jones who looked back at me and waved.

I waved bye to all of them as they left the hospital. Tyler waited till I was done waving goodbye and turned to me.

"Group in 5 minutes," he said.

He always seemed to keep things super short unless it was his monologues in group therapy. I saluted him which just made him look at me weird. I shrugged, and decided just to follow him in. There was no sense in pacing the hallways until then. When I got in, Rebecca was already there singing to her...Rosa. The blue chairs were all set in a circle. I sat on the other side of Rebecca. I figured it would be weird to sit directly near her when there was an abundance of open seats. I sat there staring at anything but the people. The white blinds on the windows, the baby blue chairs, the perfectly clean tile floor and a "you matter" poster which I couldn't help but chuckle at. Rebecca was singing to her baby "Rock-a-bye Baby" which I just realized had some violent lyrics. I mean they just let the baby fall, cradle and all? How fucked up is that?

Everyone else started filling in and Benny ended up sitting next to me and far away from Mitch. There were some new faces filing in. A very thin brunette who looked ill which looked worrisome. Another was woman who had dark skin and had her hands scorched. There was pink showing on her hands from where it was burnt.

"Everyone we have some new people miss Andrea and Tiffany. Welcome to group, this is a safe space," said Tyler in the softest tone I've ever heard his voice go.

They did not seem amused a bit which made me smile. It is funny how equally no one wants to be here.

"We are going to start with an exercise. I am going to throw you this ball and when you catch it, I want you to repeat something that was said to you that hurt you. After that, you will name something that you like about yourself that will cancel it out," Tyler said.

Benny rolled his eyes and let out a sigh. Some of the other patients looked at him confused.

"Don't worry," Tyler laughed, "I will go first. 'Your lifestyle is a sin' and my answer to that is at least I'm not pretending to be someone I'm not."

I smiled. I don't know why but you don't expect the nurses of a psych ward to have felt the same kind of pain. You sort of assume that they have all the answers in life and are just there to share their "wisdom" and not taming their own demons.

Rebecca looks up confused. "I don't get it, how is your lifestyle as a nurse a sin?"

Benny chuckled and Tyler smiled at the comment.

"He's gay, Rebecca," said Mitch.

"You are?" she looked confused.

"Rebecca, you've met his boyfriend. He came in last week," chuckled Benny.

"I just thought that was friend," she said, "well congrats!"

"Thank you, Rebecca," Tyler tries to hide a chuckle, "Why don't you go next," he tosses her the ball.

"'You are going to make a terrible mother' well obviously they were wrong because I make a great mother," she smiled.

That tug on my heart a little.

"Yes, you are. Why don't you pass it to someone?" he asked.

"Mitch, catch!" she smiled as she threw the ball.

Mitch grabbed it and looked at the ball. I could tell his jaw clenched, "'You ruined my life' well at least I have one."

"One of the new girls go," he said, passing it to Andrea.

"'You look disgusting' but at least I'm trying to get better and healthy again," she said.

She just passed it to Tiffany who was next to her.

"'If you died no one would care', well someone did care which is why I'm still alive today," she nodded and tossed it to Benny.

Benny caught it with two hands and looked at Tyler. I could tell he wanted to tell him where to stick the ball but he untensed and decided to participate.

"'You are an embarrassment to this family.' Trust me you don't need me to do that," he laughed.

He looked at me with a smile and handed me the ball. I took it in my hand, realizing I had not thought about my answer. I stared at it for a while with tunnel vision. I tried to search for the words that were scarring enough but maybe not too deep. I could feel hot tears form in my eyes as I searched my brain for the words.

My mind raced and I was little again. A very faint but still detailed memory. I just saw my father smack my mother over his dinner being cold. I ran up to him and tried to stop his hand from the next blow, but I was too light. Instead, I was thrown to the ground next to her. I looked up to see my father hovering over me. My mother's hand tried to reach for me before him, but he picked me up by the collar of my shirt and yelled, "You little shit—"

What came out was a little too dark.

"'I wish you were dead,' well now YOU are," I gritted my teeth.

The room fell silent and I could feel the whole room staring at me. I just sighed and tossed Tyler the ball who surprisingly didn't look as shocked.

"Karma's a bitch," I heard Benny say.

I looked at him and he was leaned in his chair smiling. He looked at me like he was proud of what I said.

I nodded and smiled, "Got to love her."

Tyler ended group therapy, and everyone dispersed to their rooms or the common room. He pulled me aside.

"Dr. Robinson wanted to speak with you after group," he said.

"Okay thanks, Tyler," I nodded.

A bad feeling rose in my stomach, thinking it had to do with something about my answer. Turns out it was a quick chat with the therapist about how to keep coping with schizophrenia once I got out. We talked about the medication I would have to take and how I should start keeping a tightly scheduled week. She suggested that I create a routine for myself that will get my mind off things. We started writing hobbies down that I wouldn't mind getting into. I am not much of a "hobby" person, so I just started naming things.

"Dancing, surfboarding, wait I don't live near an ocean, move to an ocean and then surfboard. Boxing! Hiking, just kidding," I laughed, "the woods give me hallucinations."

"Jessie come on be serious," my therapist said.

"I am!" I exclaimed, sarcastically.

"Really dig deep. What is something you enjoy?" she asked.

I paused and searched my mind for something I enjoyed. I used to like drawing when I was a kid, but I lost interest in that.

"Writing," I said.

"Okay Jessie. You have homework for tonight. Write something and bring it to our last session tomorrow," Dr. Robinson said.

"Alright fine. Can it be anything?" I asked.

"Yes, it can," she said.

Apart of me wanted to write something super erotic but I knew it was my last day. So, I probably should not ruin my chances of getting out because I wrote a porno to my therapist.

I walked into our room to see Benny sat up on his bed with his back against the wall, reading. Last time, he hid what he was reading so I decided to ask him.

"What are you reading?" I ask.

Benny doesn't say a word and instead lifts up his book to show me the cover.

"*The Picture of Dorian Gray,*" I read out loud.

Benny closed it and handed it to me. I started reading the back and it seemed like an interesting plot. I silently gave it back to Benny. I knew he wasn't much of a talker, but he seemed like an interesting person, and I wanted to know more about him.

"How long are you in here for?" I asked.

Benny looked at me and his eyebrows scrunched together, "You make it sound like prison."

I shrugged, "Same difference."

Benny chuckled, "I don't know, really. My parents are paying for the stay, and I don't think they necessarily want me back. So, at this point I am here until I have a plan."

"A plan?" I asked.

"Got to live somewhere, Reids." Benny smirked.

"So, are you…cured?" I hated that word.

"Is anyone really cured?" Benny asked the million-dollar question, "Are you?"

I smirked, "No I'm probably crazier now."

Benny laughed at that, "Yeah me too."

"What about you, Reids? What are your plans?" he asked sitting up straight and crossing his legs, looking intrigued.

"You don't have to keep talking to me, if you want to go back to reading about Dorian's painting that's fine."

"Nope, you interrupted me, now you must suffer the consequences of talking about your future," Benny said in such a monotoned voice.

I honestly had no answer to his question. What the hell was I going to do after this 72-hour holding? Probably nothing. I would go back to my normal life and slightly toxic ways. Forget all I have learned at this hospital. During my internal conflicting, Benny was waiting for an answer with one eyebrow raised and a bored expression.

"I have no plans," I shrugged.

Benny nodded, "My condolences."

I gave Benny an annoyed expression.

He sighed, "Just remember what you learned when it's bad and don't close yourself off from the people who want to help you. Those visitors you had, use them. Not everyone has people who would visit them in the nut house."

I was surprised at Benny and the way he was talking to me. Like he was one of the doctors or nurses that worked here.

"I think this place is rubbing off on you," I smiled.

"Yeah, I just made myself want to throw up," he mumbled with a sour face.

Benny picked up his book, went back to his reading position and found his chapter. He looked up from his book at me, smirked and looked back down to pay attention to what he was reading. I just smiled and lay down on my bed and grabbed my own book to read.

Chapter 18
Shadows in The Mind

It was the last day of my hospital stay and I wrote a very short poem. I hoped it was enough because it honestly took me forever to come up with. Why is it that whenever you have a deadline, you get writers block? We started out the day with our groups. Everyone shared something positive. We focused on the things we want instead of why we were here.

"I want to get healthy and get out of here. I want to gain a job, so, I can get out of my parent's house and create a life for myself that is just mine," said Benny.

"I want my little girl to grow up and be proud of her mother," said Rebecca, rocking her baby doll.

"I want to be a professional fighter," said Mitch, which seemed way too on point.

"I want to be healthier so I can do something with my life," said Andrea.

"I want to prove to my bullies that they can't break me," said Tiffany.

It finally got to me and I froze. I was too busy trying to come up with a poem for Dr. Robinson that I ran out of words to say.

"I just want to be happy," I said.

It wasn't a lot but apparently it resonated well with everyone because they did their usual clap. After we all filed out and Lacie the nurse stopped me.

"Dr.."

"Robinson is ready for you," I mocked her voice.

She looked at me and smiled, "I don't sound like that."

"Yes, you do," said Benny passing by us and into our room.

I laughed and walked into Dr. Robinson's office.

"Jessie, is there any questions you have for me before you leave?" she asked.

"No."

"Okay, what did you learn?" she asked.

People always seem to ask that question in almost every setting.

"That I'm not the only one with problems," I said.

Dr. Robinson nodded with a smile on her face.

"I'm proud of you," she said.

"Thank you," I responded awkwardly.

"Why don't we end this session with what you wrote," she pointed at the folded-up paper I had tucked in my hand.

I nodded and un-crumbled the piece of paper and cleared my throat.

"This is a poem I wrote, at least I think it would be considered a poem because it rhymes a bit. It's rough, but I tried. Anyways, it's called Shadows in the Mind...

As the soul looks in the mirror,

Everything in their world becomes clearer.

The shadows in the air,

Were never really fair.

Infecting the insides of a soul torn to shreds,

Drying tears as the soul lies in bed.

The truth lingers within the back of the mind,

While the soul leaves all reality behind."

I folded it back up and looked at her. She just smiled back at me.

"That was beautiful," she said.

"Thank you," I muttered as I put the piece of paper in my back pocket.

"Ready to go home?" she asked.

I nodded but a small part of me wanted to say 'no.'

Mrs. Weaver and Izzy were there to take me home. They both gave me a hug and Izzy kissed me on the cheek. I thought of saying goodbye to Benny, but he wasn't in the room when I went to grab my things. Perhaps, he was following his rule not to get close to temporary people. I am sure that included goodbyes. I waved goodbye to Rebecca before I walked out of the hospital. She waved back as she held her doll close to her.

I thought what the hell "Bye Rosa!" I shouted.

Tyler started walking down the hallway as I was holding my stuff.

"Jessie," he said, holding out his hand.

I nodded and shook it. Tyler nodded back at me and walked away. Oddly, it wasn't much but it felt like it said a lot. Like he was sending me off to the world.

We all drove home and dropped Izzy off first. I was surprised nobody asked me questions, but they probably knew I wouldn't elaborate much. After Izzy was dropped off, the car became silent. Mrs. Weaver just looked straight forward.

"I have school tomorrow, right?" I tried to break the silence.

"Yes, but you don't have to go. You can take some days off if you would like," said Mrs. Weaver.

"No, I want to go," I said. I've already had plenty of 'time off.'

We walked in the house and Mrs. Weaver asked if I wanted something to eat but I was too preoccupied by everybody who immediately stood up with looks of guilt on their faces. That hit me in the pit of my stomach. Pity, they were all pitying me. It made me miss Adeline's inappropriate flirting and Declan's anger. I looked at all of them individually without changing my expression and began walking through them.

"I'm not hungry," I muttered as I walked upstairs.

My mind surprisingly felt dead but more out of exhaustion. I went into the bathroom and looked at myself in the mirror. My face was bruised, and my neck still had slight bruises. I looked like a zombie. My eyes were red, and I had sunken bags under my eyes. Did I seriously look like this the entire time I was at the hospital?

I started to become afraid again. Something about being in the hospital made things easier. It was like the place had a force field around it, like a demon free zone. The shadows didn't bother me, and we talked about them in a metaphorical sense. My head started spinning and my skin crawled. Cold sweat started forming on my forehead. I wasn't sure what was happening, but it felt awful.

I fell to the ground and covered my head. I felt like I was going to puke. I started to feel like I was hyperventilating until I heard a knock on the bathroom door.

"Jess, you in there?" I heard Declan's voice.

I took a deep breath "yeah."

"I don't mean to be a dick right now, but I have to take a shit!" Declan shouted.

I got up and opened the door to see Declan leaning against the wall. He looked straight into my eyes.

"Just tell them your high, that's what I do," he said.

"Thanks man."

Declan nodded and brushed past me to go in the bathroom. I went into our room, grabbed my water bottle off the side of the table and crawled into my bunk. I sat up and decided to take the pills, following it with a huge gulp of water. I put the water bottle next to me. I lay down and slept the day away.

I tried to keep my mind blank but this time there were too many thoughts for my mind to catch one. They floated around my head like tiny whispers crying for help without being heard. Eventually the pain numbed my body to sleep and I could have a good night's sleep.

Chapter 19
Tabloids

I woke up feeling oddly better than usual. I couldn't tell if it was the therapy working out or a good moment before a bad episode. I got up to see that everyone was out of the room. I looked at the time to see that I wasn't running late. I went into the bathroom to see that my hair was a mess. Pieces of my hair stuck out in every direction. I quickly brushed it and put on a pair of jeans and a grey t-shirt. While brushing my teeth, I threw on my sneakers and went back into the bathroom to spit in the sink. I came downstairs to see everyone in the kitchen eating breakfast. Declan was standing against the wall with his arms crossed.

"Morning guys," I said wearily.

"You sure you even want to go to school?" asked Adeline, walking towards me.

"Yeah, why?" I asked.

"Well," Adeline paused, "things spread like wildfires around that school. I mean you see how my sexual encounter spread. You are going to be the school's suicidal kid."

"Thanks for worrying but at this point we might as well embrace our labels," I mumbled.

Adeline nodded with a smile. I went to pass her but stopped in my tracks and turned to her.

"You aren't a whore. When guys shit spread around, they don't have labels, so, why do you need a label," I added.

She sighed, looked down and looked back up at me, "thanks Jess."

I nodded and we both walked together towards the kitchen.

"Jess," Declan stopped me, "they are all going to know. It went in the paper," Declan held it up.

"The paper?" I asked.

"Former prisoner attempts suicide," Adeline read, taking the paper out of Declan's hand.

My stomach dropped.

"Well, now I need to go," I said.

"What do you mean?" Declan scoffed.

"Someone has to explain to Izzy why it says former prisoner," I looked at them.

They all froze and looked at each other with 'oh shit' expressions. Declan sighed and opened our front door, and we walked in silence to the bus. Throughout the bus ride my stomach was sick. I pictured Izzy freaking out on me about being in juvie. Once we got to school, Declan walked beside me instead of dispersing from me. As we walked through the hallway, I got a lot of stares. I glanced at Declan who was glaring back at anyone who glared at me which made me smile. My smile dropped when I locked eyes with Izzy who looked at me with a sad face.

"Izzy," I said walking toward her.

"Don't worry about them. That is terrible that someone would put that in the newspaper," said Izzy.

"So, you've read it," I said, softly, trying not to panic. My hands started sweating.

"Of course not. I find it unnerving that someone would exploit a suicide attempt like that," Izzy ranted.

"Thank God," said Declan walking away.

"What?" Izzy laughed.

"He's glad you didn't participate in the Jessie Reids roast," I laughed.

Izzy smiled, "I'm sorry people are assholes."

"Not your fault," I smiled back.

"I know your answer will most likely be 'it was stupid', she mocked my voice, "but did staying in the hospital help a little?"

I stopped walking, "I do not sound like that."

"Jess," she whined.

"Yes, I think it may have the slightest bit, helped," I said, hesitantly.

"I'm glad," she smiled.

I looked up and noticed Kyle was looking straight at me from his locker. His gaze went to our hands which were locked, and he looked at me with anger. Izzy squeezed my hand and went to her first class. I barely lasted through my classes before the English class. My stomach was in knots as I walked into class to see Kyle and Izzy sitting next to each other.

"Did you read the paper?" asked Kyle quietly but loud enough so I could hear.

"Of course not. It takes a real asshole to make money off a suicide attempt," Izzy whispered.

"Well, some people like to keep up with their town's tabloid topic," Kyle whispered.

My muscles tensed up.

"He has done it before?" Izzy looked at Kyle.

"Or something worse," Kyle muttered to her.

Izzy was silent and still through the rest of the class. I also remained in an awkward position the entire time. I was hanging onto the desk with my hands, squeezing it until my hands were turning white. My breathing was heavy, and I started hyperventilating. My eyes started to get involuntarily watery. This feeling like I was about to puke or pass out overwhelmed me. I looked down at my hands that were still squeezing onto the desk and noticed they were trembling.

The class released and Izzy turned to me but instantly her facial expression became worried.

"Jess? Are you okay?" she rushed toward me, "are you having a panic attack?"

"A what?" I said breathlessly.

I could feel a tingling sensation in my face as my head started spinning. A pain shot through my chest which caused me to clutch it.

"Just breathe," Izzy grabbed my hand.

I watched Kyle as he walked out. I could tell he sped up after he caught my glare. My breathing slowed down, and I looked in Izzy's eyes.

"I don't want to be here," I whispered to her.

Izzy's face grew worried, "Do you want me to take you home?"

"No," I said, "I'll just go outside. I need some air."

Izzy sighed, "at least let me walk you out."

I nodded and we both walked through the hallway.

"Jess, you are shaking. I am skipping my next class," Izzy said with frustration.

Izzy grabbed my hand again and led me outside to a tree. We both sat down on the grass. I stared back at the school; my body felt calm, but my mind was still in panic.

"I love you, Jess," Izzy smiled at me.

"I love you too," I said distractingly.

Izzy still looked at me with a worried face. I could tell she was thinking to herself; her mind was probably racing with thoughts. She let me calm myself down as I breathed in and out. My body stopped shaking and I could see much clearer, but the image was a puzzled look on Izzy's face. I knew she was about to ask a lot of questions which made my stomach feel sick.

"Jess, Kyle did mention that you are well-known to the tabloids, but everyone has a past. I love who you are now, and I don't want to lose you," Izzy said with tears streaming down her face.

"I don't know what's wrong with me," I whispered.

Izzy hugged me and I held her there. I didn't want to let go.

"Thank you," I whispered to her.

"For what?" she asked.

"For being my reason to live," I whispered.

I was being so selfish, and I knew that. The fact that Izzy would focus on her love for me instead of the curiosity of my mysterious past surprised me. Especially because I knew if the roles were reversed; I might not have done the same.

Kyle walked out of the school and didn't see us. I watched him as he pulled a newspaper out of the trash. I knew my reason for living would be taken from me, but I couldn't let it happen. I had to find a way.

"Izzy, can we take a nap or something," I whispered in her ear.

Izzy giggled "sounds good to me."

Izzy looked up at me and pressed her lips against mine and lays her head on my lap. It was very relaxing. It didn't matter that my back was pressed up against a tree. The sun was shining on my face as I closed my eyes and looked up. Oddly enough, I did fall asleep. There was nothing preoccupying my mind and instead it was at rest.

I felt like I could possibly see clouds floating in the sky if I focused hard enough. Everything was calm before the storm.

The peacefulness was interrupted by the sound of the bell. It was the end of school bell. We slept through half a school day or at least I did. When I opened my eyes, Izzy was smiling at me.

"What?" I asked.

"You were out of it," Izzy smiled.

"No, I wasn't," I jokingly defended myself.

Izzy laughed.

"Alright, sleeping beauty. I've got to get to a family gathering. Want a ride back home?" Izzy got up with a spring.

"I think I'm going to take the bus back today," I smiled.

"What?" Izzy looked surprised.

"Or I might walk," I smiled again.

"Are you okay?" Izzy teased.

"I am now. It is a nice day and I need some time to think."

Izzy looked confused but shrugged, "Okay."

"Oh, look there's a poetry night at a bar and grill, downtown. Would you want to go?" she asked.

"Sure, what time?"

"It's at 7. I can pick you up after my little family reunion," Izzy smiled.

"Sounds good, I will see you then," I said.

She gave me another kiss and started walking to the parking lot. She looked back at me with a smile "have fun reminiscing!" she shouted.

I smiled but my smile dropped when I saw Kyle coming towards me. He looked angry but at least he was walking towards me and not Izzy.

"I need to talk to you," he said, calmly.

He usually seemed so terrified of me but this time he remained calm. It was almost strange how calm he was.

Kyle started walking towards the back of the school without even looking back. As I followed him, I pictured myself killing him, but that image came with losing Izzy. It would be the perfect reason to turn around but what kept me following him was the thought I could lose her anyways because of him. I pictured him showing the trash covered paper to Izzy, her being horrified that she has been sleeping with a killer and what is worse is I imagined the look she would give me.

I followed Kyle till we got to the group of trees behind the school. My mind felt so fuzzy, and my sight was in tunnel vision with my only focus being on following Kyle. I stopped in my tracks once I realized Kyle stopped walking.

"I refuse to stand by and let you ruin Izzy's life," Kyle turned to me.

"I won't hurt her," I paused, "I need her."

"That's the problem, Jess. You need her to stay sane. Without her, you would probably kill the entire town," Kyle said.

"You're right. I do need her to stay sane which proves I won't hurt her. Why would I hurt the one person I need the most?" I asked.

"Because you already are! You are lying to her! You have made everyone terrified of you to the point where no one will tell her. Those letters? Death threats to students!" Kyle's face was getting red.

"Letters?" I said confused.

"It'll hurt her less if she knows soon. It'll only get worse. I mean when do you plan on telling her? Marriage? After you knock her up? What will ever happen if you two get in a fight, huh? What? If you can't have her no one can!"

"Shut up!"

"You don't scare me anymore. I am going to tell her, and I am going to make sure she is far away from you," Kyle said sternly as he got in my face.

In a sudden movement, I gripped his throat with both of my hands. I glared into his eyes and could see the fear in them no matter how hard he tried to hide it. The nobility look on his face filled with covered anger that was hiding the fact that his whole body was shaking. I was impressed by how brave Kyle was being, but I also hated him for it.

"So, your plan is to kill me," he managed to choke out.

I loosened my grip a little. I was trying to fight my own rage. I felt like there were two voices in my head and I wasn't sure which one was the right one anymore.

"You think that's going to keep Izzy from finding out," Kyle was struggling to breathe.

I let go of his throat.

"My turn," he croaked.

Kyle punched me in the face, and it was a hard-enough hit to hear a ringing in my ears. I slammed my back into the tree behind me which sent a shock down my spine. I looked up to see shadows huddling around us as if they were watching a throw down.

"How does your own scare tactic feel?" Kyle said laughing.

"You've gone mad," I said, "I've gotten into your mind, Kyle. Never let a psycho into your mind," I said, pulling myself up.

I licked my lip and could taste the blood coming from it. Kyle looked at me with both rage and terror in his eyes. The cluster of trees was giving me flashbacks of my last encounter in the woods.

"You won't turn me into a monster, and you won't suck the good out of Izzy," he swung at me again, but I dodged it, pulled his arm and made him slam into a tree.

"Izzy's strong. Stronger than me," I grabbed his hair, "and I won't let you take her away from me."

I turned Kyle around to look at me and pulled his head forward and slammed it into the tree again.

"You'll lose Izzy either way," Kyle groaned, "you're a monster."

Tears started to fall from my face. My hands looked blurry; everything looked so blurry. Kyle's eyes no longer showed any look of fear. He looked at me so blankly and closed his eyes. I felt like I was urging myself to stop but a part of me had no intention of stopping.

"Eventually, being a monster is easier than proving to people you aren't one," I whispered.

I slammed his head harder and harder until I heard the chilling crack of his skull. I let him slide down as he lay on the ground. The ringing in my ears didn't stop and everything was muffled. I felt my whole body shaking as I stared at what I did. Kyle just lays there, limp and covered in blood. His face seemed frozen in his last brave look at me. My tears started to sting, and I just dropped to my knees.

I looked up to see the little girl who was looking at me with a frightened look. She didn't say a word and instead just backed away and ran off. I didn't want her to say anything, and I couldn't say anything to her. I just thought to myself 'person number 2.'

Chapter 20
Poetry Night

I slowly lifted myself up and walked out of the woods like a zombie. I had a bit of blood on my hands but not enough to draw attention. The school remained unlocked for the detention students, so I snuck in to go to the bathroom. I rinsed my hands off and didn't dare look at myself in the mirror. Tears fell from my eyes as I breathed heavily. I could feel vomit forming in my throat and quickly ran to the toilet to hurl it up. The feeling was a burning sensation like I had strep throat. I picked myself up and decided to look in the mirror. My eyes were red, and I looked drained but other than that I looked chillingly normal. I took a sip of water from the sink and walked out of the bathroom. I looked at the time that read 4:00.

I decided the best thing I could do was somehow get back home in time for Izzy to pick me up for the poetry night. It made me feel sick that I was about to go on date night like everything was normal. I wasn't sure what else to do. I felt so messed up and had this big longing to just see Izzy's face. The detention kids started walking towards the entrance and I just filed out with them. I was relieved to see Declan walking out, maybe that means he will have a ride.

"Hey who's picking you up?" I asked him.

"Mark's coming," Declan said, getting out a cigarette.

He put it up to his mouth and lit it up.

He looked at me. "You look like shit," he said in the middle of his drag.

"Thanks," I said.

Declan looked around the outside of the school and back at me.

"No seriously, what the hell?"

"What?" I asked.

"You're still at school and not in detention and you look like you just saw a ghost," said Declan.

"Just missed the bus," I shrugged.

Declan didn't believe me for a second, "uh huh" he rolled his eyes.

I looked over to see Mr. Weaver pull up and we both walked over to him.

Declan hoped in the front, and I hoped in the back.

"Jessie, you got detention too?" Mr. Weaver asked.

"Yeah," I said.

Declan looked back at me confused and just turned back around.

"It runs in the family," he teased.

Mr. Weaver rolled his eyes and drove us home.

When I got to the Weaver's house. I just went immediately upstairs without talking to anybody. I felt like I needed to take a shower like that would wash away the murder I just committed. I quickly went into our bedroom to see Brady sitting on his bed. He watched his legs sway underneath the bed and up in the air. I picked out a nicer looking black t-shirt and one of my better pairs of dark jeans.

"Number 2," I thought I heard Brady say.

"What did you just say?" I asked him.

Brady looked at me in shock, "I didn't say anything."

"Oh," I paused, "sorry man."

I walked out of the room in a rush and into the bathroom. I felt completely wired and dizzy. I got in the shower and lifted my head to let the water fall directly on my face. The images of me killing Kyle kept rushing in, specifically the last look he gave me. It wasn't fear, sadness or anger; just bravely excepting his fate for doing the right thing. I looked down to see blood coming off my body. My heart jumped and I looked at my arms to see them bare and bloodless. I slowly let myself slip down to sit on the bottom of the shower. Tears were uncontrollably falling.

"What did I do?" I whispered repeatedly.

I almost couldn't feel the water on my body anymore. Everything was numb. The sound of the water droplets hitting the bathtub was faint. I heard a muffled knock on the door.

"Jessie, Izzy's here to pick you up," said Mrs. Weaver.

I sighed and pulled myself up in the shower and shut it off. I put on my clothes and rubbed my hair in the towel. I had no clue how I was going to keep my energy up around Izzy. Every part of me was drained. I ran downstairs to see Izzy in the kitchen chatting with Mrs. Weaver. Usually, I instantly feel ten times better when I see Izzy but this time, I felt worse. She looked at me and smiled.

"Ready to go," she said.

"Yeah, I'm ready," I managed to smile.

We both left and headed for her car. I looked back to see Declan sitting on the porch looking puzzled. He looked up at me with a sadden face and just puffed his cigarette. I shrugged it off and went in the car. We drove downtown in silence, and I just looked out the window. Izzy glanced over at me a couple times but must have decided not to say anything. We parked her car and just had a short walk to the place.

"Jess, are you okay?" she asked.

"Huh, yeah sorry. I'm just tired today for some reason," I said.

Izzy nodded but I could tell she saw through that, so I tried to lighten the mood.

"Excited to see what a poetry night looks like," I smiled.

That seemed to excite her, "oh, you'll love it."

We walked into a neat looking venue. The chairs were red, and a lot of the decorations were black. It looked like an upscale circus but still a small restaurant. We got seated at a two-seater and just a couple of tables away from the microphone.

"I'll be right back," she said.

I nodded and stared at the person talking about her period being a powerful thing. Oddly enough, it was intriguing. I feel like most guys would be grossed out, but it honestly made sense. I mean the woman's body is a wonder. Fucking bleeds out every month and survives it all.

Izzy sat down with a 'up to no good look.'

"What?" I asked.

"I signed us up," she smiled.

"What?!" I said a little loudly, a couple of tables looked over.

"You'll do fine. I'll go first. It doesn't have to be anything extravagant. It can be just thoughts you have," she smiled.

I thought it was the least I could do since I literally murdered her ex. That thought brought a sick feeling in my stomach again. The thoughts I have? Wouldn't be anything good.

"Okay fine but I don't know what to say," I said.

"Well, have you ever written a poem or a journal entry?" she asked.

"I've written a couple of things, but I don't know if I have them memorized. I should have brought something," I said.

"Just write something down now. Sometimes last-minute writings are the best," she smiled, handing me a napkin and pen.

For the next couple of people, I started jotting down whatever was coming to mind. The napkin looked cloudy and the words were jumbling together.

"Next we have Izzy," said one of the workers.

Izzy smiled and touched my arm.

"Good luck," I said.

I watched as she bravely got up on the stage. She tucked her hair behind her ear and got out her piece of notebook paper.

"This is called...Addiction."

I set down my pen, ready to listen to her.

"Warmth and poison enter your veins,
It slithers like a snake into your brain.
Your mind makes up shadows that dance.
It makes you wonder if you ever had a chance.

The chance to become clean,
But the drug is too mean.
It will never let you go,
Laying on the ground, you never felt so low.

Life seems pointless now,
Starting over, you could never find out how.
You are trapped in a dream,
So, it may seem.

The highs don't out weight the lows,
You would rather just go.
Welcoming death into your home,
Feeling utterly alone."

The applause sounds muffled in my ear as I stare at Izzy who has tears in her eyes. Here I was breaking the heart of someone who has already been hurt. Whom already felt a lot of pain and understood what it meant to lose yourself amongst the harsh world. Tears fell down my eyes as my heart physically hurt.

"Thank you, Izzy. Let's hear it for that one," the audience claps, "Now we have Jessie Reids, come on up."

The whole room was making me feel dizzy as I passed Izzy who mouthed "good luck." I faked a smile and almost tripped up the stairs. The audience all of a sudden looked faceless besides Izzy, whose face was as clear as day.

I walk up to the microphone and clear my throat.

"What is this feeling? I'm as cold as ice.

I broke a heart, and I didn't think twice.

What did I do? I used to be nice.

Did I lose my soul and didn't think of the price?

Did I get pushed too far? So, sadness became a vice.

I took my pain away, at least I was precise.

How could I do this? It isn't right.

Who will I become when I turn off the lights?

I'm empty inside like the pitch-black night.

I can't let anyone see me; I'll give them a freight."

Last thing I see is the faint microphone and all the faceless heads in the audience, until everything goes black.

Have you ever been in the middle of wanting to die and not? Like you just wish you could hop into your brain and stay there awhile and not have to witness your reality. It sounds weird but it's what I secretly wished for a lot. I knew I shouldn't die because what would I leave behind? A couple of murders and a messed-up childhood? At the same time, I wanted to and sometimes so badly.

When I came to, Izzy and a man with a braided beard was hovering over me. I could just faintly hear Izzy saying my name.

"I hate public speaking," I mumbled.

"Oh, thank god," said the man with the beard.

"Here Jess, get up slowly," said Izzy, sitting me up.

Izzy smiled at me, "You okay?"

I nodded and groaned once I felt this throbbing pain in my head. I grabbed my head.

"You fell pretty hard," Izzy said.

"Here's some water," said the beard man.

"Thanks George," said Izzy.

George…not beard man.

"Anytime, we are closing soon but take the time you need," he said.

I grabbed the water and gulped it down. It felt good to drink the water because my throat felt super dry.

"Let's get you home," said Izzy.

I nodded and she helped me stand up.

We drove to the Weavers silently at first. I stared out the window still feeling groggy from my black out. All of a sudden my hands were shaky, and my heart felt like it was pounding out of my chest. Izzy had some piano music playing that helped calm my nerves a bit.

"For what it's worth, that was a great poem you read," Izzy broke the silence.

I'm an idiot, I haven't even complimented hers yet and here I was staring at the window like I was in a gloomy music video.

"Thank you. Yours was amazing Izzy. Shit, it made me tear up a bit," I said.

"You cried?" she mocked.

"I said a bit. There was one tear," I chuckled.

Izzy laughed, "Thank you."

"Of course. You are very talented," I looked over to her and smiled.

"So are you," she said.

She looked at me like she was pitying me. Like she thought I was going through a depressional stage. When really, I was just having a little PTSD from being a murderer. I started feeling the vomit coming up my throat. Izzy pulled up to the Weaver's house and I became extremely silent. I got out of the car without saying a word, clutching my stomach.

"Jess?" Izzy said, coming out of her car.

"I think I need to puke. I'm sorry, I will see you later," I groaned, rushing inside.

"I can come inside with you," Izzy said, worried.

"It's okay, really. I'll let Mrs. Weaver know. I love you. Thanks for an amazing date," I said, walking away.

"Okay," Izzy paused, "Love you too."

I walked into the Weaver's house and immediately ran upstairs to the bathroom and puked chunks into the toilet.

"Jess?" I could hear Declan outside the bathroom door.

"Just a minute," I said between puking.

Declan barged in to see me hovered over the toilet. What a great scene that must have been to walk into.

"Seriously, what the hell is going on?" said Declan.

I got out of my hovering stance and leaned my back against the wall. Declan sat down on the floor with me.

I just stared at him while I was breathing heavily. Cold sweats were sitting on my forehead.

Declan looked down at his hands and folded them. "What did you do, Jess?"

I wanted to tell someone, but I knew I couldn't.

"Nothing," I said.

"Nothing? Tell me why you were late for school then? Correct me if I'm wrong but you aren't heavy into clubs or social gatherings," Declan said.

"I told you. I missed the bus." I was being cold and short, but I couldn't tell him.

Not after that whole speech he gave me about not becoming a monster. Plus, I didn't feel like having someone turn me in just yet.

Declan looked at me with both sadness and anger.

"That's why you looked like you just saw a dead body after school and now have your guts in a wreck? What did you do? And turned around and hung out with your girlfriend, really Jess? Are you really that fucked up?" Declan growled.

"I must've caught a bug. Nothing happened. So, quit acting like some nicotine addict therapist who needs to go to anger management classes himself," I snapped.

Declan shook his head and sat up. After he paced around the bathroom once with anger boiling, he knelt in front of me with a cold look on his face.

"I hope you get what's coming to you, Reids. You can blame it on having a shitty life or having your mind betray you but welcome to the club!" he yelled, "You are in a house full of people with the same shit and you don't see them coming back from school looking like they just killed someone. Instead, they deal with their shit! Your illness doesn't make you a monster, if it did, we all would be monsters. No, your actions are what makes you a monster. So, puke and revel in your guilt because it's less than what you deserve."

Declan got up, stormed out of the bathroom and slammed the door shut.

I carefully got myself up, groaning from the pain in my stomach. My whole body ached, and my insides felt wrecked. The worst part was how bad my heart hurt. If I could have ripped it out of my chest, I would've. I looked in the Weaver's fun house mirror and saw exactly what Declan was talking about. A murderer and…Kyle. I jumped and looked back to see Kyle standing in my bathroom.

He was pale white, and the back of his head looked smashed in. He still had the brave expression on his face that added a grimly grin.

"What?" I whispered.

"You see all of your victims and I'm the one that seems to surprise you?" he laughed.

"I'm sorry," I choked out.

"No, you're not," Kyle shook his head, "however, I have a way you can make it up to me."

I looked at him confused.

"It's come to my attention that your confusion may be real. I thought it was an act but before my untimely," he paused and opened his arms, "death. A revelation has blossomed. You have created so many barriers in your brain that you don't see everything. You've blocked the truth from yourself."

"What the hell are you talking about?" I said frustrated.

"You are more of a monster than you think, Reids," he grinned.

"I get it. You, Declan and myself have made that very clear."

"No, no, no. You see the best way you can break down this wall and reveal the truth to yourself is to see it." Kyle walked towards the bathroom door.

"See what?"

"Go to the home you truly hate and every gut-wrenching truth." Kyle looked at the toilet and back at me. "Will become clear."

After that, he dispersed into thin air, and I was alone in the bathroom. I needed to go to my old house. It was the only way to know what he was talking about. Besides, I did owe him that.

I opened the bathroom door, half expecting Kyle to be behind it, but it was just Brady looking back at me before he descended the staircase. He gave me a worried look, but I shrugged it off and followed him down the stairs. Adeline and AnnMarie were sitting at the kitchen table and Mrs. Weaver was doing the dishes.

"Jess, are you okay? You rushed upstairs so I asked Declan to check on you," said Mrs. Weaver.

"I'm fine," I said walking towards the door.

"Jess, wait," Mrs. Weaver went to grab my arm, but I shoved her away.

She backed into the fridge and I realized I shoved her a little too hard. She looked at me with shock. I looked around to see both Adeline and Annmarie frozen.

"What the fuck, Jess?" snapped Adeline.

My glance went to Brady who stood frozen in the living room. He stared at me with such a sadden but blank expression. Everything

143

about this day was becoming so strange.

"Sorry," I said blankly to Mrs. Weaver.

I rushed out of the door and down the porch steps. From the side of the house, I saw Declan and Mr. Weaver talking and walking towards me. My breathing increased and I instantly darted for the woods. Behind me I heard Mr. Weaver yell my name but when I looked back, Declan had stopped Mr. Weaver from running my way. The last thing I heard from them was Declan saying, "Let him go."

Chapter 21
The Truth

I came to a stop in front of my old house. I stormed into it. I looked around the house for some kind of clue as to what Kyle was talking about. Everything was so trashed and dirty. Half of this place is being torn down. Except my dad's office. I ran into it, and I pulled out his letters and looked up to see letters and papers taped to the walls. I didn't remember seeing them before. It was copies of letters to every student who went to the high school. I could feel vomit traveling up my throat as I looked at the walls of the office. Izzy's pictures were taped to the wall. I started breathing heavily. My mind was racing because all my blackouts were becoming clear.

I saw myself scribbling letters to every student and saying whatever threat I could to them. I remembered the photos I took of Izzy and having them developed. I remembered taping them to the wall and lining up string that made no sense. It was like I was trying to solve a case but there wasn't anything to solve. My mind started spinning and I shook my head at my work.

"Where's my control?" I whispered as tears fell.

I looked at my phone and called Izzy.

"Jess?" Izzy quickly picked up.

"Izzy, where are you?" I whispered.

"Still at home, I have something to tell you. But Jess, have you seen the news? Kyle has been killed. The killer is unknown and on the run. Are you safe at home?" I could hear the panic in her voice.

"I'm at my old house," I said.

"Jess, why are you there?" Izzy said.

"I love you," I cried.

"I love you too. I'm going to come over," Izzy said.

"Don't come," I whispered.

I looked in the mirror above my father's desk and saw him standing behind me. His red eyes glowed and he grinned an evil smile. I jumped and ran into my father's closet.

"Jess? What's going on?" Izzy cried out.

"The killers in here," I whispered.

"Stay calm. I'm calling the police. Mom, call the police!" I heard her yell.

"Don't call the police. I have a record."

"What?" Izzy sounded shocked.

"Don't call them and stay away," I hung up on her.

"Should've told her the truth, Jess," I heard my father say.

"You're not real," I whispered.

"I'm as real as you are."

I wanted to hide in that closet forever, but I knew I needed to face everything head on. I walked out of the closet to see my father standing in front of me. My heart began to race. He tilted his head at me.

"Jess, it's not our fault. It's in our genes; we are just crazy," he shrugged.

"I'm crazy, you're heartless," I quickly said.

"And you have a heart?" he laughed.

"I can love," I whispered.

"No, you can't," he said, "that's why you need me."

I looked at him confused, backing away as he walked towards me. If I backed up anymore my body would be engraved into this closet door.

"I never needed you."

"Then how come I am in your head?" he grinned.

I shook my head and started running out of words.

"You need me so you can feel like a better person than I was, because in your mind, I will always be worse than you. But I am not the one with the blood on my hands," he laughed hauntingly.

His laugh echoed as he faded.

I looked down to see blood stains on my hands. I panicked, walked out of the office and slammed the door behind me. Confusion and anger built up inside me, to let it out I began to punch the wall till my fists were bleeding.

"Jess, where are you going?" I could hear my father.

I rested my head on the doorway and let my bloody hands fall to my sides.

"There is no where you can run, no where you can hide because the monsters aren't chasing you. You are the monster haunting everyone else," his voice was muffled behind the door, but it was as clear as day.

I knew he was right; I knew Kyle was right and Declan. But most importantly I knew I was wrong. Everything about me was wrong.

"Jess!"

I turned around to see Izzy.

"I need to tell you." She paused at the sight of me and fear came before her eyes.

"Jess, why is your hands bloody?" she asked wearily.

I looked back at the door trying to hear if my father was still behind it and back at her.

"The killer, is he still here?" Izzy asked while tears filled her eyes.

She looked as if she was asking a question, she already knew the answer to. I looked at her with crazed eyes.

"Izzy, I'm insane. I was in prison until this year because I killed my father after he killed my mother or made me kill my mother, I don't know, that part is blurry. It kills me every day because I loved my mother."

I was walking towards her, but she was walking backwards with tears and fear in her eyes. My voice was shaky, and I was crying, nervously.

"I can't stop seeing those terrible images and I'm seeing people that aren't there. My father is haunting my mind and this little girl keeps visiting me. You'd like her; she is really sweet."

I paused as Izzy cried, "Stop."

"Izzy please don't be scared. You help me, you make me feel sane and you numb the pain. I love you and I'll never hurt you," I cried.

She covered her mouth and shook her head. I could tell I was breaking her heart. My gaze looked everywhere trying to soak up how she looked in this moment, feeling like it would be the last time I saw her. She was in this gray sweater and leggings. Her hair had messy curls and the moonlight seeped into her skin, beautifully. Her eyes, however, told so much pain. Filled to the brim with tears.

"Did you hurt Kyle?" she choked out.

I paused. This time it was hard thinking of a lie, thinking of something or somebody else to blame. I realized I got too good at lying and that maybe it is time to come clean.

"He was trying to take you away from me. I didn't mean to; I wasn't myself," I cried.

Izzy gasped and cried.

"Izzy," I walked up to her.

"No, stay away from me!" Izzy screamed.

"Izzy please. I'm sorry. I need you," I cried after her.

I grabbed her face and brushed her cheek.

"Get off me," Izzy pushed me away.

I forgot I had blood on my hands, and I left some on her cheek. I decided to stay away.

"I'm sorry. I never wanted to hurt you. I was so selfish. I should've stayed away from you," I sobbed.

Izzy's beautiful face was so broken. Her body was shaking, and tears were falling down her face like a waterfall. She looked terrified of me.

"You're a monster," she cried.

The words felt like a shot in the heart.

"I know," I whispered, "I'm sorry."

She put her hand on her stomach and swallowed hard. Her broken face turned into hatred. Although I knew the hatred was towards me, it held beauty because it was the strength within her that I loved.

"My baby will never be like their father," she said coldly and stormed out.

"Baby," I whispered.

"Izzy!" I yelled after her.

She ran off and I didn't go after her. There was nothing I could do, and it was better. I wanted her to hate me because it forced me to let her go. A lovely woman like her should never be involved with a monster like me.

Chapter 22
Ashes and Bars

I stood there in a trance; my mind was dangerously quiet, but my ears were filled with an abundance of whispers that I couldn't make out. I pulled out a bottle of whisky from one of the cupboards in the kitchen.

"You have a lot of alcohol dad. Cheers." I chugged the bottle and could barely feel the sting that trickled down my throat.

I slid down to the floor next to the little girl.

"Will she ever forgive me?" I asked her.

"I did," she said.

"Why?" I whispered.

"You shouldn't live your life with hate."

I nodded; it made sense.

"How do I prevent hurting you?" I asked.

"You can't," she looked down at my bottle, "you're already on the path."

I looked down at my bottle and looked up to see that she disappeared. I stood up confused.

"Well, I don't have a car," I whispered to myself.

The whiskey got to me, and I stumbled backward into the dresser we had in the kitchen and a drawer popped open. I looked in to see a photo album. I opened it to see my parents wedding but the face of one of the bridesmaids looked familiar...

"Hi Jess!" a lady said.

"Hi," I said shyly; I was so small.

My dad passed by us in this strange house.

"His mom had a work thing, so hope you don't mind him being here," my dad said.

"Oh no, it's alright, want to watch some television?" she asked me.

"Sure," I shrugged.

I remember the show being too vulgar for a child.

"Let's go," said my dad.

"Yes, sir," she laughed.

They went into a room together and didn't come out for a while.

I snapped out of the flashback and looked at the picture again.

"Mary," I whispered.

I looked more through the album but couldn't find any more information besides the fact that my father was screwing my mother's bridesmaid. I walked into my father's crummy office. I stumbled to the desk and grabbed the letter from Mary reading the address. Who would've guessed; she was a few blocks down. I crumbled up the letter and stuffed it in my pocket. I grabbed the last visible bottle of brandy and mindlessly stormed out of my house. I picked up a cigarette butt off the ash tray that sits on the porch. I lit it with the lighter that was next to the tray and stuck it in my pocket. The cigarette tasted like ash and dirt, but it settled the sting of brandy.

"Fucking Mary," I laughed to myself.

"Are you glad, Mary!" I screamed at the sky, "He destroyed us just for you!"

My vision was blurry, and my heart felt empty. I no longer thought about anything other than revenge. Revenge tasted like sweet sugar to a bitter heart. I stumbled towards the house and could barely read the letters 1509 on Lake Street. There was no car there, but I still stumbled on the porch and knocked on the door. The house was tinted blue with white shutters and white fences. All the paint was faded and the blue paint on the porch was chipped.

"Mary! Come out and talk to me!" I shouted.

"Open the door! I just need to talk to you about my father," I laughed, "you know the one you fucked, and I killed!"

I threw my arms up, "I think we'd make a great pair!"

I could feel myself losing it and started to uncontrollably laugh. Everything was fuzzy and my face started tingling.

"You screw, I kill! Be like a weird Bonnie & Clyde situation."

I paced back and forth, rubbing my face with my hands and paused again at the door.

"I just want to know if you are happy. You know because I'm not. And I'm damn sure you are one of the reasons for my unhappiness. The funny thing is, I can't even blame you because it's all me! It's all my fucked-up life!" I screamed, kicking the door.

I started to walk off the porch but spun around towards the door again.

"Can you please just answer me? I need answers. I need at least one clear fucking answer in my life."

I circled around the porch again, grabbing my hair and shaking my head. Every ounce of my body felt hot. Everything was blurry and I couldn't make out a single thing. Warm tears were falling down my face and I started to go into a panic.

Remember when I talked about feeling like someone could be controlling your every move? Like how someone could possibly die and still be moving. In this moment, that is what I felt like. I was no longer in my body and was on the outside looking in. Like I was watching television and started yelling at the main character not to go in the basement. It's that complete lack of a grasp on reality and yourself.

"No, you know what Mary! I am always to blame, so this time, I am blaming you! You are to blame! So, fuck you, you're not home and now you won't have one to come back to."

I jumped off the porch and towards the bushes that were on the side of her house. I started tearing off branches and putting them around the porch. The house was beautiful, but beauty burns in flames and my goal was to watch Mary's beautiful life burn to ashes. I used my lighter to light her letter and threw it into the branches. After that, I poured the rest of my bottle into the pile I made. The flames grew higher and I stepped back to watch the house burn.

They began to swallow the house like it was a predator eating its prey. I understood AnnMarie when it came to the beauty of fire. The orange color started to disintegrate the house.

"Now your life can burn down too."

I stumbled down the road trying to go home and laughing to myself. Faint sirens sounded in the distance which made me laugh. I guess someone heard me screaming and called 911, they just didn't get to it in time. A horrible different sound caught my attention. I heard a scream of complete torture. A chill froze my spine and my whole body panicked.

I looked back to see a fire truck pull in along with a couple of police cars. The police officers ran after me and told me to freeze but I sprinted back to Mary's house. The screaming was coming from the upstairs and the flames had already consumed the house.

"Why didn't you answer!" I yelled.

I ran onto the porch and started kicking the door. The flames engulfed the porch, so, I started looking for another entrance but was quickly grabbed and cuffed.

"Calm down, kid," said the police officer.

"No, you don't understand someone is in there! Let me go!" I yelled.

The police officer dragged me away and shoved me into their car. I watched the fire fighters run into the house and begin to calm down the mess I made.

A car pulled up and Mary got out of the car. Her brown hair was long, and they had curls at the bottom. She looked as if she came from a hospital as her outfit looked like a nurse's scrubs. She dropped to the ground in complete agony and that is when I knew who was screaming. I wanted to blame Mary for leaving her little girl alone, but I knew it wasn't in any way her fault. I told the little girl I would avoid hurting her and I didn't. I ended her life and for some reason she forgave me before I even did it. I looked straight at the seats in front of me, unable to watch Mary's reaction but I could hear every devastating scream and tear. I looked over at the seat beside me and the little girl was sitting there with her knees to her chest.

"I'm sorry," I whispered.

This time she didn't answer; she just looked down.

I heard her mother's screech increase and looked back out of the police window to see them carrying out the little girl's body. Her body was burnt, and it dangled from the firefighter's arms. Mary went limp in a police officer's arm as if the sight tore her heart right out of her chest.

My mind began to race. It was giving me images of the life the little girl could have had. It showed me her going to college, finding the love of her life and getting married. It showed me the family she could have had. It showed me the life I took away. I looked over at the little girl who was sitting next to me, but she just sat there frozen with a tear falling down her cheek. Mary and her little girl were a small family who trusted a very bad man and that was all. Mary wasn't a monster; she probably didn't even know what my father did and probably thought he just had the misfortune of having a murderous son. She was a mother who worked a lot to care for her daughter and a woman who just had everything taken away from her.

Kyle was just a guy who was in love with a girl. A guy who witnessed the woman he loved ending up with a toxic man. He wasn't an asshole, if anything, he deserved Izzy more than I did.

Maybe, I was just as bad as my father. I killed him to get revenge for my mother, but I did worse after. The real revenge would have been becoming a better person than him.

The police officer got in his car and started driving me to the station. I couldn't move or talk. There was nothing I could or wanted to say. My heart felt like it sunk into my stomach or disappeared altogether.

When they walked me in the station; all eyes were on me. I was led to the interrogation room and chained to a metal desk. I looked at my reflection in the window that didn't show who was on the other side. I truly looked insane. My hair was messy and sort of burnt and my eyes were bloodshot. I still had bloodstains on my hands and dark eye circles. I was alive but looked so dead. I wish I would've died in the fire instead of her. She would've done so much more with her life than I ever could. She would have brought happiness to people, not terror. Tears fell down my cheek when I thought about how much I wished she hated me because the fact that she was so kind as to help me, while knowing I was her killer, killed me the most. How could someone so beautiful have such a horrible fate?

"Having regrets, Jess?" said the officer as he walked into the room. I didn't answer, instead I just stared at my hands.

"Two people in one day. It's like a pattern for you," said the officer.

He leaned towards me and I looked up at him. He was a bald man who had facial hair that was perfectly kept up with. He looked about 40 years old.

"Fess up, Jess. Admit what you have done," said the officer.

"Okay," I whispered.

"What?" he asked.

"I said okay. Just take me to court and I'll plead guilty to everything," I said.

The police officer looked at the window and back at me.

"Okay Reids. Just answer me this. Why did you do it?"

"Reasons that don't mean much or justify anything," I answered.

"Is it because your father had an affair? Had another kid? You didn't want a sister, so, you decided to kill her?" he asked.

The word 'sister' shook me. I didn't put two and two together that she was technically related to me. She would have been my half-sister.

"I didn't know anybody was in there. I shouted and knocked; nobody answered but now I'm guessing it's because her mother taught her not to answer the door to strangers," I muttered.

"Well, you might want to lawyer up then," said the officer.

I looked up confused. "No."

"Reids, you are looking at a life-sentence and you don't want a lawyer?"

"What about the first kill? What are your questions for that? Pretty sure that already gets me a life-sentence. Why try to get out of the second murder?" I snapped.

"You are going to need a lawyer," he repeated.

"I don't want one," I said, coldly, "I followed Kyle to the back of the school. I killed him by slamming his head against a tree repeatedly. All because he was going to tell a girl I like the truth about me."

"What's the girl's name?" he asked.

"She remains nameless," I said.

"You can't."

"That's my deal," I interrupted, "I killed both Kyle and the little girl and I'll admit it."

"Lily," said the officer, "her name was Lily."

I looked down at my hands.

"Okay Reids," said the officer.

Lily. I couldn't think of any other name that would've been perfect. Lily was delicate and as beautiful as a flower.

The court date was the next day. I stared at the wall the entire night unable to go to sleep but I didn't want to. The feeling of the cell was cold, and the bench was hard. Look at me, complaining about the conditions of my holding cell after what I've done.

We all filed in that day to see the judge and the jury were all looking at me. As I walked up, I looked to the side to see the Weavers, Declan and Adeline. Mrs. Weaver was crying and both Adeline and Declan just looked at me with crushed faces. Declan's was angrier. I looked away from them quickly and I felt thankful they didn't bring AnnMarie and especially Brady. I didn't want him to see this and think that just because he has my illness that he is going to end up where I am. Just because you see things that aren't there, doesn't make you violent or a murderer, just like Declan said. However, I was a hell of a bad example. Truth is, he was much stronger than me and therefore will get through it.

"Jessie Reids. Do you have a lawyer present?" the judge asked.

"No," I answered.

"Offense?" she asked.

"Your honor Mr. Reids is being charged with two murders" said the attorney who I realized was standing next to Mary and a woman who looked like Kyle a bit.

"What is your plead?" asked the judge.

"Guilty," I answered.

"Your honor, a word," said the bald officer who interrogated me.

He walked over to her podium and whispered something, and she nodded.

"Jessie Reids, you are charged with the murder of Kyle Williams and Lily Miers. You are sentenced to life at the East Haven Prison with the promise that you will get psychiatric help during your stay." She slammed her gavel which made me jump out of my daze.

The police officers grabbed me and started taking me away. I looked back to notice Mrs. Jones who looked like she had been crying for days. I felt my heart shatter as I looked away from her. After all her help and selflessness. After we connected and became friends, I betrayed her by killing two innocent people. My stomach turned at the thought of Mrs. Jones realizing all of this. Tears started to fall again as I was led to the back of the courtroom. All the people I have hurt was becoming too long of a list to keep track of.

They put me on a prison bus that was full of strange people. One lady was singing to herself while twirling her hair. Some were screaming at the bus driver. It was a terrifying sight to see. The saddest part is all these people weren't going to change or be fixed. They are just going somewhere away from society for the sake of the people.

Chapter 23
Sick Bastard

In the morning, the guards go around knocking on our cells. Some were taken to the therapist while others were taken to the mess hall. A guard opened my cell with handcuffs in his hands. My first duty was going to the therapist so I could talk about my twisted mind. We got to the door which gave me a flashback to when I was little and laying on the couch speechless.

"Knock," the guard said.

"What?" I said, snapping out of it.

"Knock, day dreamer," chuckled the guard.

"Fuck you," I whispered.

The guard smacked me on the head. I groaned and pounded on the door.

"Jessie Reids," said the therapist as she opened the door.

It was a lady with white hair but the same disappointed look as everyone else and the height that barely misses the ceiling.

"Mrs. Burnett," said the guard.

She gestured for me to come in and I followed her.

"I read your files from your last therapist in juvie. So, what is it this time? Lies that landed you here? The shadows forced you?" asked Mrs. Burnett.

"Doesn't sound like a genuine question," I scoffed, what a condescending way to start a therapy session.

"Jessie, you have to let me help you," said Mrs. Burnett.

"No, that's what they said last time." I sat down. "And I let them help me. I let them in my head. They decided I was cured but I obviously wasn't."

I could feel my blood boiling as tears involuntarily fell from my eyes.

"Then let's talk about that," said Mrs. Burnett, "let's talk about what happened when you got out of juvie the first time."

"You want to get inside my head? Here you go. I saw that little girl for days before I killed her."

"You saw her?" she asked.

"She came to me and told me I would kill her before I even knew who she was," I said. I don't why I was telling her this straight away, I guess I was just tired of hiding things.

"The girl told you to kill her?"

"No. The shadow of the girl came to me and said that my fate was killing her not that she wanted me to kill her," I said quickly and panicky.

"And you listened," Mrs. Burnett said in monotone.

I got up and started pacing back and forth.

"I didn't want to," I said, crossing my arms and sitting in the corner.

"But you did," she said, sitting up and kneeling in front of me.

"You did something bad, Jess but now at least you are admitting it," she smiled.

Something about that sentence made me snap.

"Yeah, I guess I will at least have that. I'll think about the day I admitted my murders while I rot and slowly die in this prison," I said almost happily.

Mrs. Burnett sat up and looked at me confused. "Jessie," she said in a warning tone.

"Thank you, Mrs. Burnett, for making me realize that I am a great guy who admits to everybody I have put in a body bag. Well, guess what, no matter what I tell you, my ass is in here forever and all of their asses are dead!" I yelled at her.

"Calm down," she said with her hand out.

"Why? Are you worried you are my next hit?" I laughed.

"Guards!" she yelled.

I shot up from the ground. "You are scared," I said, walking towards her.

"Guards!" she screamed, backing up away from me.

"Yes, guards come in she needs you. There is a crazy man in her office! But don't worry after I kill you; I'll admit to it when you're gone," I sneered, still walking towards her.

Mrs. Burnett's facial expression was of pure terror. The guards busted into the room and quickly grabbed me.

"That took way too long," she told the guards.

I let the guards lead me to my cell and throw me in. I didn't feel like fighting them, I told the woman off and that's all I wanted to do.

They locked the cell door behind me and looked at me with the usual angry expressions on their faces. I just smiled at them.

"You're deranged," the guard in the middle glared.

"Or just lucky," I mumbled.

Making fun of my madness seemed to numb the pain but not for long. I got on my bed and lay down. My cell was empty, and I didn't have a roommate yet. I closed my eyes and thought of Izzy. The fact that she was having to be alone with a baby on the way. A baby whose father is a psycho at that. A panic hit me.

"Guard!" I screamed.

"Shut up!" he yelled.

"Is crazy genetic?" I yelled.

"I don't know was your mom crazy?" he laughed.

I rolled my eyes and he walked away. I sat silently until another guard opened my door and grabbed me.

"Where are we going?" I asked.

"Mess hall," he answered.

We walked in to see many people eating their meals silently. The guards were lined up along the walls watching. I went in the line where you get your food and the lunch guy glared at me as he plopped the disgusting food onto my plate. As I went to sit down everyone glared at me. I felt like I was little again except these guys in here could kick my ass. There were only a couple of people my age, but mostly middle-aged folks were in here with the occasional old souls that have been here forever. Looking at them was a blast into my future. I sat down next to the older people.

"Who said you could sit here?" said an old man who had tattoos all over his face. All the tattoos were sunken in and he was incredibly pale.

"I did," I said.

"Sick bastard," he mumbled.

"Excuse me?" My mind was telling me, '*What are you doing, Jess?*'

"You heard me."

"Because you're innocent? You look about 90 and you are in prison meaning you are most likely here for murder too," I said.

"Not my family," he snapped.

"So, because the people you killed weren't related to you makes you an angel? Who did you murder? How many people? Did you torture or enjoy the screams?" I asked him.

"Shut up," he interrupted.

"What? Am I getting warm? Who was it, old man? Was it a child?" I asked.

"Shut the fuck up!" he yelled standing up in his seat.

I just grinned as he freaked out. The guards grabbed him before he could touch me and were dragging him out as he was kicking and screaming. The other men were silent and didn't speak to me. I guess that was the best way to assert dominance in this prison. After dinner, we are sent to our cells again. I was moved to the solidarity rooms that had steel doors instead of cells. The one where they start giving you food through mail slots. Turns out I put that man in a strait jacket, so I was considered even more of a threat to the other inmates. I take it my guesses to the reason he was in prison were spot on.

The entire time I kept mostly to myself, my mind was too messed up to make a friend. In fact, most of them were terrified of me or just disgusted. I remember making a friend back in juvie, a young boy who robbed banks with his dad and had crazy stories. I told him I was in for stealing credit cards but when he found out the truth, he became terrified of me. The next friend I'd make would probably run away screaming. Unless they were as bad as me, I wouldn't necessarily want to be my friend. What a hypocrite I am.

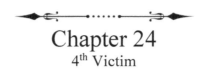

Chapter 24
4th Victim

Today I wish I could say I aged in prison and became a better man, but I am the same crazy bastard from the start. To prove this statement: I am now sitting on a cold floor wrapped in a strait jacket with blood coming from my forehead and stinging my eye. I haven't stopped hyperventilating from the awful sight of the little girl I killed, choking on blood and dying before me.

My schizophrenia has been getting worse. I am constantly seeing people; sometimes they look like anyone else and sometimes they are darker and terrifying. It is an awful feeling when you are screaming at the sight of a man hanging himself while everyone else is looking at you like you're mad because they don't see what you are looking at.

I have been in solitary confinement and have been seeing the therapist regularly except ever since my first encounter with her; she asks that I have handcuffs. I have choked out inmates and put a couple guards in the hospital. I am a mental case, but my therapist told me to write everything down during our library times. I can't bring it in the cell with me because they are afraid, I'd get too creative with the pencil. The truth is, I don't think I am ever going to get better and I've accepted that.

So far, I have been keeping track of things the little girl has said. Looking back and tracing my steps. She told me five people were going to be my victims. I came into prison with 3 victims. My father, Kyle and Lily. During my stay, I was the reason for a death because it turns out the old man who was dragged away and put in strait jacket after I taunted him; found a way to end his life. The guards wouldn't say how. I guess they didn't want any of us getting ideas. The worst part about finding this out was that this time I didn't cry. I didn't shed a tear for the man I pushed to the brink. It scared the shit out of me because the more I think and the more I realize; I am truly a monster.

It made me think of something I blurted out to Kyle before I killed him. "Eventually, being a monster is easier than proving to people you aren't one." I think I decided to follow that way too religiously. I honestly am tired of trying to fix myself and correct my mistakes. I'm a terrible person and a part of me is just accepting that. I am here for life, why try to be a decent person now? That probably sounds crazy, I know it does and maybe I don't mean it but for now I kind of do.

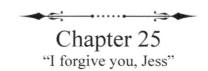

Chapter 25
"I forgive you, Jess"

"**R**eids." The guard smacks my cell. "Wake up."

I just lie there not wanting to budge.

"Hey nutcase, get the fuck up," yells the guard.

I shot up off my bed while the anger boils up inside me like chemicals reacting.

"What did you say?"

"What? Don't like the truth? You are bat shit crazy."

The guard has a shit eating grin on his face, the way he enjoys getting under people's skin, makes you wonder who is the crazy one here.

"You don't have room to talk," I smile back.

"Oh really? Who killed mommy and daddy? Who burned a little girl alive? How cold hearted do you have to be to kill both your mother and a little girl?" the guards face was getting red, "What about the little girl, what the fuck did she do to you? Didn't get into your fucking car when you said you have candy?"

My arms move and wrap around his neck.

"I may be crazy, but I am not sick. You on the other hand, I hope one day karma beats the shit out of you. I hope you suffer, and karma tears you limp by limp or you fuck with the wrong people, and they cut your fucking dick off," I say with crazed eyes.

I watch with a smile while his face starts turning red and he desperately attempts to break free of my grip. The other guards start to race over to my cell in panic; one of them carrying the strait jacket I have been acquainted with too many times. It was something I used to fear but in a sick way it has started to become a comfort to me.

"I hope it happens when your little buddies won't be there to save you," I smile.

The guards break him free of my grip and open my cell in such a rage that I know I am once again fucked. They drag me out of the cell and immediately start trapping me in the strait jacket. Once they got me trapped, they hold me still while the guard whose neck is still purple starts kicking me in the gut. You would think the amount of times this has happened to me that I would not feel the knife-like pain of a man's foot to the stomach. I took a lot of punches to the face as the other guards joined in. They were taking turns like I was a piñata at a kid's birthday party. Instead of screaming and grunting in pain, I laughed at it. I remain laughing as the guards' stare at my bloody face.

"Fuck you all," I say during my laughter.

They started dragging me to the padded room while my legs dangle in front of me.

"Fuck you all!" I keep screaming repeatedly until they silence me with a slam of the door.

The worst part about getting your ass kicked in a strait jacket is that you can't even stop the blood from dipping into your eye. This padded room has become way too familiar to me. It's smell of death is a little extra strong today and they still haven't cleaned any of the blood stains that are most likely mine. I rest myself up on the wall and wait for my visitor. For some reason, the little girl seems to come to me when I am in this room. She comes in and we talk about the shit I've done and how I can get better. After that she turns into a corpse and leaves a pool of imaginary blood. It is our routine.

"Jessie."

I look beside me and instead of the little girl, it is my mom.

"Mom?" I croak.

"Look at you, you look like you haven't taken a bath in ages. How is my baby doing?" she asks.

I looked down at my strait jacket.

"I'm doing great mom," I lie. "I miss you."

"I miss you too baby."

Tears start to roll down her cheek.

"Mom, what's wrong?"

"I failed you," she mumbles.

"Mom, you didn't fail me. None of this is your fault," I say desperately.

"Baby, look at you. Look at where you are at. You wouldn't have gone to juvie as a little boy if I would've gotten away from him sooner and maybe you wouldn't have done all the stuff you did."

"I wouldn't have gone to juvie if I didn't murder dad and instead tell people what he did to you."

"How old are you know?" she asks.

"I'm 32."

"I've missed everything," she says.

"Don't worry mom. You didn't miss that much."

"You have a kid?" she asks.

"Yes, I think so. Izzy mentioned it," I say.

She nods and smiles at me but frowns. Her beautiful face starts to change, the wounds my father made start to show and her eye slowly blackens. She begins to look like the last time I saw her. My heart tightens at the sight.

"Mom?" A tear runs down.

"Be there for your kid," she says.

My mother vanishes. It is funny… for these hallucinations to be all in my brain; you would think I'd have more control over them. Instead, the hallucinations seemed to come and go as they pleased.

I lean back and stare at the spot my mom was at. I look over to the corner to see if the little girl is stopping by now, but she still isn't here. So, I doze off.

I walk into a room with red walls and a tiled black and white floor. My ears are ringing as I hear a faint sound of someone crying. People with animal heads are lined up against the wall. Goat, horse and cow headed people are staring at me. My heart is racing, and tears are forming in my eyes. Everything about the scene is telling me something awful is about to happen. At the end of the room there is someone I notice. Her dark hair is blocking her face a bit as she cries in her hands.

"Izzy?" I gasp.

"Jess," she says, looking up at me so coldly.

She is standing behind a tiny casket and looks at me with such anger and hurt. I approach the golden casket that has blood stains on the side and look in it to see a tiny boy as cold as ice. He looks almost blue he is so cold. I know exactly who he is supposed to be. The way I can see myself in his face. My chest is heavy as my heart feels like it is being punctured with a needle.

"You killed him." Izzy looks at me with hatred.

"Him? No, no I would never kill our son. I love him," I say. Those words shocking me, considering I haven't met him.

"You are a murderer. You don't feel love, Jess," she scoffs.

"I didn't hurt him Izzy!" I yell.

"Murderer!" she screams an ear-piercing scream that starts to bring down the walls.

I look up to see that ink was coming out of her mouth as she screamed at me. Her cry echoes throughout the hall. She picks up the ice-cold little boy out of his casket. The little boy dangles in her arms as she wails. The ceiling starts collapsing above us sending a crack through the lights like a river. As the ceiling collapses onto her, the animal headed people start walking closer to us.

"Izzy, watch out!" I scream.

I am too late, pieces fall on her one by one, as I watch with horror. I fall to my knees and cry for myself to be replaced for them both. The boy falls out of her arms and she lies there crushed by one of the pieces of the ceiling. I can only see her hair covering her face and her arm reached out as if to hold the boy one last time.

I scream out of agony and the room echoes it. I see the shoes of one of the men and recognize it as something Kyle wore. I look up to see a man with a goat head slowly lifting a gun and pointing it at my head.

"My turn," he says and pulls the trigger.

I woke up quickly, lying in my sweat as I breathe heavily but it feels like there are a million weights on my chest.

"Jess."

I look over to see the little girl in the corner all burnt up. She is huddled there with her knees pulled up to her chest and her scorched hair in her face. The shadow of the room heavy in the corner she is in.

"I'm sorry," I cry.

"Jess," she pauses and smiles a sweet smile, "I forgive you."

You would think I would feel relief, but the words hurt because here is this little innocent girl whose life I have taken, and she still forgives me.

"Why?" I ask.

She just smiles. She doesn't give an answer, maybe she doesn't know or maybe I keep hallucinating her saying she forgives me just so I can hear it from somebody. I can't explain why I want to hear "I forgive you" so badly because I knew out of all people, I am the least to deserve it. I hate the things I have done and yet I keep repeating it. I don't change, I just regret.

Chapter 26
New Roommate

After being returned to solitary for a couple days, a guard comes to open my door. He motions for me to grab my stuff and walks me out of the room. I can't tell if I am grateful for moving rooms or disappointed. He takes me to a different cell without saying a word to me. This time there is another bed in it which shocks me. Never once have they given me a roommate because they are always afraid I'd off them. I guess things were a little too overcrowded to make exceptions.

"A roommate?" I say.

"Looks like you're no longer special," says the guard, "drop your things."

He nods for me to walk down the hall.

"You're not going to be my escort?" I mock.

"Just get your ass in the hall for breakfast," he says with a dull face.

"Love it when you talk dirty to me," I say as I walk down the hall by myself.

I feel free walking by myself. There always seems to be one guard watching me. Come to think of it, there isn't that many guards in the hall at all. A part of me wants to take advantage of that but I should probably be a good little boy and eat my breakfast.

When I get in line, I hear some of the inmates gossiping to each other like a couple of teens about all the newcomers. Sounds cheesy but they are considered "fresh meat" which makes it sound kind of sexual in my opinion. I go to sit by myself as usual until I recognize one of the newbies. I look around and sit in front of them.

"Benny?" I whisper.

Benny looks up at me with a five o' clock shadow on his face, a couple more wrinkles under his eyes and his hair cut that makes the curls just sit on the top of his head. Other than that, he looks very similar to the Benny I remember from the hospital.

Benny scoffs, "Looks like we both ended up locked in the same place, once again."

"Yeah, looks like we did," I say.

"How have you been, Reids?" he asks.

His facial expression has a grin but one that sort of seems like he is tired of this world or generally pissed off.

"Not good," I shake my head.

"Me too," he huffs, tossing one of his peas off his tray.

I watch as the pea rolls fast off the table.

"So, what happened after the hospital? What did you get into after that?" I ask.

Benny stabs into his piece of meat. "What did you?" Benny seems pissed.

"Um…" I say, looking around.

Something is telling me this is not the same Benny I remember but then again, I'm not the same Jess. Benny knew pre-murder me; it makes me think who is Benny now?

"Never mind, I know. I am here for my part in a gang. One I joined after spending a year in a home that wouldn't pass child labor laws because my family didn't want me. I was too much of an embarrassment for their brand. I wasn't allowed to live by myself yet, so, I joined a new family. Sold drugs and now I'm here," Benny laughs.

"I'm sorry, Benny."

"You're sorry? I'm in the same place as you for selling some weed and you murdered a little girl," he says coldly.

I just stare at him speechless.

"Don't start talking to me like we are friends just because we spent time together in the looney bin, got it?" he snaps.

Hot tears were forming in his eyes. Normally I would punch a guy or attempt to slit his throat with a plastic spoon for talking to me like that, but I can't do that to Benny. I don't want to do that to him. For the first time, I am not picturing myself choking this guy to death. There is no sudden urge to launch at him because I am just shocked. It's been a while since an inmate has even tried to talk to me like that. Hell, some of the guards stopped talking to me like that.

"Okay," is all I manage to say.

I get up and walk away from the table. I immediately go to my cell after breakfast is done, shaking my head at myself. I just let Benny make a fool out of me in a place I have finally gained credit. I will admit I have been always on the fence about having such a bad

Phillips

reputation in the prison. Half was always pride and the other shame because it is just another reminder of the person I am. However, the worse you seem in the prison, the more likely you are going to be left alone. After that, I realize the worst. I look back to see Benny being let into my cell. Shit. I am roommates with the guy who just chewed me out in the lunchroom. Benny looks at me pissed and sighs.

"Can I get some paper and a pencil from the commissary?" Benny asks the guard.

"Not with psycho as your roommate. Don't want him stabbing his wrists with a pencil. Although, it wouldn't be the worst thing," the guard chuckles, "or of course stabbing you."

The guard walks away, and Benny just plops on his bed. At this point, I'm not sure if I should say anything. So, I just lie down on my bed and stare at the ceiling. The biggest thing I'm worried about now is having an episode in front of Benny. When I am by myself it decreases the number of people seeing me screaming at nothing. Now I have an audience, great. Grab some popcorn Benny and get ready for a show.

Chapter 27
We Aren't Broken

They open the cell door like it is nothing. It is almost like having a roommate made the guards act differently. There are so many newcomers that the guards seem too busy to terrorize me. I am not about to question it because I plan to enjoy it while it lasts.

It's Sunday which is usually when I have my library time. I'm afraid to talk to Benny but at the same time the guy wants to draw. I look over to see him lying in his bed with his arms behind his head just staring at the ceiling. He seems so focused on it that I look up at the ceiling to see if maybe there is something I am missing. I shake my head at that, I am the one who sees shit that isn't there, not him.

"What are you doing?" he says.

I look back at him and clear my throat, "Nothing."

"I'm going to the library if you want to come," I say.

"Are we starting a book club?" he mocks.

I roll my eyes. "They allow you to draw and shit in there."

Benny nods. He shrugs and gets up out of bed.

"Sure, why not," he sighs.

We both walk out of the cell and through the halls. I look over at him and he gives me a weird look which makes look ahead. It feels weird having someone walk next to me down these halls that isn't a guard. I look around the whole prison just to see everyone either roaming or the guards walking like they have a purpose. Their chests puffed out to look more intimidating.

"You okay?" asks Benny looking at me with one eyebrow raised.

I look at him. "Does it seem a bit different to you in here?"

"It's my second day here," Benny says with a monotoned voice, "so no."

"Right," I chuckle awkwardly.

We both enter the library which doesn't fully look like a library. It looks more like a doctor's waiting room with a couple of bookshelves.

"This is the library?" Benny scrunches his nose.

"Yeah," I chuckle.

Benny sighs and we both sit at a table. I'm surprised he didn't sit at another table with the way he talked yesterday. I get out a piece of paper and a pencil. What I normally do is write down shit and stuff the paper in my pocket. If you look underneath my cell mattress, you won't see something badass like a knife. No, you will find idiotic sappy poems and journal entries like I am one of those lovesick writers. Benny rumbles through all the pencils and pulls out some colored pencils. He slams them down on the table next to a sheet of paper all while mumbling to himself, but I can only make out "I feel like a kid" which makes me laugh.

Benny pauses and I immediately stop laughing.

"Sorry," I cough out.

He looks at me with a dead straight face and opens the box of colored pencils. I try to hide my grin as I write, and he starts scribbling something out.

An inmate passes by us and scoffs, "Queens."

"What did you say?" I look up.

It is a bald man with a tattoo reaching up his neck to his chin that looks like a dragon. His eyebrows are dark, and eyes are small and beaty. However, he is the same size as me which proves I would have a fighting chance.

"You heard me. Which one are you, Reids? Bottom or top. I bet bottom," says the inmate.

I jump out of my chair and instantly grab his throat. The guy just laughs.

"And who the fuck are you?" I ask.

"The only guy who isn't scared of the famous psycho in town," he chuckles.

Should have known, letting one inmate talk back to me unharmed would make others want to try. I squeeze his neck harder that makes him involuntarily whimper.

"Not so manly now, are you?" I grin.

"Hey Reids." Benny grabs my arm.

I look at him with rage and he puts his arms up as a surrender.

"Look I don't care if you kill him, he's obviously some homophobic dick but is he really worth being thrown into solitary for?" asks Benny.

I scoff at the comment, when am I not in solitary?

Every inch of me wants to squeeze this man's neck harder but I sigh, "Fine," and let the man go.

"Yeah, listen to your girlfriend," the inmate chokes out.

I punch him in the face so hard that I feel the pain in my fist travel up my arm. It knocks the inmate clean out. This causes enough commotion to cause the guards to come in. They grab me and start dragging me out. I look back at Benny who is picking up my sheet of paper. Shit, that is not exactly my target audience.

Instead of throwing me in solitary they decide that me seeing the therapist is better. Seems strange, I just knocked someone out and they want me to see the therapist that is terrified of me? What the hell is going on? I realize a lot of these guards are unrecognizable. Huh, maybe they are making changes in this prison. Firing the bad eggs.

They walk me into Mrs. Burnett's office and put some cuffs on my arms. These guards don't say a word to me. I look at both of them with surprise. They just dragged me out from punching a man and yet they both seem relatively calm. I sit down in her chair and the guards disperse from the room.

"What happened in the library, Jess?" she asks.

"A fight," I say, slightly still distracted.

"Why?" she asks.

"It's a prison, is that really the most surprising thing that's happened here?" I ask, snapping my head around to look at her.

"I guess not." Mrs. Burnett put down the coffee in her hand. "They were going to put you in solitary, but it looks like one of the guards stood up for you."

I scoff, "The guards stand up for me?"

"There's been a reform in the prison. Got rid of the ones that seemed to abuse their power a little too much. With this many new inmates being transferred here; we can't have that many fuck ups."

I look at her shocked at the choice of words and nodded.

"How is your new roommate?" she asks.

"Fine," I shrug, "I know him actually."

"I know, I mentioned that to the warden. I talked to him when he entered; apparently both of you are into the arts too. Perhaps you artists can work together to better each other and fix yourselves," she smiles.

I remain quiet but something about that irks me. Us artists can FIX each other. I snap.

"You know what's funny about people today?" I say, calmly.

Mrs. Burnett looks at me confused. "No what's funny, Jess?"

"They almost wish they were mad because it would explain what they were feeling deep inside. It's become normalized, an aesthetic even. It has made people realize how many minds are sick and twisted. The madness of the masses and it's great…" I laugh.

"Finally, the whole world isn't pretending that everything about humans is normal and sane. Humans aren't sane and the ones who pretend to be are boring as hell. It's the people who gave into their madness that are the most interesting," I remain calm.

"Everyone is dying inside; it's either embrace it and live with what you got or suppress it so much that you rot." I could feel the tears fill my eyes. They are boiling hot. Mrs. Burnett just stares at me with a confused expression.

"The people who spend their normal, perfect life still end up as a rotten corpse in the ground. At least the ones who go mad leave something behind. Artists? A scribbled-out journal, a painting that needs a translation, music that saves the depressed from offing themselves. The very art you enjoy!" I shout.

The fear returns to Mrs. Burnett's eyes, which makes me grin.

"That is what comes from madness, and I can feel it, it's spreading. Like a disease infecting every hurting mind," I calm my tone again, "it's great because it scares the shit out of the pretenders and resurrects the mad, unstable, brilliant people you are so desperate to cure." I sit up out of my chair and lean my cuffed hands on her desk.

"Well guess what? We don't need to be cured because we've realized we were never broken."

Mrs. Burnett looks at me with a mixture of anger and fear.

"Guards!" she yells.

They burst in and guide me a little more forcefully out of the room as I look back at her with a grin. I am back in my cell in no time to see Benny sitting on his bed with his picture next to him. It is more realistic looking than the cartoons he drew in the hospital. I sit down on my bed and the guards come in and take off the cuffs. They leave Benny and I be. I just stare into the abyss while smiling, a part of me already forgot what the hell I just said but I remember the shocked expression on Burnett's face. Finally, my mind and vision focus on the drawing Benny is creating.

"Nice drawing; looks real. Who is the woman?" I ask.

I stare at it. It is this woman drenched in blood and in some sort of prom dress.

"Carrie," he says.

I nod, unsure of who Carrie is.

"Looks badass," I say.

"She is…you've never? Never mind. Figured you'd be in solidarity," he says.

"Me too. They took me to the therapist instead," I laugh.

Benny nods and takes out a piece of paper from underneath his paper.

"You left this," he says, handing me the paper.

I look down at what I began to write:

Don't worry now,

It's hard to explain how…

I'm no longer filled with dread

Because inside I'm already dead.

I crumble up the piece of paper and toss it underneath my pillow without saying anything.

"It's not bad, you know. Kind of relatable," says Benny.

"Thanks," I mutter, lying down on my bed.

Chapter 28
What. The. Fuck

I wake up early to see that Benny is still asleep. Our cell door has been open, so I decide to take a shower. It's best to try and go when no one is there. This place has stalls but still they aren't very tall. I go in to lucky only hear a couple of shower heads running. I don't shower as much as I should but here lately with everything being calmer, I've been able to at least every other day. I don't take long showers because my mind begins to race in them and often times, I'll start seeing shit. One time I was in the shower and I swore all the lights turned off. I felt like a shadow was lurking behind me and I screamed which was embarrassing because the asshole guards came in just to laugh. There I was screaming in a towel while the guards laughed and walked away. Luckily, they decided I was too pitiful to throw a punch at during that time.

After my shower, I wrap myself in a towel. I normally get dressed in the shower, which is difficult with the ground still being wet. It beats your naked body being stared at by a whole bunch of strange men. My body in my opinion isn't as good as it used to be but I'm also not too embarrassed by it either. Not to sound cocky, but it didn't change as drastically as I'm sure these other guys have. However, that still doesn't mean I want an audience expecting a prison strip tease. I walk out in the towel and look around to see that no one is there. I quickly remove my towel and grab my underpants. Once I got them on, I hear someone walk in before I could start putting my pants on. I look over to see Benny just frozen and paused with his toothbrush in his mouth.

In the midst, of awkwardly trying to pull my prison pants up over my still damp legs, my dumbass just says, "Hi."

"Hi," Benny awkwardly says and walks into a stall.

By then my pants are on and I've begun to put on my shirt. I start to brush my teeth. I am not sure why I feel so embarrassed. It's not like he saw my entire bare ass or anything. I walk out and back into our cell. Soon, it would be breakfast.

I go to get up and Benny walks in.

"Going to breakfast," I say.

"Alright I'll meet you there," he says.

I walk out of the cell and towards the mess hall. Why am I acting so weird around him, who cares if he saw me in my underwear? What am I 16? I walk into the mess hall to see an abundance of newbies. What the hell is happening? It looks like there was some kind of nationwide criminal group that all got imprisoned at the same time. Was there another Manson family I didn't know about?

I grab my food and sit at a table. I watch as Benny comes in looking as intimidating as possible. That is something he does a lot when he enters big groups. He makes sure they know that he doesn't want to talk to anyone. Benny grabs his food and comes to sit across from me.

"Hi," he mocks in my awkward tone of voice.

"Ha okay," I say as I stab my ham.

He just chuckles.

A random inmate comes and sits next to us which surprises both Benny and I.

"Hey guys have you heard the news?" asks the inmate who is this small Mexican man.

"News?" I ask.

"They are tearing down this prison," he says.

"Really?" asks Benny.

"Yeah, apparently family members have been complaining about the bruising they've noticed during their visitations. They tried to fix it by switching guards out but now the overcrowding is becoming an issue. Not to mention this place looks like a shit show," he says.

"Huh," I scoff.

"Anyways pass it along," he says and continues to a different table.

Benny and I look at each other. We both shrug and continue eating our food. I watch the man go to the next table to surprise those inmates with the news. He is literally just delivering the news from table to table. There is one table that throws a chunk of ham at him the minute he sits down which makes me chuckle.

Today we are allowed recess time which makes us sound like kids in elementary school, but it is great to get fresh air when you can. Benny and I decide to just walk. For a bit we walk in silence.

"You seem the same," Benny says.

I look at him confused. "The same?"

"As in the person I knew in the hospital. I figured you'd be different after reading about what you did," he elaborates.

"Trust me, I'm different," I say.

"Well yeah a little more tempered," he scoffs.

I laughed, "yeah" but I just stare at the ground. That is probably not a good thing to seem the "same" after murdering people. Kind of makes me sound like a sociopath.

"I'm just saying that maybe you aren't as much of a monster as I thought," he says.

I stop walking and he pauses to look at me.

"I am," I say angrily.

"Okay whatever you say man, just trying to I guess apologize for freaking out on you," Benny says.

"Don't apologize, you were right," I keep walking, "once you think I've gotten better, I'll do something so don't get your hopes up."

"Okay," he laughs.

"What's funny?" I ask.

"Nothing. Looks like they want us back inside," says Benny a little coldly.

After dinner, we are back in our cell and going to bed. Things have been relatively quiet since our discussion outside. I know I was a little annoying, but I don't want to hurt another person that's expecting me to be a decent human being. I'm not and the less I pretend to be, the better.

I close my eyes and instantly regret it. The thoughts spiraling in my head about making this new friend has the room spinning. I realize I fell asleep as I stand in an empty prison cell. Except this prison room is lit green with black and white tiled floor and some strange doctor table.

"Worried, Jess?" I hear.

I look back to see Kyle.

"You should be. After all, you have one kill left," he chuckles grimly.

"Benny's my friend," I say.

His laugh echoes, "And Lily was your sister."

"That was an accident," my voice cracks a little.

"Keep telling yourself that," Kyle picks up one of the tools on the table.

"Kyle, I'm sorry."

Kyle nods as he stares at the sharp pliers he picked up and in one swift motion stabs me in the stomach. I grunt at the striking pain such a quick motion brings a pain that feels like it could last forever.

"Sorry isn't good enough, Reids."

I pull out the pliers and drop them on the ground. I fall to my knees, clutching my stomach.

"What more do you want, Kyle. I can't bring you back," I cry out.

Kyle kneels next to me.

"No but you can pay for it over and over again." He looks at me with cold tears in his eyes.

The desperate anger in his eyes, hurt me. How come I only cared about this person after he was dead?

"Kyle," I plead again.

He picks up the pliers and plunges it in the side of my head. I feel the bursting of my skin and the immediate ache in my brain.

I wake up screaming in my cell. Sweat has drenched my shirt and sheets. Benny jumps up and is by my side.

"Hey man, calm down. You're alright," Benny says in a panic.

I push him away and fall off my bed. I look up to see shadows have entered the cell. The cell has the green tint too.

"I'm still dreaming," I mumble.

"No, you're not, Jess. This is real." Benny gets up from where I pushed him.

"No, no, no," I whimper as the shadows hover over me with similar pliers.

My attention to them is distracted when I feel hands on my face. I look in front of me to see Benny close to me. He looks blurry but I can make out some of his features.

"Look I don't know what you are seeing but whatever it is, it isn't real," he says.

My vision begins to clear, and I see him completely, but the shadows are now behind him. I look up to see one of them raise the pliers towards him.

"Watch out, it will kill you," I say sternly.

"Nothing's there, nothing is going to kill me," Benny replies.

"Something will," I whisper.

Benny looks at me confused but does something that completely shocks me.

His lips press against mine. Everything that is fuzzy begins to clear up. I can't tell if I felt something as he kisses me but for some reason I kiss back. Whatever it is, it's helping me calm my nerves by focusing on something else. I slowly kiss him for a bit as his hands are still on my face and I have moved my hands to be on the back of his head. He stops and looks at me. I just sit there on the floor of the cell in shock. My body is still covered in sweat from waking up from my dream. I have no clue what my facial expression looks like.

Benny raises his eyebrow. "You okay?"

I just nod. So, Benny gets up from the floor and lies back in his bed like nothing happened. I get up and slowly soak into my bed. My mind starts spinning again but from something more subtle and confusing. I look over at Benny whose eyes are closed, and he has tossed over to his side to go back to sleep. I begin to wonder if maybe I am still dreaming and decide to just close my eyes until it is morning.

Either I dreamed of kissing a guy or I just did. What. The. Fuck.

I wake up staring at the ceiling. At first, I forgot the details of yesterday until I look over to see Benny sitting up and putting his shoes on.

"You hear what's happening next week?" asks Benny.

"No what?" I ask.

"There is a new prison called East Haven correctional institute. They plan on transferring all the inmates there before they tear this shit hole down," he says.

"No shit?"

"Yeah, planning all these buses and the best way to transport all the inmates," he gets up.

"Huh. Finally," I mumble.

"Yeah, anyways I'm heading to breakfast. See you there," he says, walking out of the cell.

"Yeah," I practically say to no one.

I lift myself up and put my head in my hands. Everything just oddly went back to normal. It happened right? I really don't think it was a dream or me imagining things. That seemed way too real for that. I shake my head and walk out of the cell.

Benny is right. This is all everyone is talking about. The transfer of all the inmates to this new prison. Guards are talking amongst themselves about what they should do if things go south. Obviously, a lot of inmates are seeing this as a good time to escape. One giant prison break. I don't plan on trying to escape. To be honest, it is better I am here than out in the world causing chaos as I did when I was a kid. Unfortunately, I might be the only prisoner thinking that way.

In the mess hall, guards roam and pay attention to the conversations of inmates because too many groups are whispering amongst each other. I can tell the guards are prepared for anything. It is becoming a waiting game as the prison is officially closing but the question is: will it be better? It is hard to tell because prison inmates can still learn how to make shivs and guards can still be corrupted but at least the 'living conditions' and 'overcrowding' might be fixed. It is funny because that might just be one of the least of my concerns.

I would rather be stuffy and dirty than kicked in the stomach and socked in the face. Of course, that is just a personal preference. However, a new warden is going to be hired. It's this man named Mr. Sanchez according to Benny. Our entire breakfast is spent talking to inmates. It is the first time I really have mingled with the other inmates. Benny and I look like a couple of teenagers soaking in all the gossip of the school. I got a lot of information. It is surprising how knowledgeable some of these inmates are.

Warden Williams has been the warden here since I was put in prison in 1996. Detectives came in one day and found out a lot of the guards he was hiring had past records from other states. It's ridiculous that instead of firing a guard or an officer, they just transfer them to another state. As if no one would find out or they would suddenly change their behavior. Anyways, this new Warden Sanchez has been transitioning us into the new life we are going to have in this new prison. Which is why we have new guards and almost all the old guards are gone. At least the ones that gave me weekly beatings. That is also why we have been having more free time. I mean, I have written more than I have been able to recently. I was always in solitary or a padded room over every little thing.

As I watch the whole room of gossipers with tattoos and orange suits, my gaze goes to Benny. I am not someone who can't admit when a guy is attractive, but I never fully saw a man as...I don't know how to explain it. Anyways, for what it is worth, I'm glad he is in my life again but as a friend of course. I like that he is into art and interested in my writing too. It's always nice to share common interests with people; it makes you feel less lonely.

I have learned a lot of writers tend to be able to explain more with a pen or pencil than they can with their voice. It's so hard to explain how you feel unless you are doing it anonymously. Writing feels like you are an anonymous writer you see in the newspapers. Telling your dirty secrets or answering questions about how to get their woman back after they cheated. News flash, you won't. A lot of writings tend to make zero sense because my mind travels too quickly to stay on one subject. However, I made something that might be better…

Peace. What would it feel like? To truly feel the happiness that comes with peace. Would it feel like floating in the water? Or flying high in the sky? Does it only come after surviving the pain and finally being relieved of it? Life is an everlasting heart ache that breaks us down to the very bone but perhaps finding peace makes it all worth it. Perhaps falling in love makes falling out of love worth it. Smiling makes the tears we shed worth it. Finding people makes it worth losing people. Perhaps living makes it worth dying. In the end, peace is all everyone is looking for in whatever form they please. They're looking for everlasting happiness that makes them want to dance within their skin. I truly think everyone can find this but unfortunately, we must die a little inside to get there. We must hurt to truly find peace.

It is not perfect but it's what I've been thinking about recently. Not that I think I deserve it but I sure as hell know some people that do. Nobody visits because I refused any visitations. I felt like if they kept seeing me it would deny them peace and stop them from moving on. I ended up regretting this decision when Mrs. Jones passed away a year ago. It hurt like hell to find that out from a guard that told me in the most racist way possible. I won't tell you what he said, it's too upsetting, and I will never repeat it. They didn't explain how, and I didn't want to know. I was hoping it was in a peaceful way, but I was afraid it would be something violent and I couldn't hear that happening to Mrs. Jones. I still haven't changed my visitation rules though because even though it hurts; it's for the best. I am not sure they would even want to see me anyways and I would not blame them.

I told myself I would spend this prison time alone and away from the world. Of course, I have kind of broken that rule. I gained a friend which is something I have been avoiding. It is like Benny forced his way into my life without even trying.

We walk back to the cell in silence just walking near each other.

Inmates brush past us accidentally knocking me into his arm.

"Sorry," I say awkwardly.

"It's fine," he laughs.

We walk into our gray cell with two steel beds just sitting across from each other. A strange feeling entered my stomach and I stood frozen. This cell is horrible and dirty looking. Why the hell did it feel like home all of a sudden?

I sit down on my bed quietly and stare at my feet.

"You okay?" asks Benny walking to his bed.

I nod.

Benny starts taking off his shoes. He doesn't seem to like wearing them anytime he's in the cell. It is the first thing he does like it is a house.

"Are you doing it?" Benny asks.

I look up confused. "Doing what?"

"The great escape?" Benny says dramatically.

"No," I laugh.

Benny smiles, "Why not?"

I look at him. His head is tilted like he is ready for me to go into a huge speech.

"I don't deserve to escape," I say.

Benny's face oddly looks hurt, but he nods.

"I have a feeling it'll go terribly anyways," he says.

I nod. "A massacre."

Benny leans his back against the wall. I watch his facial expression that seems like he is in deep thought. His thick eyebrows are concentrated.

"Are you okay?" I ask, hesitantly.

"Why don't you seem evil?" he blurts out.

"A lot of evil people seem normal on the outside," I say.

Not sure why that is the first thing that came out of my mouth.

Benny shrugs, "Maybe there is no good and evil. It's just living. There's bad and good in all of us."

"You delt drugs and joined a group. I murdered people," I say coldly.

"And it kills you inside. If you were some sociopath, you wouldn't feel bad about it, but you are Reids, sick to your stomach and having night terrors. And you want to know what's worse?" Benny says sternly.

"You secretly wish they never changed the guards."

I look at him confused but my stomach drops.

"Why would I wish that?" I protest.

"You like being beaten up because you feel you deserve it. You believe you deserve endless torment because of what you've done," Benny says.

"So, what? Because I feel bad for what I've done means I'm not evil? What the hell is that logic, Benny? You just don't want to see it!" I stand up from my bed. "It scares you that you get along with someone like me, so, you justify it but telling yourself that deep down I'm a good person. Well guess what! Deep down I'm still the piece of shit you see on the surface!"

"Fuck you!" Benny stands up and gets in my face, "I don't have to justify anything to myself. There's nothing wrong with me."

"I never said that. There isn't," I pause and shake my head.

"Why do you push everyone away that could possibly lo—" Benny stops.

He just storms out leaving me alone in the cell. I look up to see his shoes still there. Great, you pissed the man off so much that he is walking around the prison barefoot.

Something inside my gut is turning so much that is unbearable. I drop to the floor and hug my knees on the floor. Everything starts spinning and my skin starts to tingle. A chill runs up my spine as everything starts to numb. I start to panic because it feels like I am becoming paralyzed. I stumble out of my cell and bump into an inmate.

"Watch it," the man says.

I look up to see the bald man with the dragon neck tattoo.

"Fuck you," I whisper.

"What the fuck did you say?" He gets in my face.

"I said go fuck yourself you bald, brainless, piece of shit," through my teeth.

In one stinging swing the man punches me in the face. Suddenly, his body is crushing mine but all I can feel is the coldness of the floor and faint stings of every swing. I can't help but laugh because Benny is right. Something about a sock in the face creates a twisted form of justice to a guilt-ridden soul.

"Get off of him!" I hear a faint yell.

The man is pulled off me and another guard starts helping me up.

Another guard joins him to wrap my other arm around his shoulder. They start taking me away and my blurred vision focuses on Benny who looks at me with pain.

Chapter 29
Justifying Something

After medical I head to the showers. My face is fine, just a couple of marks and a black eye. The swelling is down on my right eye. I look in the mirror to see my beat-up face. To work on my face, they shaved off the scruff and all that is left is a shadow. All I can think about is how desperately I want a cigarette and I've never smoked. It reminds me of Declan and his cigarette addiction. I understand it now. I haven't thought about Declan and the other kids for a bit, but I wonder how they are doing. I step into the shower and let the water fall on me. When I put some soap in my hair, some falls on my face and stings. I grunt at the sting and quickly wash it off my face.

"Great," I mumble, turning off the faucet angrily.

I start drying myself and put on some pants. I walk out of the shower still drying my torso mumbling to myself.

"Get your ass beaten by a supervillain and now you can't even take a damn shower without lighting your face on fire," I mumble to myself.

"What an interesting monologue," Benny says.

I jump and drop my shirt onto the bathroom floor. I slowly pick it up to see it has gotten a little soaked.

"Gross," I say disappointed.

"My bad," scoffs Benny.

I try shaking it like that is going to magically make it dry.

"How is your face doing? Besides being light on fire," Benny mocks.

"Better," I say looking in the mirror.

I look over to see Benny right near my face which makes me jump again.

"You are very jumpy," Benny mumbles.

"I'm a schizophrenic," I say monotoned.

"Right," Benny smiles.

His smile drops and he looks at me in a way I can't explain. My muscles tighten as he gets closer to me, but I can't seem to back up. I

184

just stand frozen.

"What are you doing?" I ask.

"Justifying something," he smirks.

I look at him confused and he presses his lips against mine. After he kisses me, he looks at me and up and down, smiles and walks out of the bathroom. I stand there once again confused and idiotically holding my damp shirt.

"Justifying something," I mock.

I throw on my shirt that feels uncomfortable as the damp spot clings to my chest. I walk out of the bathroom to see guards just walking around and talking amongst themselves. It makes me think for a second I missed more days than I thought. I rush into our cell.

"Wow speedy," Benny laughs.

"Are we getting transferred today?" I ask.

"Yes, you slept through the entire rest of the week," Benny says.

"Holy shit," I mumble.

"I'm kidding," he laughs.

I glare at him and sit down. "You know that day is going to be a shit show. What day is it exactly?"

"Friday and I kind of hope so. I haven't seen a show in a while," Benny smirks.

I shake my head and laugh.

"Let me guess some kind of play," I mock.

"Don't mock a good Shakespeare play," he grins.

We went outside for recess and just walked along the trail that most inmates use to run. It is silent for a while after our second awkward kiss. I'm not sure what I am doing and why I'm not stopping him. I can't tell if I feel for him that way or if I'm lonely. That thought makes me feel sick to my stomach, Benny is not someone I would want to use just because I feel lonely. However, I can't help but remember feeling something that intrigued me when I first met him too. His focus on the book he was reading and his short sentences and monotoned demeanor. The man interested me even then.

"Wow, Reids, you look like you are in some deep thought," Benny chuckles.

I look up to see him stare at me and I blush. What the hell, I'm in my 30s and I am blushing like a teen. The blush makes me feel a little guilty when Izzy all of a sudden comes to mind. That is obviously over but who knew I would feel anything for another person after her.

"Just thinking," I say, distracted.

"About what?" Benny asks, kicking a rock.

"Wouldn't you like to know," I mumbled, mocking Benny's sarcasm.

"Stealing my lines," Benny mumbles back with a slight smirk.

There is silence again and Benny clears his throat, "Why did you start a fight with dragon?" he asks.

"Dragon?" I ask.

"We never learned the assholes name, so I'm calling him dragon," he shrugs.

"No reason," I say quietly.

"Uh huh. Nothing to do with our conversation before?" Benny pries a little more.

"Oh, you mean where you told me I'm some sicko who enjoys pain?" I smirk.

"That's not—I meant, it seemed like you enjoy being punished," Benny stutters out.

I stop walking and turn to look at him. "Is that how you meant it to sound?"

Benny stops and his face gets a little red.

"Yeah, now that I said that out loud, it sounds bad," Benny's voice falls monotoned.

I just chuckle and we continue to walk until we are called back inside.

We get inside the prison for dinner and eat silently. After all the inmates exchanged the information of what's happening on Friday, they went back to the normal routines and cliques. Yes, I am saying cliques. It's seeming even weirder between Benny and I. You would think we would be more comfortable around each other, but it is getting awkward. I can't tell if it's tension or guilt. I don't even know which one it was in the pit of my stomach let alone his.

We get back to the cell and as usual Benny slips off his shoes and sets them nicely by his bed. I don't know why but something came up in my mind.

"What did they diagnose you with back at the hospital?" I randomly ask.

Benny shrugs, "Severe depression."

I nod. "Oh sorry."

Benny smirks, "It's fine. I dealt."

"Does it still get bad?" I ask awkwardly.

All of a sudden I am feeling very nervous around him. He has a different facial expression on that I can't narrow down.

Benny moves to sit on my bed with me and my body stiffens.

"Sometimes but that's depression for you. It never goes away," Benny sighs.

He leans back onto the wall and just stares forward. It confuses me for a second, does he just want to sit on my bed? I just scooch back and match his stance.

"The girl who visited you, what was her name?" Benny asks.

"Izzy," I say, my voice sounding sadder than I meant to.

"Not together anymore?" he asks.

I pause, "I murdered people."

Benny scoffs, "Sorry I shouldn't laugh at that."

I nod and smirk a little. It is funny in a terrible way, I guess. Poor girl, most people break up with their significant others over normal things.

"She's going to have the worst ex story," I mumble.

Benny laughs but stops when he sees my face. He elbows my arm.

"Sorry, I just...I think she has a kid, mine," I gulp.

I look at Benny whose eyebrows are raised in shock.

"Shit," he mumbles.

"I'll never see it and don't want to because it's just for the best." I stare at my hands. "But it still occasionally hurts that I will probably never meet it. I don't even know if it's a son or daughter."

"Sorry man," Benny says now staring at his hands and it slowly slides to hold mine.

I look at him and he looks up at me. He still has those super indented cheek bones just with more scruff. I never noticed his eyes before; they are this gray blue tint. I feel myself staring too intensely. I don't know why I do that to people. It hits me, I don't just do that to people, I do it to people I feel attracted to. This scares me for a second, it is just going to be another casualty. Another heart I was going to either kill or break. Benny starts to lean towards me.

"I can't," I mumble.

Benny freezes and leans back.

"People who get close to me either die or get their heart shattered and it's always my fault. It's always my doing and I don't know how to stop it," I say.

"I don't care," Benny says.

I look at him confused. "You should."

Benny smirks and chuckles, "Don't tell me what to do."

He takes my face and presses his lips to mine. I start to feel a sensation that is warming the numbness I constantly feel in my brain. Like when you are drunk and try to focus on something or smoke a cigarette to feel grounded when the room spins. As my thoughts whirl, I am opening the kiss and deepening it as I let my hand rest on the back of his head. Benny oddly smells like pencil shavings and some sweeter musk. Our bodies have gotten closer and without realizing, I've swung his legs around to rest against mine, so he is facing towards me. I know any second someone could walk by this cell and see a guy practically on my lap, making out with me but I don't want to stop. I just keep kissing him until two inmates having an argument outside breaks us apart. We just stare at each other for a second breathing heavily and when footsteps seem to come closer, he hops off me and sits on his bed. A guard walks by and glances in at us but moves on quickly. We both watch the guard slowly walk away and glance back at each other. The curls in his hair are wildly sticking out which makes me chuckle and he just joins me in the laughter.

For a moment we sit there in silence and I look up to see Benny in deep thought. It makes me want to find a way to read his mind, to open his brain and see everything.

I go for the next best thing, "What are thinking about?"

"The hospital," his smile is faint.

I look at him confused.

"Do you remember when you left?" he asks, softly.

I nod but realize he isn't looking at me to see me nod. He is just gazing into the hallway.

"Yes."

"I hid from you. I don't know why I did it. It was rude of me, but something told me that it would hurt like hell saying goodbye to you. I didn't understand why at the time. So, I just hid behind the door to the empty group therapy room," he chuckles.

He turns to look at me with glossy eyes, "I'm sorry I didn't say goodbye."

I smile, "It's okay. Turns out it wasn't goodbye."

Benny just smiles.

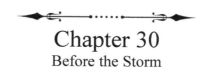

Chapter 30
Before the Storm

I wake up half asleep to hear Benny ruffling around on his bed. All of a sudden, I feel his breath closer to my face and open my eyes to see his eyes looking back at me.

"Morning," he says but his face has some weight to it, something is bothering him.

"Morning, what's wrong?" I ask.

"You are way too observant," he mutters.

I laugh and find myself lifting my arm and putting it through his hair.

"It's Thursday," he sighs.

"Good job you know your days of the week," I tease.

He looks at me very unamused. I sit up a little bit to see he is sitting on the floor near my bed. So, I grab his hand and lift him up onto my bed. He sighs and lets me.

"Tomorrow we are getting transferred. I wasn't nervous about it till now," Benny explains.

I nod. "Yeah, at this point I'm not sure what to expect."

I grow worried, what if our room changes?

"Shit, what if we aren't roommates?" I ask.

Benny frowns at that.

"Well, maybe we still will be. Apparently, the warden did that on purpose," I mutter.

"What?" he asks.

"Oh, um yeah. My therapist actually I guess did it on purpose since you knew me," I say hesitantly, scratching my head, "something about artists sticking together."

"Artists sticking together?" Benny laughs.

I shrug my shoulder. "Yeah, she doesn't make sense most of the time."

For a second we are silent until Benny breaks it. "Food?"

"Food," I agree.

Phillips

We both walk out, and I have to fight back the urge to hold his hand whenever I see anyone look at him. Another thing I hate about me and relationships, I am way too protective or maybe it's not even that. The thought of me being territorial over a person sickens me but if I am honest with myself that is probably it. We go and sit to eat our food and the Mexican man who delivered the news to us comes back.

He playfully punches Benny in the shoulder which makes him wince and goes a bit in a defense mode.

"Easy there, tiger," he teases.

The horrible thoughts of grabbing a man's throat passes through my brain and every single one of my muscles tighten as I resist the urge. It is a simple joke, a playful punch that is it. The man didn't fucking kiss Benny in front of me. God, I hope Benny isn't seeing my reaction. I realize everything is silent at the table and focus my vision to see both the man and Benny staring at me. Shit, I need a recovery.

"Hey man," I manage to fake a smile.

"Reids," he says awkwardly, "anyway you guys ready for tomorrow?"

I shrug and try to look around the prison to focus on other things. Every bone in my body wants to scream for him to leave this table right now.

"Well, I'm going to go. Bye Reids and—" he pauses.

"Davis?" Benny says in a question which makes me look over confused.

"Moreno, nice to meet you man," he pats him on the back and walks away.

I look at him confused.

"I figured he called you your last name, so I said mine," he smiles.

"Benny Davis." I smile.

Benny rolls his eyes at me which helps my muscles loosen.

After we ate, we went outside for a little and do our usual walk.

"So, Moreno seems nice," Benny kicks a rock with an odd facial expression on his face. It's a smile that makes my blood boil a bit. Was Moreno flirting making him smile?

"Sure," I scoff.

That makes Benny's smile get bigger and he slowly turns to me with a smirk on his face.

"What?" I ask, annoyed.

"You were jealous," he laughs.

I roll my eyes and walk a bit quicker but it just eggs Benny on.

"Oh no no. You are not running from this one," he chuckles.

"I'm sorry," I mutter, walking quicker.

Benny puts out his hand and puts it on my chest to stop me.

"I'm just teasing you man," he looks at me concerned.

"I shouldn't be like that though. He just gave you a pat on your back and I reacted like he was fucking you in the lunchroom," I mutter, my eyes going wide at what I just mentioned.

Benny's eyebrows shot up.

"I shouldn't be that controlling," I say. "I wanted to—"

Benny backs up a little and I know he knows what I was going to say. Knows that I wanted to kill yet another person. I wait to see tears form in his eyes or his face go angry, but he just looks at me with such confusion. He just walks away, and I can feel my heart hurt a little, he should though. He turns to me.

"You coming? Guards are bringing people in," he says.

I look at him confused, why is he so calm? I just shake my head and follow him inside. We walk silently to our cell, and I can't help but keep looking over. His face is so focused like he is contemplating his whole life. It's like his face has every emotion and not just one that I can make out. Is he mad at me? Disgusted or sad?

We get in the cell, and he just sits down with his eyebrows creased. I sit on the edge of my bed bouncing my leg up and down.

"I don't mean to be insensitive right now, but do you want to think out loud?" I finally ask.

"I think something's wrong with me," he mutters.

I can't help but laugh, it comes out in such a burst that Benny looks up at me in shock.

"Something's wrong with you?" I ask, "Benny I just said I wanted to kill somebody because they touched your back and you think there is something wrong with you?"

Benny looks up at me with another facial expression I can't make out. He is at the edge of his bed with his hands folded together. He visibly swallows hard and all of a sudden looks very nervous.

"Benny?" I ask, wanting to fill this awkward silence.

"I," he paused, "I liked it."

My face gets hot, and my mind gets so confused.

"What the fuck do you mean?" I ask.

"I know it's fucked up. That should have scared me that you'd want to kill a man because of me but for some reason a part of me was," he paused for a while not wanting to look at me, "flattered."

I have no clue what to say. Am I flattered about this?

"Oh," is all I can say.

"What are you judging me now?" Benny snaps.

"What? God, no. I am the last person that would ever judge you," I quickly say, "I'm just surprised. I don't know what to say. I thought you'd run."

We both are silent, and Benny shifts on his bed and clears his throat.

"What did you feel at that moment?" Benny asks.

"Just anger boiling when I saw his hand touch you and just wanted to launch at him. It's hard to explain," I mutter, confused on why he is carrying this conversation on.

"Because you would rather it just be you?" he asks quietly.

"What do you mean?" I ask nervous, unsure of where this is going.

"Touching me," Benny slightly smirks.

I blink my eyes quickly at that and gulp. Finally, Benny looks up at me with a bit of mischief in his eyes. The sound of a buzzer and the doors locking up makes me jump out of my tunnel vision on his face. I look out into the hallway and when I look back Benny is sitting up from his bed and walking up towards me.

He lightly pushes me back further onto my bed and straddles my lap. Every inch of my body is suddenly burning up. Benny is now looking into my eyes with such intensity that I can't say a word. What the hell is happening? He leans down and presses his lips on mine. I open my mouth a little to let him do whatever he wants. Benny took that as an invitation to start French kissing me. A shock hits my tongue as I reciprocate it. My skin crawls at every sound he makes. He pulls away and whispers in my ear, "I want to be only yours."

After that, I grabbed him with a soft force and shoved him underneath me. I swear we continued all night, and I did what I didn't want that man to do and that's touch Benny anywhere I could. Forgetting about tomorrow's events and any other trouble I have had for that night.

Chapter 31
Friday

A loud ring sounds off and guards start getting all the inmates ready. Benny and I groan and realize we are still in my bed. We laugh at each other and quickly get up to look more in order before a guard sees. Benny slips on his shoes and starts gathering up his stuff. Figures they would do it straight in the morning, giving inmates as little of time they can. They line Benny and I up with the rest of the inmates. We all get our hands cuffed just in case we get creative. All of us are huddled in a line while holding pitiful pillowcases with our clothes.

We begin to walk out, and the guards are ready for anything. It looks like every guard is on duty in the same area with their guns ready. We are all being loaded on buses to move not that far down. Benny and I get put in line behind two guys that seem certain they were getting out of here which makes me nervous because we could easily get caught in the crossfire. Benny and I look at each other worried. We start walking outside of the prison and towards the buses. It is a very dull day, so the sun isn't blinding but the fresh air feels amazing. I close my eyes to take in the fresh air even though it smells like mud. My peace is instantly interrupted when I hear someone yell which seems random, until a big group of inmates start to run off.

Guns instantly go off and my first thought is how insane these people are until I notice a hole in the fence big enough for even the largest man to fit through. Men in orange suits are running so fast and are coming together like a heard of zombies who finally found a human.

Benny looks at the hole and to me. "Run."

Before I could feel anything; my legs are moving. We slip in the middle of the group. It is difficult running with my hands cuffed, but I run as fast as I can. People are being shot down around me which makes me feel guilty. However, the only person I am worried about is Benny. I look over at him every couple of seconds to see he is still beside me. We are close to the hole in the fence and I look over to see Benny smiling at me until a bullet busts through his head. My heart drops and every inch of my body becomes sore. He falls to the ground limp making me stop in my tracks. Bullets are still flying, and it is a miracle they are missing me. I want to stay with him but everything in me is telling me he is gone. It instantly killed him. Every part of me wants to drop down to him but I'm also afraid to see the wound so close. His eyes remain open but completely still. I dart away and through the fence. I keep on running and not daring to look back.

Right where the hole was is a big group of trees. To get to society, you have to run through the trees. I haven't been in the woods since 1996. Of course, I think the shadows entered my body and followed me to the prison because this is no longer the place where my shadows were worse. However, I can tell they are getting stronger. It is like the woods give them power. I run and run until a cramp on my side shoots through my ribcage. I look back to see no one but I hear a lot of rustling. It's got to be the prisoners or at least I hope it is. I walk fast with my hands still cuffed. The trees start to bend oddly as I stare harder, I realize they are breathing. They expand in and out in unison. My vision starts to get shaky, and I try to shake my head to clear it. I close my eyes.

"Focus," I whisper to myself.

I open my eyes to see a woman with hair in her face and jump back. It causes me to fall to the ground onto my handcuffs. The handcuffs feel like they just cut into my skin. I have to toss myself to the side with my knees up to pick myself back up. I look back to see the woman in the distance. She is just weeping in the distance with her hair in her face. The hair is almost black and curly. It reminds me of Izzy's hair except, it is in tangles.

"It's not there. Nothing's there," I whisper.

I walk slowly towards the woman who is walking closer to the opening of the woods. All of a sudden a little boy cuts in my path. I freeze to stand before this pale blue boy who just stands in front of me, silent. He looks about 5-years-old.

"Hi kid. Where is your mommy?" I ask.

The little boy tilts his head and gives me a sad look.

"That's creepy," I chuckle nervously.

The little boy slowly turns to look at another child who is coming from the bushes.

"Lily," I whisper.

She walks towards me slowly with the same expression as the boy and her head tilted.

"No," I gasp.

They both look at me silently as smiles show on their faces. Their eyes glow yellow as I hear a faint roar. I look back to see multiple shadows behind me all lining up like an army. I look in front of me to see the kids have disappeared.

"Jessie," the shadows seethe.

I look back again to see all of them turn into dark and twisted versions of myself. They all have red eyes and evil smiles. Cracks like rivers are formed on their faces. I start to back away from them and break into a sprint once I realize they are running towards me. The weather is cool, and the cold air is entering my lungs as I run. It stings but I don't want to stop. I can feel the shadows on my neck as the hairs on it stand up.

Finally, I enter the town, trying my best to stay in alleys rather than sidewalks. I realize the main thing I need to do is to disguise myself. I run into a dark alley that has a couple of apartment doors leading into it. A man comes out who seems a bit bigger than me but not too much. He is paying attention to his paper, and I quietly approach him and instantly head butt him. My head starts throbbing as I see the man fall to the ground instantly passed out and I walk into his house that he didn't lock up yet.

In there I find a hammer and other tools. I begin trying to use whatever I can to bust out of my handcuffs. I walk over to the saw on his desk and scrap my handcuffs against it; hoping nothing hits my hand. After a while it finally busts off. I sigh out of relief and lie my head on a table.

My mind feels so fuzzy that the numbing sensation is sitting on my neck and traveling down my arms. Images rush through my head. I haven't given myself a chance to think and I don't want to, but something is pushing its way through. Those pale kids, the shadow army and Benny...Benny. I fall to the ground in tears.

"Fuck!" I scream. I realize I need to be quiet, so I cover my mouth to muffle any more screams.

My whole body is shaking as the image of the bullet hitting him passes through my mind. How could I let that happen? I should have stopped and let a bullet enter my brain as well, died next to him. At this point, I am so fucking tired of people dying on my account. I crawl towards a mop bucket as I feel a warmth travel up my throat. To add to the pathetic picture, I vomit into a bucket. Unsure of what to do next, I slowly get up and start looking for different clothes.

I grab a flannel and a pair of his blue jeans. I pull them on and look in the mirror that sat on the man's dresser. My hair is uncontrollable. I shave the rest of my scruff as I watch hot tears fall from my eyes. I pull on some old tennis shoes the man had, not wanting to touch his nice work shoes because it is the least I can do since I head butted him.

I come back out of the house and see the man still lying there. "Five victims" pop in my head so I quickly go to check his pulse and a huge rush of relief runs over me when I realize his pulse is still there. I try not to think about if Benny counts as the fifth victim, shaking my head, I pick the man up with all my might and drag him back into his house and plop him on his rug. His house looks like he is a hunter which explains his clothes and his decoration of a deer head on his wall. I look down at his table that looks like he chopped a stump and set it on the middle of his floor and saw a jar of change. I grab the jar and fish out a lot of quarters and go on my way. I make sure to close his door and lock it behind me because god forbid the poor man gets robbed twice in one day. My next stop is the bus stop.

My plan is to escape Connecticut and get as far away as I can. I don't mind running because I don't have much keeping me here anyways. It would be nice to find a place where I am not in the tabloids. A place no one knows the story of a child killer named Jessie Reids.

As I walk, I pass many farmers and nothing but hayfields. My mind is running through different ideas. Do I even try to run away? Do I let myself get caught and thrown back in prison? No, I need to get away. Far enough away that no one will have connection to me, no more deaths. Perhaps mine will be the last death from my own hands. That is what I'll do, run away and get myself buried in an unmarked grave. Be known as a man with no name rather than the murderer I am. A smirk runs across my face as I think of it.

I find the nearest bus stop and next to it is a small gas station. A part of me knows I shouldn't go in because I should avoid public spaces, but I can hear my stomach rumbling. It is easier to get in and out of a store without being noticed rather than a restaurant where multiple people study your face. I walk into a gas station and go to look in the snacks isle. The cash register man is just chewing on a toothpick as he spins a pencil in his hand. Everyone seems to mind their business and not stare. There is barely anybody at this gas station. The news of a prison break might still be new, and I will admit I look very different from the Jessie Reids they all knew. I stare at the different Pringles as my stomach makes the loudest noises it possibly can. I am so confused by all the different choices. Why would someone want to eat chips with a ranch dressing flavor? I scrunch my nose as I look for a flavor I recognize.

"I like the BBQ ones," I hear a voice say.

I look over to see this young man who stands like he is wise beyond his years. My heart feels like it stopped. He is tall and has tan skin with bright green eyes. His jawline sharp and hair shaggy brown. To me he looks so familiar and there is this gut feeling that I know him somehow.

"The what?" I ask.

"Barbecue, BBQ for short," he smiles.

"Well, I'll take your word for it because there are some weird ones here," I mumble.

I look at his shirt that has a yellow smiley face on it with x's as the eyes. All I can think to myself is how relatable the shirt is.

"I like your shirt," I say.

"Thanks. It's my favorite band," he grins.

"Who is it?"

"Nirvana, you never heard of them?" the guy chuckles.

"No, but I haven't listened to that much here lately," I laugh.

"Well, give them a listen," he says.

"I will."

"Are you just passing through here?" he asks, pointing to the bus stop.

"Yeah," I chuckle, "you?"

"Yeah, kind of. My mom and I are moving to New York. You'd think I wouldn't want to leave this town because it's my home but it's New York, what's a better place to go to college than that?" He kept going on.

I am surprised by how open he is and how easily he talks to people. I would have scurried away if a stranger started talking to me about pringles.

"Well, good luck," I say.

He nods. "Thank you and good luck with your travels."

"Ben, did you grab your snack yet? We need to get back on the road."

I become speechless. The woman has long black wavy hair and tan skin with a similar, slightly diminished accent. Her hair is half pulled up and she has a long skirt on with a black jacket. A bottle of coke hangs from her hand. I swear she hasn't aged a day. Izzy looks the same and her son looks like her but with eyes like mine. A part of me wants to tell her who I am or ask her if she knows. Tears start to form in my eyes as my heart aches.

"Uh...BBQ Pringles," he laughs, quickly grabbing one of the Pringle cans.

I can't speak and I just stare but Izzy looks at me confused. She looks as if she is solving a puzzle or doesn't know how to react to me. All of a sudden the doors burst open with a roar that breaks our concentration. A man appears with a gun in his hand and a ski mask. His jacket is bright orange, for a second, I forgot that I wasn't the only one to escape. I watch as everyone panics and puts their arms up. Izzy immediately covers Ben. A loud ringing forms in my ears, muffling the sound of panic and fear.

"Give me the money!" he shouts at the cashier.

Ben pushes past Izzy and says, "Dude, calm down" and immediately the robber points the gun at him.

By then, I have made my way near them both and quickly go in front of Ben in time for the man to pull the trigger. A hot pain dashes through me as I feel myself fall on the ground. There are many screams but luckily, I can hear one of them yelling "police" as they arrested the shooter.

I look up at the blurry tiled white ceiling. My breath is shortening, and I can't feel most of my body. I hear "somebody call an ambulance" and other various voices. All I can see are the two faces hovering over me, Izzy's and Ben's. I watch their horrified faces and the tears in both of their eyes. A hand on my chest to try and stop the bleeding. A Faint, "mom, what do we do?" My eyes start to blur but I can still see the silhouettes of the two and I think to myself 'there isn't a better way to die.'

I slowly close my eyes and smile faintly at the fact: perhaps my fifth victim has always been me.

Dear Son,

You are probably never going to read this, so I don't know why I'm writing it, but I didn't want to leave words unsaid... or rather unwritten. I don't think I'll ever get to meet you and that might be a good thing because I am a piece of shit. There is not a day where you and your mother don't cross my mind. I hope you two are doing okay and I regret hurting your mother, resulting in me never being there for you. I am sorry and although you don't owe me anything while I owe you the world; I do ask for one thing... Please don't end up like me. Surprisingly I met someone here that taught me something...Live a life worth living. Laugh, fall in love, hurt and cry. Succeed in life and fail. Learn and make mistakes. Have confidence and insecurities. Meet people who take your breath away and leave people as a stronger person. Scream on mountain tops and get caught in the rain. Shatter into pieces so you can put yourself back together again. The most important thing is to feel everything. Feel joy, sadness, anger and fear. Feel every part of life through every bone. Because the only way your life will ever be wasted is if you feel nothing. Numbness would ruin the adventure. And after everything is said and done, don't be afraid of dying because there will be nothing you wished you did.

I love you,
Dad

Printed in the USA
CPSIA information can be obtained
at www.ICGtesting.com
LVHW041406280723
753393LV00003B/572

9 798218 194727